I0557923

The Green Dress

By Michelle L. Rusk

CHELLEHEAD WORKS

The Green Dress

Copyright © 2015 by Michelle L. Rusk

All rights reserved. No portion of this book may be reproduced—mechanically, electronically, or by any other means, including photocopying—without written permission of the publisher.

ISBN: 978-0-9837776-2-5

Library of Congress Control Number: 2015935352

Chellehead Works books are available at special discounts when purchased in bulk for premiums and sales promotions as well as fundraising and educational use.

For details, contact the Special Sales Director at:

info@chelleheadworks.com

505-266-3134

Albuquerque, New Mexico

Printed in the United States of America

First printing June 2015

Designed by Megan Mickey

Edited By Elizabeth Hadas

Photography by Pamela Joye

To Gregory, for the days ahead

Chapter One

"What do you mean my Aunt Sally left me her entire house?" Audrey asked her mother, who was holding a manila envelope.

Shirley Thomas peered at her daughter through her silver-wire-rimmed glasses. "We never told you that your dad had a sister?"

Audrey stared at her mother and closed her laptop. She was sitting at the round kitchen table, the same one she grew up eating at outside Kansas City, Kansas. She placed her hands on the top of the case and shook her head. "I don't get it."

Sitting across the table, Shirley pulled a stack of papers out of the envelope. "Sally and her husband, Patrick, were estranged from the family. None of us were never really sure what happened, but not long after they married, we never heard from them again. Your father was angry at his sister for leaving his life, so he never spoke of her again."

Audrey peered right back at her mom, her gray hair glistening in the early May sun that soaked the kitchen through the sliding glass door. "What does all this have to do with me?"

Shirley took a deep breath and shoved the papers over the table to Audrey. "Apparently Patrick died some years ago and Sally died three months ago. Your father. . . ." She trailed off and put her hand over her heart, Audrey knowing her mother missed her father more than anything. "She left everything to him. The stipulation was that if he died first, it go to his children."

"And I'm his only child," Audrey murmured. She pulled her long hair into a ponytail, securing it with a hair band from her wrist, a habit she had developed years ago as a teacher. When the day got rough, putting her hair up always seemed to give her new perspective.

"The house and everything in it is yours."

"Where is this house?" In her mind, Audrey pictured a ramshackle house built a hundred years ago in the middle of a Kansas cornfield.

"Albuquerque."

"Albuquerque! As in New Mexico?" Audrey threw her head back, her ponytail bouncing from side to side, and laughed. "That's not a place I've ever been. Or ever wanted to go."

"I'd advise you to go. And now!" Shirley sounded serious.

Audrey looked at her mother. "What if it's a shack?"

"It's not," her mother assured her. "The Parsons, Sally and Patrick, were very wealthy. They lived in a very exclusive part of town."

"But you hadn't talked to them in years. How do you know they didn't lose all their money?"

"You'll see in these papers the money she left you. And that doesn't include what she left charity."

Audrey began to flip through the pages and saw *$500,000* next to her name. "On top of the house and its contents?"

Her mother nodded. "Yes. It's all yours." Her mother paused and continued, "I don't believe in coincidence. Your life has changed a lot in the past year. I see this as an opportunity for you. Take it."

"You aren't saying that because you want me to move out so you can start dating?"

Shirley laughed. "No. You have an opportunity most people will never have. Your marriage ended. Life is handing you a new start. My chance for a new start is over, and that's okay. I'll see your father again when it's my time. In the meantime, I'm going to play a lot of bridge at the senior center with my friends and tend to the flowers in my yard."

She looked out the window at the plants that had begun to spring to life after several days of late spring rain.

Audrey felt as if she didn't have much left in her life. She'd walked away from the house she loved—and most of the contents—after Rick announced he had never loved her. It had taken her six months to absorb the shock, the sadness that everything she thought was true—the life they lived in Whispering Grove with the four-bedroom house they planned to fill with kids, the neat green lawn that Rick mowed and tended to on weekends, the neighbors they spent Saturday evenings talking and laughing with over dinner and drinks—it was all a big lie. The suburban lie, she called it.

She walked away from the house one day with just her car, filled to the brim with what would fit. She packed her clothes and anything else meaningful to her, thankful it was at least a large SUV, and drove to her mother's house, where she planted herself until she could figure out where she wanted to live.

She never thought it would be Albuquerque.

Leaving at three in the morning, Audrey knew she would arrive in late afternoon. She had never driven that way across the heartland of America. Usually she and Rick bypassed it by flying to Arizona for their vacations. Lying vacations, she thought, realizing how much corn grew in Kansas.

With hours to kill while she drove, her friend Mandy called her several times. "As long as the cell coverage holds up, we're good," Audrey joked, looking around and seeing . . . nothing.

"I don't even know anyone who has been to New Mexico, much less lives there," Mandy said, laughing slightly. "What do you know about New Mexico?"

"That the roadrunner was always trying to beat the coyote and headed to Albuquerque?"

"That's probably all any of us know about it."

Audrey had done a Google search but wasn't able to come up with a photo of the front of the house. She thought maybe it was because the Google cars hadn't it made it to that part of the country.

As she watched the green interstate exit signs pass, she thought about turning around. But turning around to what?

"Don't come back," her mother had warned with a wagging finger, just as she had when Audrey went off to college. "I hear too many stories from my friends about their kids coming home and never leaving again. I want you to have fun and build a life."

Only my mom, she laughed, thinking of her mother content to play bridge, laugh with her friends, and watch her flowers grow now that her dad was gone.

Her mom loved her, she knew that, and she wanted Audrey to be happy, but she definitely wasn't like most parents. Even though she was okay having Audrey back, she seemed ready to be alone. Maybe it was because she had had time to accept that Audrey's father was going to die, time to prepare to move on.

As Audrey entered New Mexico the landscape became barren. As she drove, she thought of adjectives to describe it, something she knew only an English teacher would do.

"I'm going to sell the house," she told her mother. "I'll be back at the end of the summer— in time to start school. I'll buy a house for me with what I sell Aunt Sally's house for."

Shirley laughed at her daughter. "No. Why don't you take a year off?" she suggested.

Audrey looked at her. "Why? What would I do?"

Her mother shrugged her shoulders and gave a funny smile. "You have money. And since you were ten years old, you've wanted to write a book. Why don't you take a year off and live in Albuquerque and write that book?"

"What would I write about?" Audrey asked, realizing the book dream had long been squashed by so many other parts of her life, mostly the big lie with Rick. She didn't have that dream anymore. Her dream had been to live happily ever after, and she thought that the day she and Rick married, the dream had come true. She liked teaching and coming home in the afternoon with Rick not far behind her from his job at the bank in downtown Kansas City.

"I'm sure you can think of something," Shirley said, getting up from the table to retrieve her mug of coffee from the black granite counter behind her. "Albuquerque is a beautiful place. It will inspire you."

"You've been there?" Audrey asked her mother, eyebrows going up. "I thought you had no communication with Sally."

3

"I've seen photos," her mother said. "And Cynthia down the street used to visit Santa Fe once a year. She always came back to tell us all about it."

"Then why don't you go and do this?" Audrey suggested.

Her mother laughed as she sat back down at the table. "No thank you. I'm quite content right here. Cynthia always felt so inspired when she went there. I'm sure it will do the same for you."

"I hope Albuquerque will," Audrey muttered, looking at all the empty land and sagebrush that filled it, "because this is not very inspiring. Even a cornfield is more inspiring than this."

But once she drove through the canyon, the interstate putting her on the west side of the Sandia Mountains, Audrey was surprised. A little. The city unfolded in front of her as if she had climbed a big hill and could now see the other side. Buildings and life extended for several miles in front of her with the mesa out west reminding her how much open land still existed in the United States.

She took the first exit into the city to Sally's house, though, and didn't get to explore more.

"I believe it's called Aspen Hills," her mother had told Audrey. "Patrick was stationed there in the Air Force, and Sally went there for nursing school. After he was discharged, they met and he became a well-respected insurance agent as the city grew around them. I'm not sure why they never had children."

Down a hill into a canyon and back up to a neighborhood, Audrey let her phone tell her where to find 1610 Tumbleweed Drive.

"Even the streets have barren names," she thought, entering an area with sprawling ranch homes and rock front yards peppered with juniper and pine trees.

"Oh my," she mumbled, her eyes opening wide when she saw the house. At first glance it didn't look like much, but she noticed a three-car garage, which meant something. The one-story brick house was on a hill with a white painted wrought iron railing leading up to the front door.

The key in her hand, Audrey walked up the steps, feeling numb, not fully realizing this was hers. Or at least until she sold it and bought herself something in Kansas City. What would she do in Albuquerque anyway?

The smell told her the house hadn't breathed any fresh air in some time. The front door opened into a tile foyer. Dishes were arranged on the dining room table, as if Sally were expecting guests for dinner and had a heart attack before they were to arrive. The living room, filled with furniture, was decorated with mirrors. For a moment Audrey didn't realize she was looking at herself.

"That's because I'm not sure who I am," she muttered. "I lived the lie too long."

"Helllooooooo!" a voice called, interrupting her thoughts. Audrey walked to the front door and saw a silver-haired woman smiling at her. "You must be Sally's niece! The attorney told us you would be coming. We're so excited to have you here." Audrey let the woman in. "I'm Betty. I live across the street. Your aunt and uncle were our friends since, well, the day we moved in. And we all moved in about the same time. Our houses were brand new."

Audrey swallowed, realizing she knew nothing about the woman who had given her everything. But she also knew the gift was really for her father, who had died too young of a brain tumor. "Oh," was all she could say.

Betty was holding a dish. "These are for you. My famous chocolate chip cookies."

Audrey accepted them graciously but reminded herself that she had to lose some weight while she was there. She had planned to avoid cookies until she got her weight down.

"I hope you didn't bring much. Your aunt has a house filled with stuff and there won't be room for anything you brought," Betty laughed. "She was quite a woman you know."

"Yes, I'm sure she was."

Betty didn't catch it: Audrey had no idea who Sally was. Audrey let it go.

"Well, I need to go," Betty said. "We have water aerobics at the country club pool at 11 and Esther always makes fun of me because I'm chronically late." Before she closed the door, she looked back at Audrey and said, "We'll have you over in the next day or two. The ladies and I are comparing schedules."

"Instant senior friends," Audrey muttered watching Betty walk across the street. She hoped there were some women her own age nearby.

She began to walk through the house. She wanted to tiptoe, as if Sally and Patrick might be around the corner. She kept shaking her head, waffling between not knowing where to start and feeling that she was in a house where she didn't belong.

"This is mine," Audrey started to whisper. "This is mine."

She hoped eventually she would believe it.

The halls were filled with paintings, the closets filled with clothes. The dining room had more dishes than a department store bridal registry. There was stuff everywhere. All Audrey could do was continue to shake her head. Four bedrooms, three bathrooms. A yellow and dark brown kitchen stuck in 1982.

"At least the washer and dryer are new." She ran her finger across the front loaders in the laundry room off the kitchen.

Audrey poked her head in the garage: a nice sedan sat in one bay, the other one empty, everything organized. The car would be the first thing she would sell.

Back in the house, she stood in the kitchen for a moment, feeling too overwhelmed to do much else, when she realized she hadn't scoped out the backyard.

Audrey's eyes opened wide as she came around the corner by the bedrooms and saw the low wrought iron fence with a gate surrounding the pool. While the house sat on a slope, it was flat, enough for a pool. The gate squeaked as she entered the pool area. The water looking amazingly clear considering no one had lived in the house for a year.

As Audrey stood there in awe, looking down at her own shadow in the water, she couldn't believe it. No one told her there was a pool and Google hadn't been much help. "That sucks you can't scope it out before you go," Mandy had remarked when they went out for one last dinner before Audrey left.

She didn't hear the side gate open. When she looked up, a man in a New York Yankees baseball hat carrying a big white bucket and a long pole with a net on the end of it looked just as surprised as she was.

"Uh, hi," Audrey said, waving awkwardly and once again forgetting that the house was hers.

"Hi," he said putting the bucket and pole down and walking over to her with his hand extended. "I'm Bert. I'm the pool guy. You must be Sally's niece?"

"I am," she said, wondering if all of Albuquerque knew she was moving in.

He waved his hand at the pool. "I kept up the pool after your aunt died. It was the most important thing to her. She swam every morning, even in the winter. The lawyer told me to keep it clean and bill the estate until you got here."

"Doesn't it snow here?" Audrey asked, craning her neck toward him.

"It does," Bert laughed. He pointed to a rolled-up blue plastic cover extending across the deep end of the pool, under the diving board. "Sally kept the solar cover on and the heater running." Then he pointed to the roof. "She had solar panels put on the roof two years ago to heat it."

Audrey felt as if her head would never stop shaking. There was so much to learn. "I'm from Kansas. I'm not sure the sun shines enough there."

"It does here. Welcome to the Land of Enchantment."

Audrey watched him get to work and it took her a moment before she realized she better ask questions. After all this was her pool now. "How often do you come? What do I pay you? What do you do when you're here?"

Bert stood back up and wiped his hands as he laughed. "Don't worry. I'll fill you in on everything. I saw Sally the day before she died. She never told me what the plans were for the house; we all thought she would live forever with the energy she had. But I'll make sure you feel like you are taken care of."

Audrey bit her lip before she spoke. "Well, if you were that important to her, just fill me in and we're good."

She watched him for a few minutes: skimming the pool, vacuuming the bottom, checking the chemicals.

After he left, Audrey sat down on one of the chairs near the shallow end, simply watching the water. She looked around and realized there was grass to be cut. Surely there were landscapers, too.

Her mother had told her that Patrick died in 1990. Sally had lived alone all these years, taking care of a big house and living a life without her husband of forty-some years. When Audrey walked back inside, realizing the easiest access to the pool was from the master bedroom, she headed back toward the kitchen looking for a glass of water. That's when she realized she had missed something: sitting on the wet bar in the den was what looked like an open tool kit. Instead of tools though, the yellow plastic box held paint tubes and brushes.

Audrey looked behind the bar to find several paintings leaning against the cabinet. She walked back into the hallway where paintings adorned all the cream-colored walls and realized they had all been painted by Sally. Audrey ran her right index finger across Sally's initials in the bottom left corner of one picture.

She spent a moment looking at the paintings, most of them of mountain scenes although there was one beach scene with a cliff behind it. Probably Northern California, Audrey thought. And then when she returned to the den and picked up the two paintings leaning against the cabinet, she saw that one was of some flowers and the other was the pool. It wasn't finished; it looked as if Sally had started and had set it there to dry while she went to do something else.

Everything she saw told her that Sally didn't know she was going to die.

"What the attorney told me is she was found in her bed, as if she went to take a nap and didn't wake up," Audrey's mother had said. "She was supposed to have some people over for dinner that night and when she didn't respond to the phone, one of the neighbors who had a key went inside and found her dead." She shook her head. "She was alone for so long and she died alone."

But none of that had meant anything to Audrey until now. She was getting some idea of who Sally was, the woman who left her everything, even if it was by default.

Once again she didn't have long to think about it. The doorbell rang.

"I don't think I heard my doorbell ring in two years," Audrey mumbled, feeling as if she were in a time warp where people didn't text first.

"Hi, dear!" exclaimed Betty, waving. She was wearing a bathrobe. At first Audrey was surprised but then she remembered Betty had said she was going to the pool. "I would have called but I wasn't sure if the phone was still working. I know you young people only use cell phones so maybe you had the phone turned off."

Audrey wanted to laugh. She had only been there an hour. She hadn't paid much attention to the push button phone by Sally's bed or the yellow wall phone with the long cord hanging in the kitchen.

She let Betty in and once again they stood in the hall together. "The ladies are free tonight if you are. We thought maybe you could use a good meal since we're sure there are no groceries here."

Why not? Audrey thought. Let me them feed me and start telling me who Sally was.

"Sure," she said, not hesitating.

"Great!" Betty pointed across the street. "My house is right there. Is 5:00 okay? We like to eat early."

Audrey smiled. Maybe this was how things were done in Albuquerque.

After Betty left, Audrey glanced at the grandfather clock in the living room and realized it was already 3:00 p.m. She brought her belongings in from the car—what little she had brought, since she didn't plan to stay. School started August 22, and she planned to be back.

"Did you tell them you were going away for the summer?" Mandy had inquired.

Audrey had shook her head. "No reason. I'll be back for school to start and tell them all about my big summer adventure then."

She took her belongings down the hall, not sure which bedroom to use. She stopped at Sally's and stood there, a bag in each hand and her pillow under her arm.

The bed had no sheets on it (surely they had been removed with the body), but it felt strange knowing that was where Sally died. Audrey reminded herself she didn't plan to stay and went back down the hall to a room that appeared to have been a guest room.

When she opened the walk-in closet, she craned her head around the corner and saw that it was filled with dresses. Not just any dresses but vintage dresses from the sixties. Audrey began to pull them out one by one.

This is definitely a time warp, Audrey thought. It was as if someone had moved Jackie Kennedy's closet to Albuquerque: sheath dresses, party dresses, brocade, cotton, linen. But mostly simple lines.

A green dress caught her eye—the color of a Granny Smith apple—and Audrey hung it facing her on the rod. It looked more like Kate Spade than the sixties. The brocade pattern gave it a sense of depth, much like the pool water Sally had painted on the canvas in the den. The sleeveless top with a high neck looked as if it needed a set of pearls.

I'm sure there are some around here, Audrey joked with herself. She ran her fingers across the fabric, across the plastic buttons, raised with matching green paint on them, and down the flared skirt to the hem.

"Kate Spade in my time warp," Audrey said softly. "Maybe Kate's mom."

She pulled the dress down from rod and turned behind her where a full-length mirror had been attached to the back of the closet door. Audrey held the dress in front of her and ran her hand along it.

Two years ago, she knew, the dress would have fit. But now Audrey would need to lose weight to it zipped up. For the first time she was upset that she had cared so little about herself over the past year. She sadly put it back in the closet and got ready to take a shower and dress for dinner with the ladies of Aspen Hills.

Chapter 2

When the door opened at Betty's house, another woman answered. "Hi!" she exclaimed, her hair so gray it looked almost blue, like Marge Simpson in the cartoon. She reached out to hug Audrey. "I'm Esther Smith. We are so glad to meet you."

Audrey smiled and let Esther lead her to the kitchen, where Betty was standing over the oven. "The lasagna needs about twenty more minutes," she said. "But Mary Ellen isn't here yet anyway."

While the two houses were not of the same design, both kitchens were stuck in a previous time, though Betty's had undergone a relatively recent renovation. Maybe 1990. The white tiles offset the black appliances. Audrey saw a pool out the window over the sink.

"We want to know everything about you," Esther said, folding her hands together in front of her. "Sally never told us she had any family."

There's a reason for that, Audrey thought, one I thought you would know better than me. But she didn't want to spoil their excitement and bit her lip, smiling instead.

"Yoohoo!" a voice called as the front door opened. "I'm here!"

"We know you are," Betty called back, shaking her head and taking the dishes, flatware, and napkins to the dining room.

Mary Ellen burst into the kitchen and made a beeline for Audrey. "We're so glad you're here!" Audrey didn't even get a chance to turn the hug down. When Mary Ellen backed away, she pushed her glasses up on her nose and took a good look at Sally. "You have her eyes!" She turned to Esther who was still in the kitchen. "She has Sally's eyes, doesn't she?"

Esther came over, looked, and nodded. "I didn't even realize it."

"Ladies," Betty called from the dining room. "Let's have some salad."

"Oh Betty," Mary Ellen said, taking the attention off Audrey for a moment. "Do we always have to have salad? Why can't we go back to the days when we used to have Jell-O?"

"There is no nutritional value in Jell-O," Betty reminded her friend, serving up the plates around a dining room table that could easily have seated ten. "We may have eaten it all those years but it certainly didn't help us."

Mary Ellen leaned over the table to Audrey. "She's always trying to get us to eat better. Ever since she gave up smoking."

"I heard that, ME!" Betty called out.

Audrey looked around her. Betty didn't have as many dishes and as much glassware as Sally did. Her dining room was simple yet elegant. Before they could start asked questions, Audrey had one for them. "Where are your husbands?"

All went quiet.

The timer went off on the oven and Betty left the room.

"Saved by the bell," Esther laughed under her breath, watching her friend leave, before turning back to Audrey. "Betty's Warren walked out on her years ago." Mary Ellen shook her head. Audrey looked over and Esther was staring at her salad. "The louse wanted to be with his twenty-something secretary."

"Who promptly left him after about two years," Esther contributed.

"Betty got the house and a nice monthly payment," Mary Ellen said.

She held her hand to her heart. "My Gene died two years ago." She began to shake her head and Audrey felt bad she asked.

"My Larry is in a nursing home. He has Alzheimer's and has no idea who I am." Esther's sadness permeated the room. The last husband left, but having no idea of the life they had shared together.

Audrey gulped, feeling sad for all of them.

"And you know Sally's Patrick died so many years ago. Had a heart attack on the eighth green of the Aspen Hills golf course at fifty years old. I still remember that day." Mary Ellen continued to shake her head.

Audrey hadn't known. Fifty. Shirley had told her that Sally was three years younger than Patrick. At age forty-seven she was widowed.

"Why didn't she ever marry again?" Audrey blurted out.

Esther laughed and looked at Audrey. "We come from a different time. We had an obligation to our husbands, even when our marriages were over."

Betty had returned and set the lasagna near her own place at the table so she could serve everyone.

In a short time, Audrey began to see how much the four women meant to each other. They had been through a lot. She knew they missed Sally and they probably were scared that Sally's death was a reminder their own lives were nearing the end. Audrey was a breath of fresh air for them, yet a connection to a past they couldn't have back.

"That's enough gloom and doom," Betty said, handing Audrey a slice of lasagna. "We want to know about you."

"Yes, you aren't in Kansas anymore," Mary Ellen said, bursting out laughing. "I'm sorry I just had to say that."

"What do you want to know?" Audrey wasn't sure what to say or where to start. Or what was interesting.

"You didn't come with a family," Betty noted.

"I don't have one." Audrey played with the noodles and tomato sauce a little. "He left me. He said he didn't love me and that he never did. We lived the big suburban lie for ten years."

All three women gasped.

"You poor dear," Mary Ellen said, holding her hand over her heart.

"I wouldn't wish that on my worst enemy," Betty said, putting her fork down and shaking her head. "Was there another woman?"

"I don't know if there was then but there is now," Audrey admitted.

So much for going to Albuquerque to start life anew, she thought. It's all coming up again.

But the tone soon changed. While Audrey was taking a bite of lasagna, the three woman looked at each other.

"Well, we're going to have to find you a new man," Esther said.

"Oh no," Audrey told them, holding her hand out in front of her as if that would stop them. "I don't want a new man. I don't want a man at all."

"You're just saying that because you're exhausted from the journey," Mary Ellen interjected. Audrey wasn't sure what journey she was referring to—the drive from Kansas?

She thought of the green dress and her weight. And her hair gone dirty blonde. She was sure her green eyes didn't sparkle anymore. Audrey tried not to look in the mirror anymore, for fear of what she might see. Someone she didn't like, someone who wasn't the woman she used to be.

No one gave her a chance to speak, though. They were clearly plotting. Audrey kept eating, slowly. The others had forgotten their food.

"I know exactly who we need to set her up with," Esther said.

"That handsome young man that lives next to Gloria and Sam!" Mary Ellen exclaimed.

"Yes!" Betty agreed.

"Nooooo," Audrey told them.

"Yesssss!" they all agreed.

"We don't know his name," Mary Ellen started to say. "He lives down the street. He's a doctor." She turned to the other two women. "Has he ever been married?"

"I'm not sure," Betty admitted, putting her elbows on the table. "Maybe he was during medical school. Didn't he tell someone he was married for a short time?"

"It doesn't matter," Esther said. She turned to Audrey. "He's a primary care physician. He works normal hours. He has a dog."

"And he's very handsome!" Mary Ellen reminded her.

"Mmmhmm," Esther agreed.

"No way," Audrey told them.

Later that night, in the bed in the guest room, she couldn't sleep. As tired as she was from the long drive, arriving at Sally's house, and then dinner with "the ladies," as she kept wanting to call them, she thought about how much easier it would be to be on her own. Being with someone wasn't on her radar.

There was something else no one knew. Audrey got out of bed and walked around the house in the dark, finally going outside and sitting by the pool. The pool light had gone on; probably on a timer, she thought. Audrey lay in a lounge chair by the pool, not realizing how cool Albuquerque nights were. She walked inside, found a blanket in the hall closet, and went back to the lounge chair, watching the water.

She didn't like herself. Seeing that dress, and knowing that two years ago it would have fit, made her angry and depressed.

"Don't let yourself go," her teacher friend Donna had warned her. "It's much harder to lose the weight than it is to put it on. I know from experience." She pinched her side. "I call this my divorce flab. It's the lasting gift Ronnie so kindly gave me when he left."

"That will never happen," Audrey assured her.

And then it did, without her even realizing what was happening. The margaritas and chips on Friday nights with her friends came first. She thought getting out was important—part of her healing. She didn't realize that it was the wrong kind of getting out. She should have been getting out to the gym with her friends. Or getting out to eat a salad.

And each time she was invited to a party she always made sure she ate.

"You need to keep up your strength," her grandmother had told her the first time she saw her after Rick announced he wanted a divorce. And as Grandma McLatchen walked away she muttered, "That bastard."

"I heard that, Matilda!" Grandpa McLatchen called from across the room, where he was watching golf on television.

"Oh, stop with your holy ways," Grandma called to him from her spot in the kitchen where she was getting dinner ready. "He hurt our granddaughter. He doesn't deserve any forgiveness."

And that was a whole different ball game, Audrey thought.

She worried that not forgiving Rick would keep her from moving on. While she understood her grandmother's emotions, especially because she felt the same way, she knew that her grandfather was good at forgiving people and moving on. He lived the most peaceful life of anyone she knew. Whenever Audrey saw him, he would greet her with a big hug and a kiss and when he pulled back, his blue eyes held such kindness.

It was not the same on the other side of the family, the parents who had raised her father and Sally. Audrey still didn't know what had happened, and it was apparent that the ladies didn't know either. Sally must never have talked about her family.

Audrey didn't realize she had drifted off to sleep until she woke up to the sun coming over the trees in the yard. She sat up and yawned, taking a moment to remember where she was.

As she walked inside, thinking how good a cup of coffee would be, she remembered that no one had lived in the house for some time. There probably wasn't any food. In the kitchen she spotted an old Mr. Coffee machine on the counter by the sink but the cabinet looked as if someone had cleared out the food; she hoped this had kept mice away.

"Grocery store," Audrey said to herself, remembering that she saw it coming down the hill before she turned into Aspen Hills. Sharp's.

At 6 a.m. the store was deserted except for the red-polo shirt wearing employees who were stocking shelves and adding produce to the depleted piles.

"Coffee, sugar, milk, fruit," Audrey mumbled, trying to remember her list. She had a pen but had found no blank paper in the house. "Greens. Lots of greens." She forgot to look and see if Sally had a blender. Surely there was no juicer.

She filled her cart with the items she knew she would need for the day, wanting to reach for a frozen pizza but pulling her hand away and walking down to the low-calorie frozen dinners instead.

While a woman with a cart full of items, probably buying for a family with several children, checked out at the only open register, Audrey looked at the tabloids.

All the perfect marriages . . . not so perfect, she thought. But maybe some still were and the writers and the public were stirring up something that wasn't really there. As the old song said, no one knows what goes on behind closed doors.

As the woman's items were placed in bags, room opened up on the conveyor belt for Audrey's groceries. Audrey looked next to the magazines: the candy bars. She found herself wanting to grab one. Then she did.

She hadn't realized someone was behind her. As quickly as she had grabbed the candy, she put it back. She looked again, wondering if it was her own shadow scaring her. Or maybe it was her conscience. No, it was just a man standing there with something wrapped and a banana.

"You don't want me to see you're buying a candy bar?" he asked.

Audrey looked up to see he was smiling. "I thought you were my conscience reminding me I don't need one," she said sheepishly. "Especially at 6:30 in the morning."

"I would recommend the breakfast burritos, personally," he said, placing his items on the belt. "I'm not sure where they come from but they are some of the best in town."

Audrey nodded, unsure what a breakfast burrito was. She decided not to ask. Immediately he would know she didn't live there.

"They are just as good as the ones at Frontier," he added. "Have you had those?"

"Um, no," Audrey told him, trying to sound like she had a clue.

She looked at him—the salt and pepper thick black hair cut close to his head; brown eyes. He wore a long-sleeved blue shirt with a blue-and-white-striped tie. She was wearing a green sundress with her hair pulled back—the most presentable outfit she could muster without knowing where most of her stuff was.

"Good morning," the checker said, an older lady. "Do you have a Sharp's card?"

Audrey shook her head. "I don't."

Now he surely knew she wasn't from there.

"You can use mine," the man said, handing the woman his keys. "Then I get your rewards," he teased.

"Thank you," Audrey said, reminding herself that she would need to get one next time. At least she could use it for the summer.

As she pushed her cart away from the checkout stand, the man called to her. "Have a great day."

Audrey waved. "You, too."

When she arrived back at the house, she found the newspaper in the driveway and sat down by the pool to read it while she drank her coffee and ate a container of Greek yogurt with strawberries. Before long she heard male voices and then the hum of lawn mowers. Audrey walked around the corner from the pool to see the landscapers.

A man in a hat almost jumped when he saw her. He took his hat off and bowed.

"Hi," she said. "Are you the landscapers?"

"*No inglés,*" he said, pulling out his cell phone and making a call.

It all sounded like gibberish to Audrey as she stood and watched. Then the man handed the phone to Audrey.

"Hello," a Spanish-accented voice on the other end said. "You must be Sally's relative," he said.

"I am."

"We've been taking care of the yard for years. I always send her a bill once a month."

"Okay," Audrey said meekly, unsure when the people who took care of Sally's house would stop showing up. Sally had a team to take care of everything around her.

Back inside the house, she happened to glance at herself in the mirror as she walked by. She backed up and stood there for a moment. The sundress flowed under her breasts so no one could see the belly she had accumulated during the unraveling of her life. When she had packed her car, also thinking she would be back in Kansas in the fall, she hadn't brought all the shapely clothes she had worn for years. Instead, she filled it with the shapeless garments helping her to hide what she had initially not cared about and later came to hate. She sighed and walked back outside to retrieve the newspaper and coffee. Placing them on the kitchen table, she peeked out the front of the house to see the landscapers driving away.

In the guest room she found her bathing suit. She wasn't sure why she had thrown it in the bag. She knew it was hot and dry in New Mexico—one of the few things she remembered about the state, probably from what she learned in elementary school. She always pictured it filled with desert and cactus; she was surprised that there was so much grass at Sally's house. And that what she saw so far looked like a city. When she drove in she could see the downtown, looking more like Kansas City than a southwestern desert city.

She didn't bring the bikinis. They were in a box with all her tight clothes; tops, bottoms, and dresses that had fit at one time. Now she would spill out of them. The bathing suit she brought was a two-piece, one that would cover everything but still in two pieces. She slipped into it, not looking in the mirror, and walked to Sally's room to enter the pool area via the sliding glass door.

But before she opened the sliding door, Audrey peeked in the closet and saw four one-piece swimsuits on the left. Two in blue, one black, and one red. Audrey touched them, realizing they had been well used. And next to them was a long white cover-up. It looked crocheted, with big holes, not really a cover-up to get warm so much as a cover-up because one needed to cover the swimsuit. A pretend cover-up.

From what Audrey had learned about the ladies on the block, she pictured them sitting under umbrellas by their respective pools talking on the phone to each other—although they lived across the street from one another. Then there were the water aerobics classes they attended at the country club pool. She also knew that Sally was a big swimmer.

"She swam every day," Bert the pool guy had said. "There could be snow but as long as the heater worked, she was good."

Audrey saw some slip-on sandals below the white cover-up. She pulled the cover-up off the hanger and slipped it on, hoping it slimmed her figure a bit. And hoping it would help her to understand something about Sally.

Outside at the pool, she removed the cover-up and climbed onto the diving board. It was stiff, not the kind for doing tricks off, but the kind most found in backyard pools just so people could say they had a diving board.

After standing there for a moment, looking down at her distorted figure in the water, she dove into the pool and let the water consume her.

For a brief moment, she felt freedom that she hadn't experienced in a long time. There had been a freedom when the judge had signed off on the divorce, but not like the freedom of her life before—the life when she thought she had the security of a husband who loved her and a life with him that was the envy of so many other people. The lie.

Audrey came to the surface in the shallow end and pulled herself against the wall, resting her chin on her arms folded on the pool's edge. The dry air was cool, not like the humidity of the Midwest.

She stood there for a moment thinking about how good it felt in the water. She wondered if maybe swimming had been Sally's freedom, too. Once she had read that Rose Kennedy swam in the ocean or a pool frequently. Maybe that was how many people found their peace: in water.

Audrey looked up and saw a clock near the deep end on the wall by the house. She looked ahead of her at the length of the pool. It wasn't that long but it was long enough. It could be a start.

Twenty minutes, she told herself. I can do twenty minutes.

She set to swimming laps, cutting through the water and letting it move around the pool as she moved along. She swam a few laps freestyle, going back to her high school competitive swimming days. And then set to backstroke, the one she had been best at. She loved freestyle, a simple way get to the other side of the pool as quickly as possible, but her coach, Dan Roberts, knew she could backstroke like no one else.

"You will win relays and make it to state," he would tell her after she saw the lineup for the meets. "And we will win state."

"All because of my backstroke?" Audrey would ask doubtfully.

A big smile lit up his face.

It had been true. They won state her junior year because she swam the last leg of the medley relay, where they had been two points behind going into the race. Audrey pulled them ahead of two other teams, and it was enough to secure the title.

For years she had hated seeing the ceiling of the pools she swam in: probably the reason she was so good at it. She hated it. It was the reason she didn't want spend the next four years of her life looking at ceilings.

But now as she set into the backstroke, she saw the sky above her. Audrey had forgotten that part about backstroke: the few outdoor pools she swam in where she got to see the sky. The Albuquerque sky was so blue! She thought of sky blue, the color in the Crayola box of sixty-four crayons.

Peace in the sky, Audrey thought, flipping around under the diving board for another lap on her back.

She switched back to freestyle and enjoyed the quick pace that came with it, wondering why she had avoided a pool for so long, but then went back to the backstroke. Seeing the sky made her feel good.

"I don't know why I haven't swum in so long," she lamented to Mandy later that day in text.

"Because you felt so crappy," Mandy reminded her.

"Thanks for beating around the bush with that."

"Any time."

It was true though. She hadn't felt like doing anything for a long time. It was as if someone had zapped her zest for life out of her and wouldn't give it back. She wanted to blame Rick for taking it away, and it had taken her some time to realize that he didn't care about her. No matter what she did or said, it wasn't going to change anything. She had to let go of the past, find peace, create a new happiness .

After she and Mandy ended their conversation, Audrey walked back to the guest room. The green dress hung on the closet door where she had left it the previous day.

"I'm going to get back there," she told herself. "Somehow I will."

And then she went back to the pool with a pen and a pad of paper—she finally found one in the kitchen drawer by the phone. The ultimate goal was to wear the green dress. But really Audrey knew it was much more than that. She could have her freedom back, her peace, her happiness. She was not bound by what had happened in the past.

And she knew it wasn't just about the weight. It started with her head. It was her outlook on life that kept her from working out, that stopped her from taking care of her skin, that kept her from making the healthy meals she had long thought were so important. No more chips, chocolate bars, or extra margaritas.

This is my chance to start over, Audrey thought, watching the sun move over the pool and the light dance off the surface. Mom was right. Maybe that's why she had been brought to Sally's house. While Sally surely had no idea when she left everything to Audrey's father, maybe this was the way it was supposed to be.

Audrey walked back inside, used a magnet from a local bank to attach her list of goals to the yellow refrigerator, and started to open cabinets, taking inventory of Sally's life.

"Make this house yours," she pictured Sally telling her. "Don't worry about the future. Just make the house yours."

"I will," Audrey said, pulling out green and yellow dishes with flowers on them that made her think of split pea soup. "I mean, I am."

In the garage she found a few empty boxes and began to fill them up. It was going to take a long time but it was a start.

Chapter 3

It still felt odd to rifle through Sally's items. Maybe some people would believe it was easier because Audrey didn't actually know Sally, but it was quite the opposite. Audrey felt as though she were a burglar in the house or a babysitter looking through the parents' belongings.

Audrey stood in the door of the master bedroom and looked around. She walked into the bathroom where tubes, jars, and various other beauty items filled the drawers. Sally also had a dressing room table topped with makeup and perfume and drawers filled with jewelry.

"Patrick always bought her the most beautiful jewelry," Mary Ellen had lamented with a sigh at dinner. "He had the best taste."

As Audrey started to pick through the items, she wanted to know more. She wanted all three women to come over and tell her stories about who Sally was and the life she lived.

"And she always looked perfect, like she could walk out the door and go anywhere at a moment's notice, even when she got out of the swimming pool," Betty had added.

Audrey sat down on the dressing table stool, cushioned with a faded pink fabric, and thought for a moment. She would have to throw a lot of it out. She had no use for it and she didn't know anyone else who would. She pulled open a drawer, one filled with jeweled necklaces, bracelets, rings, earrings. Audrey rubbed her face with one hand and closed the drawer with the other.

This won't be easy, she thought.

In the next drawer down a book and some pens rested on top of some scarves. Audrey opened the book to find it was a journal. The first entry was dated two years ago. She flipped the pages, looking for the last entry: the morning Sally died.

Before she started to read, Audrey opened the bottom drawer, where she found a stack of identical journals.

Sally's life.

Sally had written her own personal history. Audrey pulled them out and put them on the floor. She opened the bottom right drawer and found a few more. These looked older. Sure enough, when she opened them, they were from the 1950s. The next drawer up held several blue Tiffany boxes. And the top drawer was filled with tissues, cotton balls, and cotton swabs.

Audrey took the books outside to the table by the pool and opened the umbrella. She glanced at the ending dates in each one and put them in order, starting with the oldest. At first she looked at the most recent one, wondering what Sally's last day was about, wondering if she knew she was going to die. It appeared to be just another day.

"A beautiful fall morning in Albuquerque. Going to swim for a bit and then paint this afternoon."

If she was going to figure out who Sally was, Audrey knew she would have to start at the beginning.

"September 5, 1955. Albuquerque

I took the train from Kansas City, saying goodbye to my parents and my brother at the station platform. Here I am in Albuquerque, New Mexico, far from the corn and instead surrounded by cacti and tumbleweeds. I'm in my room at the St. Elizabeth School for Nurses and start classes tomorrow."

Audrey couldn't read line for line, though. She found herself looking for a clue as to what happened between Sally and the rest of the family.

Mostly in the beginning the journal was about the other nursing students and the challenges they faced learning to become nurses. But then she met a man named Reuben and the entries changed.

"He came here from Wisconsin although really he is from South Texas. After serving in the Korean War he went to the University of Wisconsin to get his engineering degree. He's working for Sandia Labs. All that stuff I don't understand that went on in Los Alamos to build the bomb. But I like him. A lot. I might even love him."

Reuben was not Patrick, Audrey thought, turning the book over on the table for a moment. What happened? She wondered, staring at the pool and wishing that Sally were right there with her, swimming laps. She pictured Sally with her hair tucked under a swim cap, wearing her one-piece navy blue bathing suit, swimming back and forth while Audrey tried to ask her questions.

"Let me finish," Sally would say.

Audrey would sit on the steps of the pool, waiting for Sally to end her workout. And when she did, she would join Audrey on the steps.

But at first she didn't give her any answers.

"I loved him," was all she would say.

Audrey shook her head. She made that conversation up in her head. Totally silly and not realistic. Instead, she picked the diary back up and started flipping through it. Sally saw Reuben as much as their schedules would allow. Reuben lived with an aunt and uncle and their family. He was twenty-three. Sally was twenty.

She knew she needed to do other things. While time felt endless, Audrey had no intention of staying in Albuquerque. If she was going to get the house sold, there was a lot of cleanup to do. She took the stack of books inside and put them on the kitchen table.

Audrey walked back to the bathroom with a black plastic trash bag and started with what was easy: the makeup and all the beauty supplies, stuff Audrey wouldn't dream of using. Or least until she was Sally's age, she thought jokingly, looking at every formula for getting rid of lines and spots.

"We can't do anything about it," Betty would laugh later, running her fingers across her cheek over her own lines. "We live in the desert where the sun shines over 300 days a year. But Sally never gave up the fight."

After filling one trash bag, she walked into the garage and opened the door to outside, seeing it was garbage day.

"I can throw out this one bag," she mumbled to herself, dumping the bag into the heavy plastic can and rolling it to the street.

As she did, she saw an older man walking toward her. He was accompanied by a well-behaved chocolate lab who meandered on his leash near the man. As he got closer, Audrey could see the man was Hispanic, his hair gray and his skin dark from the sun.

She thought of her dad and stood there for a moment to wave a hello.

"Hello," he called back, waving as the dog turned toward Audrey.

"Can I say hi?" she asked the man, before bending down to pet the dog.

"Sure," the man said.

"You sure are cute," Audrey told the dog who was trying to lick her face.

"Oh thank you," the man said, making Audrey laugh.

Audrey looked at the dog. "You're cute, too."

It's my son's dog," the man said. "He has to be at work early so I try to walk him before I go golf a round here at the country club."

"That's good of you," Audrey said.

"You're from Kansas?" he asked, tilting his head toward the license plate on her car.

"I am," she said.

"Visiting family?"

"Um, no," she said. "My aunt lived here and left the house to me."

"No wonder I haven't seen anyone around here in a long time," he said. "My son just moved up here last year. It's a long way from my house but I joined the country club hoping we could spend more time together."

Audrey stood up and wiped her hands on her shorts. She got a good look at the man for the first time. His deep brown eyes radiated a kindness that made her feel happy. Whoever his family was—his son, his wife, and everyone else—they were lucky to have him.

He looked at his watch. "We better scoot," he said. "I have a 1 p.m. tee time. Come on, Sadie." He tugged at Sadie's leash and off they went before Audrey could say goodbye.

At least people are nice here, she thought, wondering if anyone her age really existed. There was the guy at the grocery store, she remembered, but figured she would never see him again. What were the chances she would shop that early in the morning?

Inside the house she found another black trash bag and kept loading up the things she knew she couldn't donate. She'd get to those next.

Audrey stood for a moment in the bathroom in the hall off the other bedrooms. She then put the bag on the counter and walked out the front door and over to Betty's house. She felt as if she were in a time warp: the others hadn't shared their phone numbers with Audrey, just their house numbers and all the details about where they lived.

"My house is the white one with the red trim and the basketball hoop that looks like it's going to fall over," Mary Ellen had said, pointing in the direction of her house.

"Hi," Betty said, looking surprised to see Audrey standing at her door. Betty was dressed for tennis: she wore a white polo and a white tennis skirt trimmed in navy blue.

"Hi," Audrey said. "Would the three of you like to come to dinner tomorrow night?"

"Oh," Betty said, her smile getting wide. "I'll ask the other girls but I'm sure they would love to. Friday was usually our Canasta night."

"Canasta?" Audrey asked, looking confused.

"You haven't ever played Canasta?" Betty put her hands on her hips and laughed. Audrey knew she was pleased to have something to share. "Then we will teach you. We haven't been able to play since Sally died; she was our fourth person. We tried to include Iris down the street, but she's just a little different." Betty's face turned slightly. "We were never comfortable with her so we just told her we weren't playing anymore."

Audrey nodded and acted like she knew exactly what Betty was talking about.

Canasta sounds like a type of soft drink, Audrey thought as she walked back across the street to grab her keys and drive to the grocery store.

The three women arrived together the next evening. Audrey stopped Betty and Esther waiting for Mary Ellen walking up the street before they rang her doorbell. Betty carried what looked like the Canasta cards, Mary Ellen had a coconut cake—"I hope it's okay," she said, sliding up to Audrey and slightly whispering as if the others had no idea what was going on, "Dessert was always my job for Canasta"—and Esther held a wooden bowl filled with chips.

"You had appetizers?" Audrey asked, remembering what Betty told her each one would bring.

Esther nodded. "And the dip is in my purse. I couldn't carry them together."

She handed the bowl to Audrey and went digging into her purse for the dip.

"It shouldn't be that hard to find," Audrey teased her. "It's not like it's a lipstick."

Betty and Mary Ellen were walking around the house; Audrey spotted them out of the corner of her eye. She could see the sadness on their faces as they stood in the living room, one of the rooms Audrey had yet to touch.

"It looks as if she just went out to the store," Betty said to Esther.

"Or to swim."

Audrey swallowed hard and began to think she shouldn't have invited them over. Maybe it was a mistake.

"Let's go outside," Audrey said, grabbing a tray of drinks from the counter and pointing at Mary Ellen to grab her chips and sour cream and onion dip.

"Oh, the times we spent out here laughing," Mary Ellen said, sitting down at the patio table by the pool.

"And eating Sally's Jell-O!" Esther reminded her.

Betty looked over at Audrey. "Sally loved to make Jell-O. She had every Tupperware mold possible."

"So that's why the cabinet was filled with Jell-O boxes!" Audrey dipped a pretzel in the sour cream mix. "It was the only food left in the house."

"Yes," Betty laughed, taking a sip of the lemonade that Audrey had handed her. "Oh my. This is wonderful. Girls, did you try the lemonade?"

The others nodded as they took sips. "Wherever did you learn to make lemonade like that?"

Audrey patted herself on the back. "I'm a Midwestern girl. And we used to entertain all the time." What she didn't tell them was that it was even better with tequila. She would introduce that later as she got to know them better, She was beginning to be sure they did their share of drinking around each other's tables over the years.

"Maybe some lemon Jell-O might be good," Audrey suggested.

"Remember that one that Sally would make with the marshmallows?" Esther asked the other two. She turned to Audrey. "Did you ever have your aunt's Jell-O concoctions?"

Audrey took a deep breath. "I never knew my aunt." She said it simply as if the statement were supposed to stand alone with nothing around it.

"You didn't?" Betty asked. She waved her hand around. "And she left you all this?"

"She left it to my dad," Audrey corrected Betty, knowing that Betty had no idea.

"Then how did you get it? The attorney told us it was yours."

"My dad died of a brain tumor five years ago. The will said that if he died before Sally, it was to go to his children and I'm his only child."

"But you didn't know Sally," Betty said again.

"I didn't even know my dad had a sister."

All three took a deep breath and looked shocked.

Audrey decided to turn the tables. She leaned forward, her arms folded on the table in front of her. "Did you know that Sally had a brother?"

The three of them thought for a moment and looked at each other. "I guess not," Esther said.

"I don't recall her ever mentioning family," Betty added. "She only talked about Patrick's family. They spent all their time with them. I figured that Betty's family lived too far away to travel here."

"That's my point," Audrey said. "Sally didn't talk about her family and my family didn't talk about her. But does anyone know why?"

The three women again looked baffled.

"Do you?" Betty asked Audrey. "You must know something."

Audrey shook her head. "That's why I'm asking you three. My mom doesn't even know and she is the last tie to my dad's family now that Sally is gone. Their parents died about twenty years ago when I was in junior high."

"I don't understand," Betty kept saying. "She and Patrick had everything."

"Except kids," Mary Ellen reminded her. "That they never had."

"Sally always said there was something wrong with one of them but she would never say more than that," Esther added.

Betty turned to Audrey, who was on her right. "You don't understand. They were the couple we all wanted to be. They had everything but the kids, but that never kept them from having our kids over. They did everything together outside of when Patrick was working. Sally wanted to keep working as a nurse, but Patrick encouraged her to stay home and work at her painting."

Audrey felt some sadness for her aunt. And that was just about all she knew. There was still a missing piece and no one seemed to know what it was. Audrey wasn't ready to tell them about the diaries. Not yet.

Instead, she got up and went to the kitchen to get the burgers to put them on the grill.

"Do you have green chile?" Betty asked, looking over at Audrey starting the gas grill.

"What is green chile?" Audrey asked. "That's about as foreign sounding as Canasta."

The three women laughed. "I bet Sally had some in the freezer," Mary Ellen said, getting up and going to the kitchen.

"If you don't know what green chile is, then you haven't been introduced to New Mexico yet," Betty said.

Mary Ellen returned with a plastic bag with something green that was frozen inside it. "This is green chile. I'll run it under the faucet and defrost some."

"What do we do with it?" Audrey asked no one in particular.

"Put it on the burgers," Esther said.

Mary Ellen returned with the strips of the long green roasted pepper in a white bowl. "I thought about putting these in the Waterford bowl," she said, then laughed.

"Sally would haunt you over that!" Betty laughed and three women shared a giggle.

"Um, what do you mean?" Audrey asked, bringing out the buns and condiments from the kitchen. She stood by the table as they kept giggling.

"Patrick used to do that to annoy her," Mary Ellen said.

Audrey walked back to the grill. As the voices of the three women remembering all their times together drifted toward her, she thought she was finally learning more about Sally. Still, she had no idea what would make Sally and the family not acknowledge each other for all those years.

Setting the platter of burgers on the table, Mary Ellen immediately put a bun on her plate and reached for a cheeseburger. "I'll show you exactly what to do with the green chile." She looked over at Audrey, who sat watching, her hands in her lap. "Be ready to be addicted," Mary Ellen warned. "It's a type of pepper that's roasted and peeled. We freeze it so we have some all year round. The best part is the fall when the roasters are out and you can smell it in the air."

"I love fall here," Esther sighed.

Audrey smiled as Mary Ellen laid several strips of the chile on her burger and then added the rest of her chosen condiments.

"You like ketchup on your burger?" Betty asked, turning up her nose at her friend. "I don't remember that."

"That because we haven't had burgers in so long," Esther reminded her gently.

The three of them nodded in unison. "Not since Gene died," Mary Ellen said quietly, setting her burger back on the plate and putting her hands folded in her lap for a moment. The other two did the same out of respect and Audrey joined them.

"But now," Betty said, ending the silence and picking her burger back up, "we can have new traditions with Audrey!"

Audrey still hadn't taken a bite of her burger. "But I'm not going to stay," she protested. "I plan to sell the house and go back to Kansas."

The three of them were quiet as they looked at her. "And what are you going back to Kansas for?" Esther reminded her. "Why don't you stay here and start a new life."

The others nodded. Audrey let it go. She knew they were going to do everything they could to keep her in Albuquerque. As she took a bite of the burger, wanting to finally try this green chile they kept talking about, she figured they were looking at each other, as if they were plotting about how to keep Audrey there.

"Oh my," Audrey said, covering her mouth with her hand and looking at the others. "This is incredible."

She wasn't sure how she would describe the chile taste to anyone in Kansas. It definitely wasn't a green bell pepper. It had some kick but not much.

"And that's the mild version," Mary Ellen teased. "We've gotten soft in our old age."

"Wait until you try the red chile."

"It has a kick but it's . . . perfect."

"We'll turn her into a New Mexican yet," Betty teased, looking at her friends. Esther and Mary Ellen nodded their agreement.

Audrey had put up the yellow umbrella she found in the garage and the four women continued to sit there after finishing their burgers, then eating the cake that Mary Ellen had brought with her.

"You have to eat a bigger slice," she kept saying to Audrey who insisted on something smaller.

"I'm sure it's wonderful," Audrey said. She ran her hand in the air across the swimming pool to her left. "But I'm trying to get back to bikini form."

They all ahhhhed. "We get it," Esther said. "Those string things you women wear now don't leave much to be hidden."

"Every inch of fat can be seen," Betty sighed. "I'm glad ours had more coverage."

"But you don't look like you need to lose anything," Mary Ellen noted, looking Audrey up and down.

"It's all here," Audrey said, patting her belly. "Trust me. It's been a difficult time but somehow I have to get past it."

"How Sally loved to swim!" Betty said, looking off into the distance as if she were watching Sally in the pool. "It didn't matter how cold it was or if there was snow. As long as the heater worked, she was out here in the pool."

"It would be too humid for this in Kansas," Audrey reminded them, changing the subject without realizing it.

The sun had begun to set, the shadows hovering larger over the yard.

"Oh my, it is much too humid in the Midwest," Mary Ellen said. "I grew up in Michigan and we'd be swatting mosquitoes left and right."

"Are all of you from somewhere else?" Audrey wondered.

"Oh yes," Betty said. "We came here with our husbands. Mine was in the Air Force and so was Mary Ellen's. Esther's came as an engineer out of college."

"But Sally came to become a nurse?"

"She did," Esther piped in, crumbling her paper napkin on her empty plate. "She said she wanted to see the world, and New Mexico was as far as she got."

"How did she meet Patrick?"

They looked at each other. "I don't know. We all came here after being married so I'm not sure we ever talked to her about it. I believe Patrick came here with the Air Force. It's hard to leave after you experience New Mexico weather."

"And green chile," Betty added. "I have to send some to my kids every year."

"Many people moved to the desert for the dry air because it was thought to cure TB," Esther explained.

After the women left—Mary Ellen making sure to put the rest of the cake in the refrigerator. "You enjoy it. You'll get into that bikini soon enough," she said with a smile. It was hard to say no to the white hair and blue eyes that twinkled. "I'll get my dish another time"—Audrey thought about Sally as she brushed her teeth.

It still wasn't adding up. Audrey thought back on her own life with her family, particularly the interactions with her grandparents. Everyone seemed normal to her. She loved when they came to her swim meets, her grandmother always baking chocolate chip cookies for the team.

"That's the one thing I remember about swimming," her teammate Marla had once commented on Facebook, "your grandma's cookies!"

"We are your biggest fans," her grandfather would boom after a race, no matter how Audrey had done. Audrey always knew she was loved by them. He would lean over and whisper, "Bigger fans than your parents but don't tell them that," sending Audrey into hysterics, especially after she hadn't done well. She would quickly forget as they all went out for pizza, usually taking several of her teammates with them.

And now she was left wondering who they really were. Or was it Sally? Her dad was much like her grandparents. As she climbed into bed, happy she had the trio over, as she now referred to them, she was tired but the wheels kept turning about Sally. Yet there was still a lot of reading. Maybe the answers were waiting for her in the journals she hadn't opened yet.

*****

Audrey stood by the pool at 7 a.m., looking at the sky, wondering if there were ever any clouds in Albuquerque. She wasn't sure she had seen one in the two weeks since she moved there. She stepped onto the diving board and set to swimming her laps, let her mind wander as she cut through the water, stopping only when she heard the timer she set by the pool playing a funky dance tune.

When she came up for air, she felt as if a shadow were standing above her and she jumped at first.

"*Dios mio!*" It was an older Mexican lady with her hair pulled up in a bun, her hand on her heart.

"Um, I don't speak Spanish." Audrey climbed out of the pool and pulled Sally's long white coverup over her bathing suit. It didn't matter who—she didn't want anyone to see her body. She followed the woman into the kitchen.

"Oh, okay," the woman said. She stood for a moment, looking past Audrey, and then pointed at the kitchen counter and grabbed a sponge. "I clean. *Limpio.*"

"Oh," Audrey said, smiling and laughing. "You are Alicia?"

"*Si*. Yes. You are Senora's . . . granddaughter?"

"Yes," Audrey smiled at her.

The woman's eyes lit up. Her face looked as if life had been hard but she still held a lot of spirit. Audrey grabbed a towel and wrapped it around her head to dry her hair.

"I speak some English," Alicia said, holding two fingers together. "*Un poquito.*"

"Ah, *un poquito*. A little." Audrey laughed. She had taken French in high school and knew not a word of Spanish.

Realizing that Alicia was probably not going to understand anything she said, Audrey spoke anyway. "Go ahead and clean. But I am cleaning out the house so it's a mess."

When Alicia didn't respond, Audrey took her arm and waved for Alicia to follow her. They walked into Sally's dressing room, which looked as if it had been hit by a tornado. While the trash had been removed and black garbage bags of donations filled half the garage, there was still a lot left. Audrey had no idea what she would do with the jewelry or the handbags and had left them where she found them.

"She had exquisite taste!" Betty had said when Audrey had shown them the bathroom the night before. "None of us could rival that nor how much she saved each time she went to Kistler's and got something on sale."

"I don't think she ever paid full price for anything," Esther remarked, looking around the room.

"Yet she looked like she spent too much on everything," Betty said.

"*Oh, amo!*" Alicia picked up a chocolate brown Coach bag and stroked it. "*Esplendida.*" She held it next to her as if it were a puppy. "*Señora adora la bolsa.*"

"The bag?"

"Yes," Alicia said.

Audrey didn't flinch. "You can have it."

Alicia looked confused. There she stood in her t-shirt, jeans, and flip flops with the expensive Coach bag in her arms. "Yes? Me?" Alicia pointed at herself.

"Yes, you." Audrey said, seeing how much the bag meant to her. "It's yours."

"*Gracias! Gracias!*"

Alicia hugged Audrey, her smile radiating throughout the house. She sang as she worked, making Audrey happy that she had done something for the woman who clearly cared about Sally.

Before she left the dressing room, Audrey stood for moment. Everyone loved Sally yet something had come between her and the family. Audrey still didn't know what it was.

After she showered, Audrey took the journal she was reading outside and sat under the umbrella by the pool to stay out of Alicia's way. Alicia was happily vacuuming and singing when she wasn't talking rapid-fire Spanish on the phone.

The shadows lingered over the pool, shading the yard from the desert sun. Audrey opened the book and found the grocery store receipt she was using for a bookmark. She didn't dare dog-ear a corner and ruin the journal. As she began to read, she felt herself slip back in time and Sally seemed to be right there with her, telling her the story.

"He used to take me to a restaurant downtown," Sally said, dressed as if she were going to church, wearing a peach shift. She looked about thirty. It was as if she were stuck somewhere in time and that's where she had to be tell Audrey this part of the story.

Audrey looked around, thinking about pinching herself. She squinted her eyes. Was Sally really with her? Audrey shook her head as if that would make her see better. Sally didn't go away. She kept talking.

"It was actually a diner. Since I worked at the hospital, it was just a few blocks for me to walk. But he had to drive from the base where he was working. Oh my. Central was such a different road."

"Central?" Audrey asked.

"Route 66. Central is the road here." Sally pointed in the sky. "It takes you all through Albuquerque and beyond."

Audrey nodded. She kind of knew what Sally meant.

"He would go into work at 5 a.m. just so he would have enough time to spend my entire lunch with me and still drive back and forth to the base." Sally looked out at the trees that lined the back of the yard and then took a sip of the glass of iced tea in front of her.

There was so much Audrey wanted to know but she kept her eyes on the words, her focus on Sally. She had to let Sally tell the story on her own time, at her own pace.

"Oh dear," Sally suddenly said. Audrey jumped a little, worried that something was wrong. "I just realized I forgot to tell you how we met."

That was true, Audrey realized, flipping back in the journal. How had Sally forgotten something so important? She talked about Reuben but not where she met him.

"There was a place on Central downtown called the Flamingo. It had a tropical theme, which we loved since we were in the desert. It was a great place to relax with a drink on a Friday evening after work and maybe find someone to dance with. I went there with my friends Susan and Evelyn one October evening. It was still warm, and I had on this beautiful green brocade dress. Oh, how I loved that dress! It was sleeveless and the skirt flared out just enough that it made a statement when one of the boys would twirl me around. Oh, but it was still demure. I was not one of those, how would you modern girls say it? Hoochie girls?"

Audrey giggled. "Yes, that's how we would say it." And then she realized that Sally was talking about *the* dress. No wonder she had kept it.

I had just sat back down with the girls when a nice-looking dark-haired man with the most beautiful brown eyes walked over and said, "I'd love to dance with you."

Sally looked at Audrey. "It was love at first sight. While I always hoped it would happen to me, I was still surprised when it did."

"Tell me about Reuben," Audrey blurted out. She sat back realizing she shouldn't have said it.

"It's okay," Sally laughed. "I love to talk about him since I never get to anymore. He was such a wonderful man. Those farm boys in Kansas had no idea how to treat a woman. Reuben was there for me, he worried about me, he cherished me. No one ever loved me as he did."

Audrey placed her elbows on the patio table and leaned forward again. She wanted to ask Sally what happened, why she didn't marry Reuben. She remembered what her mother had told her, though. "Don't ask too many questions," Shirley warned. "If someone wants to tell you, they will."

And so Audrey kept listening instead. "We were inseparable after that first night together. I could only go out for lunch three days a week because of the way my shifts at the hospital worked. But he was there each of those three days.

"We would go to Ida's Diner on Central." Sally stopped and looked back at Audrey. "Have you been there? It's still there."

Audrey shook her head, not sure if Sally was in present time or somewhere around 1970. She would look up Ida's Diner though.

"Well, make sure you get the grilled cheese. I never figured out what they did but I could never make one as good as that."

"Señorita?"

Audrey was startled from the journal. She looked up to see Sally gone, Alicia standing around the corner. Alicia waved. "Bedding? Do I *limpar . . .* ?" she stopped to think what the next word was. "Wash? Sheets?"

Yes, Audrey nodded. Alicia disappeared back into the house.

Audrey shut the journal and sat for a moment, taking a deep breath. Sally had been right there with her, telling her about Reuben. She loved him, yet there was so little Audrey knew. Audrey stared at the pool, a shadow cast over half of it as the sun came over the property. By afternoon it would fully be in the sun, feeling more like the desert than it did now.

She picked up the journal and walked inside to Google Ida's Diner. If it was still there, she knew where she was going to have lunch.

Chapter 4

Downtown Albuquerque appeared to be in a period of revitalization. It wasn't crowded but there were enough people to say it wasn't dead. Audrey drove the entire way on Central, starting at one end of the city, where she lived, and going all the way to the center.

"Oh my goodness," Betty said later. "We did that in the old days before the freeway but now I wouldn't dream of going that way. It would take way too long."

"Gene would never take the freeway," Esther lamented, "if he could still take Central he would."

She passed by motels that had been boarded up, a few that appeared to offer hourly rates, and then the area of town near the University of New Mexico called Nob Hill. It was lively in Nob Hill, much more than downtown, as if it had a head start.

While Nob Hill was filled with boutique stores and retro restaurants, downtown still had a few open slots where the building was waiting for someone to come along and take it over.

"I hear they have quite a few bars downtown now," Mary Ellen had said. "I suppose that's good for the young people."

"As if we never drank," Betty snorted and the three women began to laugh.

Ida's Diner sat on the corner of Central and 5th St., with a big pink sign over the door.

As Audrey drove around the block to park and then walked to the diner, her bag in one hand and the journal in the other, she wondered if Ida was still alive.

"Hi," the waitress who happened to be clearing the table by the door greeted her. "Have a seat wherever you want and I'll be right over." The older woman in the vintage brown dress and apron picked up the coffee mugs and placed them on a tray.

Audrey slid into a red booth halfway across the restaurant, making sure she faced the front and the light streaming in from the windows. Everything felt as if it had a layer of not grime but history on it: the vinyl booths, the table, the plastic-coated menus. The black-and-white tiled floor.

"Definitely the grilled cheese," Audrey mumbled to herself, halfheartedly looking at the rest of the menu. She wanted to connect with Sally and that's what Sally told her to have.

"What can I get you, hon?" the waitress asked, pulling out her worn pad and a pencil she had stuck behind her ear.

"The grilled cheese, please," Audrey said, trying to sound confident, as if she had been there before.

"Would you like green chile on that?"

Audrey looked at her and quickly lost her confidence. "Does everyone here put green chile on everything?"

"You aren't from here are you?" The woman smiled and laughed, not in a way to make Audrey feel stupid but wanting to help her feel at home.

"I'm from Kansas."

"Yeah, that explains it. I'll tell you what. Get it with the green chile and if you don't like it, I'll have them make you a new one. But I guarantee you'll be hooked."

Audrey nodded and pulled out the journal to start reading after the waitress had left, not paying much attention to her surroundings as she dove back into where she left off.

"If you don't like it, I'll take it and have it as a snack," a voice from behind her said.

Audrey was startled and almost asked, "Is that what strangers do here? Offer to eat the food of people they don't know?"

But when she turned to look, a familiar face smiled back her from the next booth over. There weren't that many familiar faces to her, especially outside the house. The guy from the grocery store!

"Hi," she said, grinning at him.

"You're a long way from the store," he said. "And I don't see any candy bars."

"And I don't see a burrito on your plate," Audrey said, peering over at his empty dish.

"That's because I ate it. But you made a wise choice: the green chile grilled cheese is great here. Like no other." And he leaned over toward her to whisper. "But the breakfast burritos at Frontier are still the best."

"Do you come here often?" Audrey raised her eyebrows. "Why didn't you go there?"

He pointed east. "I work at the hospital about five blocks away. I'd have to drive to go to Frontier."

The hospital. "Is that the only one nearby?"

"You don't know?"

Audrey laughed. "Um, no."

"It's the only one downtown." He stuck out his hand over the back of the booth. "I'm Vince Montoya."

"I'm Audrey Matthews. I mean Thomas." She shook her head and immediately felt stupid.

"I really do know who I am," she said, looking at him. "I got divorced a year ago and I thought when I moved here I would change back to my maiden name."

"You're new here?"

"From Kansas."

"Welcome to Albuquerque," Vince said, standing up. "New Mexico is the Land of Entrapment, so don't plan on ever leaving."

As he left the tip on the table, Audrey thought about how kind everyone was. It wasn't that she expected them to be mean or indifferent, but she felt welcome in New Mexico. It was like the state was wrapping its arms around her and taking her in, making her feel comforted in a way she hadn't experienced since her marriage ended.

The waitress placed a plate with the grilled cheese sandwich, chopped green chile spilling out of it, and a stack of potato chips off to the side, in front of Audrey.

"Maybe one day you'd like to meet me here," Vince said, standing over Audrey's table. He pointed his head at the plate in front of her. "Providing you like the grilled cheese, of course."

She grabbed a napkin from the dispenser and wrote her cell phone number on it.

"Must be a Kansas area code." Vince joked. "It's not 505."

"That's right," she laughed.

Audrey wasn't sure what she thought as she watched him walk out of the diner. When she called Mandy back in Kansas later, Audrey flopped back on the guest bed and felt like she was back in high school. She was scared, she was insecure. But she was also excited.

"Is he cute? If he works at a hospital, what does he do? Tell me more."

Audrey realized that in all her excitement, she had no idea what Vince did at the hospital.

"He's Hispanic?" Mandy asked after Audrey told her his name. "Like tall dark and handsome?"

"OMG, so tall dark and handsome!" Audrey giggled. "With a tie and a chiseled face and salt and pepper hair."

"Oooh lala," Mandy laughed. She got serious for a moment. "It's about time you had something to look forward to. Or rather, someone to look forward to. After all that asshole did to you. The right man is going to come along. I believe that. You never did anything to deserve what he did to you."

Audrey felt herself sober up. The free moment of peace dissipated as she looked around the room. She had a lot to do; she had no idea what the future held. She tried to tell herself it didn't matter. She was here in Albuquerque for now.

"Life puts you where you're supposed to be," Audrey remembered someone telling her.

And life has me here, she thought. The big arms of New Mexico were comforting and maybe that was what she needed: to finally feel some peace.

Still, she didn't feel settled. And seeing the green dress hanging, she so badly wanted to try it on but felt her stomach and knew it wasn't the time. It would come, and she hoped she had a place to wear it.

Chapter 5

As Audrey swam her laps the next morning, she felt a newfound purpose. A man had taken an interest in her. Not just any man but a handsome and interesting man. Not the cashier at the gas station. She felt lighter as she swam her laps and thought of Sally swimming next to her before they would finish together and sit on the steps and have a conversation.

"Oh, he's not like any boy you know from Kansas," Sally said.

Audrey thought for a moment. That was true. Most of the males in her life had been, well, white. There had been few Hispanics in Kansas when she was growing up. She began to swim again and thought for a moment. She remembered Roberto Santiago.

In eighth grade, Roberto, called only that on the first day of school until he asked the teachers to refer to him as Rob, had moved from Arizona to Kansas City with his family. The girls instantly swooned over him. He was exotic, being from Arizona and all, with his dark eyes and dark skin. And unlike all the other boys, he loved to play soccer.

"Football is okay," he would say shrugging his shoulders, "but the real football is where it's at."

They all felt a little bad for him, though.

"Dude, why did your family move to Kansas? That must suck for you," Chris Braun asked one day before social studies.

"My dad got transferred," Rob sighed. "He says we're going back in two years. I'm hoping to go live with my aunt in Phoenix, though."

While he had never seen snow, he wasn't that interested in it and at lunch Audrey and her friends Katie and Marcy talked about how cute he was.

"This morning I heard him tell Chris Braun he might go live with his aunt," Audrey said.

"How did you hear that?" Marcy asked, surprised, taking a granola bar out of her paper lunch bag.

"Duh, she sits in back of him," Katie reminded her friend sarcastically. "Thomas, Santiago."

Marcy nodded and didn't say anything. Katie smirked, knowing she was right.

"I couldn't bring him home anyway," Marcy said trying to act disinterested.

"Why not?" Audrey asked.

"He's Hispanic. My dad would have a fit if I brought home a boy who wasn't white."

"Seriously?" Katie asked.

"Yeah, seriously."

"I would do it anyway. He's human. He's cute. My dad would get over it." Katie waved it off.

Audrey watched her friends go back and forth like a Ping Pong ball and then thought about her own family. She had no idea if it mattered or not until she talked to her mom a few days later.

"Mom?" Audrey finally got up the nerve to as while she did her homework at the kitchen table and Shirley stirred the spaghetti sauce.

Audrey took a deep breath. She felt nervous but she wasn't sure why. This wasn't a big deal. Or was it? She tapped her pencil against her math book.

"If I wanted to date a Hispanic boy, would it be okay?"

Shirley didn't answer right away. Audrey stared at her mom's back, surprised. She thought her mom would instantly tell her it was fine. Audrey knew something wasn't right.

"Mom? Would it be okay?"

Finally Shirley turned around and faced Audrey. "Why do you ask?" She looked uncomfortable. "Where did that come from? It's not like there are many Hispanics here in Kansas." She let out a soft laugh. "Unless of course there is an influx from Mexico I don't know about."

"A boy named Rob just moved from Arizona." Audrey shrugged her shoulders. "I was just asking. Marcy said she would never be able to bring home a Hispanic boy."

Shirley looked relieved.

"Why are you acting weird? Is it a big deal? I didn't think it was."

Shirley picked up her cup of coffee and walked over to the round heavy wood table where Audrey sat and smiled. "It's not. You can bring home whomever you want. He can be purple and we'll like him just the same."

Audrey didn't know what it was about and let it go. Rob did move back to Phoenix in the winter anyway and it became a moot point.

"That was a bummer," Katie lamented at lunch after he left. "He sure was cute. And I bet his mom made awesome tacos."

Now Audrey sat on the pool steps resting after her swim.

"Oh how Reuben's aunt could cook," Sally said. "Mmmm, the best *huevos rancheros.*"

Audrey watched Sally, wearing her navy blue swimsuit and not looking much over fifty as she relaxed on the pool steps.

"What are *huevos rancheros?*" Audrey asked shyly.

"Oh dear, they kept you in Kansas much too long!" Sally laughed. "Take a corn tortilla lightly fried and then top it with an egg, I liked my egg fried. Add some hash browns and cover it with green chile sauce. How I loved spending Sunday brunch with his family because she always made us each a plate of *huevos.*"

Sally's journal talked a lot about Rueben's family and how they took her in and treated her as one of their own. She felt as loved by them as by her own family back in Kansas.

"It was hard for me to get home to Kansas especially with work. But they came to visit, finally, and I thought it was going to be this great time for all of us." A look of sadness came over Sally's face. She sat for a moment staring at the diving board and then got up, pulled on her coverup, and went into the house, leaving Audrey sitting in the pool by herself. As she walked away, she called, "I need go make a bowl of Jell-O."

Whatever had happened, either she had not reached that point in the diaries or Sally never wrote about it. Audrey got out of the pool herself, not feeling as graceful as Sally was, and got into the shower, letting the hot water run over her as she thought about Sally. What could have been so bad that Sally shut down like that? And why didn't she want to share?

Audrey wrapped her bathrobe around her and sat in bed, wanting to read more. What was she missing?

But while she turned the pages, going past mundane details about patients and their ailments, a text chimed in on Audrey's phone from a 505 number.

"Maybe you want to meet me for lunch on Tuesday? I'm sure you're already craving another green chile grilled cheese."

Audrey laughed out loud, her legs crossed, the diary on top of her lap.

Vince.

"I am!" she wrote back." I hope I can survive until then."

"You have a date?" Betty asked, her eyes getting wide that Friday night when they all met at Mary Ellen's house for dinner.

"She has a date?" Mary Ellen asked, coming out of the kitchen with a platter of fried chicken. "Audrey has a date?"

"I do," Audrey said, feeling excited to share it with the three women, knowing how pleased they would be.

"Well, that was easy," Mary Ellen said, looking at her two friends as she sat down at the table and placed a paper napkin in her lap. "We didn't have to do anything."

"Tell us about him," Betty said.

"There's not much to tell," Audrey admitted. "I don't know a lot yet. His name is Vince and he works at the hospital downtown."

"How did you meet?" Esther wanted to know, three sets of eyes staring Audrey down. They were relentless with their questions.

"The grocery store the first time," Audrey said.

"The first time?!" Mary Ellen exclaimed before Audrey could continue. "There was more than one meeting?"

"Um, well, yeah," Audrey said, shifting slightly in her seat as if she were being judged by her mother's friends. "Then we met at Ida's Diner."

"Oh my," Betty said, her eyes opening wide. "You've been busy. I guess I haven't been looking out my front window enough. I thought you were in there sorting through Sally's life, not out running around town."

"I hardly call that running around town," Audrey laughed, sipping her wine.

"I haven't been to Ida's Diner in years," Esther said, and turning to the others added, "We should go there sometime."

"We should go there and spy on Audrey is what we should do," Betty said, looking confident.

"Oh no!" Audrey laughed. "I don't need the three of you following me around."

"You will have to let us meet him," Esther said.

"We assume this will go far and we need to put the Aspen Hills seal of approval on him," Betty said.

Audrey laughed until Esther added, "We have to be your family since Sally isn't here."

For the first time, Audrey felt that Sally was really related to her. Finally she was beginning to feel like Sally, whose house she was living in and to some extent whose life she was living.

What she didn't tell anyone of them was that she had begun to paint.

Audrey had found the laundry room cabinets filled with paint while the laundry detergent, dryer sheets, and stain remover sat on the counter next to the washing machine. It was as if Sally got tired of doing laundry in there but had nowhere to paint or do her laundry and forced them to coexist in one place. She wasn't sure why all the paintings and the box were in the den by the wet bar and moved everything into the laundry room to keep it in one place.

Later, Audrey would find the clothes line and the clothes pins in the garage, most likely having been forced out of the laundry room to give the paint and other supplies more space.

The walls were painted a light yellow, enough to give the room color against the white cabinets and white washing machine and dryer. Betty had explained one day that Sally had bought a new washer and dryer just a few months before she died.

"The washing machine started to leak and she finally gave up and got a front loader," Betty had said, running her hand across the top of the washing machine. "She never thought she wouldn't be here. We all thought we were going to live to 100 and still be in our houses." She laughed lightly, not looking at Audrey. "The joke was on us."

Audrey moved the canvas Sally had started off the easel and looked around the room for a place to put it. She finally leaned it up against the wall on the counter.

"I don't want to put this away," she said, as if Sally were there listening. "I still feel like I shouldn't be moving things around. But I do want to start something new."

"You should," Sally said suddenly standing next to Audrey. She wore an old floral shift dress that looked vintage but also timeless.

"She had these old dresses from Lilly Pulitzer," Betty joked. "If you haven't found them in the closet, you will. She and Patrick took a trip to Florida and it was not long after Lilly opened her store. Sally fell in love with the dresses, having no idea how big Lilly would become one day. They would go to Florida once a year in the winter so Patrick could golf and I think Sally would buy out all the dresses in her size."

Audrey had opened all the closets but hadn't spent much time looking in them.

Sally saw Audrey looking at her dress. "You can wear them. I'm sure they will fit you. I just love the big pockets. And you know that story, right? Lilly was selling orange juice by the side of the road, using the fruit from her husband's citrus grove, and she found the orange juice was leaving a mess. She created these shift dresses in bright floral colors because you can't see the stains." Sally chuckled. "And that's how it all started. For me, they didn't show the paint I would spill on myself."

Audrey stood and looked at the painting Sally had started. It was far enough along that she could see it was of the pool in the backyard.

"It's okay," Sally said. "Start another one. Let's see how the pool looks to you."

Audrey wanted to talk to Sally, but something always stopped her. The two women stared at each other and Sally spoke again as if she knew what Audrey was going to say. "You can finish my painting later." Sally shrugged her shoulders. "Or maybe you never will. That's okay, too. You're forging a new path."

Audrey looked around the room, trying to remember where she had seen blank canvases. She spotted them between a cabinet and the wall. She pulled out a smaller one and placed it on the easel.

Then she stared at it.

And stared at it some more.

"Oh dear," Sally said, now sitting in the chair by the window. "Don't worry about anything but painting. Don't fear anything. The more fear you have, the less you enjoy the beauty around you."

Audrey opened the plastic container of paints and squeezed a bit of blue on the palette. She stared at it a minute, knowing it wasn't the blue of the pool. It was too royal blue. She found the white and added a tinge, using the bottom of the brush to mix the two. Now it looked like the water in the backyard.

And then she began to paint, not thinking about anything other than creating what she saw, maybe not what Sally or anyone else saw, but how her mind saw in the backyard. Then she added trees around it, using varying shades of green.

But when it came to the patio furniture and the umbrella, she walked outside, surveyed them for a moment and went back in the house.

"It's okay," Audrey told herself, "I can stop there. Better to let it dry and let me think for a while."

Audrey cleaned her brushes and took another look at the painting before leaving the room. As the sun continued its way over the house, the light in the room had begun to shift.

"I always liked to paint in the morning best." Sally had reappeared. "There is the most light in here."

Audrey nodded and walked down the hall to the bedrooms. There was one room she hadn't spent much time in and it was the one that appeared to hold Patrick's things. Maybe it had been Patrick's bedroom while Sally resided in the master. Or maybe that was where Sally put Patrick's life, unable to let it go after he died.

Opening the closet, Audrey saw clothes that she was sure had been new in the 1970s or 80s. That made sense, since Patrick had died at fifty. Sally had been a widow for thirty years. On the shelf above his clothes sat boxes of golf balls, tees, and various hats, mostly the floppy kind.

"Oh Patrick and those stupid hats," Sally laughed. "I hated them. But after he died I couldn't bear to part with them."

Something in Audrey didn't feel connected to Patrick. But it wasn't the same way she hadn't felt connected to Sally. Now she felt connected to Sally yet Patrick was an unknown, a man who existed only in photos and the stories of the women across the street. While the trio talked as if Sally and Patrick had the most amazing marriage, Audrey wasn't so sure.

Something had happened to Reuben. Why didn't Sally marry him? All her diary entries said how much she loved him, how she wanted to marry him and spend her life with him. And it appeared he wanted to be with her, too.

Audrey looked around, expecting Sally to give her the answer. She was nowhere to be found. Audrey closed the closet door; she could deal with Patrick's stuff another day. She found the diary by her bed and walked back into Patrick's room, where she settled into the overstuffed chair with the ottoman.

If Sally wasn't going to tell her, maybe it was because she needed to read more. The answers had to be somewhere. Somewhere something had gone awry in Sally's life, and Audrey thought it was still ahead. As far as she could tell, after glancing through all the books, there didn't appear to be in any lapses in writing that lasted more than a few days.

Sally didn't drone on about how much she loved Reuben; it was a real love for a man who cherished her and spent time with her. Sometimes Audrey felt jealous of what Sally had with Reuben because it forced her to reflect on her relationship and marriage with Rick. And the more she read, the more she realized she was lucky it was over. There had to be a man out there who would really care for her.

She placed the open diary face down on her stomach and shut her eyes for a moment, thinking about Vince.

What am I going to wear? She thought, her eyes flying open.

It was one thing to run into him at the grocery store and another at Ida's Diner, but this was a planned experience.

"How can you not have anything to wear?" Mandy asked on the phone when Audrey called her in a panic. "You have the cutest clothes of anyone I know."

"Did," Audrey reminded her, sitting on her bed against the pillows. Slowly things were becoming hers, not Sally's anymore. "I can't fit into most of what I own so I didn't bring it."

"You left all your cute Kate Spade dresses at your mom's?" Mandy sounded not just surprised but horrified.

"What was I going to do with them?'"

"Your mom won't get rid of them, will she?"

Audrey laughed so hard she almost snorted, feeling embarrassed. "My mom? Heck no. She'll call me up one day and ask me when I'm coming back to get them."

"You're not coming back, my friend," Mandy said.

"I am," Audrey countered. "Once I clean out this house I'll sell it and come back."

"But why would you come back? It sounds like New Mexico is a happier place for you. At least you sound better than you were here in the grassland."

"Don't you want me to come back?"

"I do," Mandy said. "But if I had to pick between you being happy and you living here, I'd pick you being happy."

A true friend, Audrey thought. She looked around the room and changed the subject without realizing it. "I found the most amazing dress in my aunt's closet. It's like a Kate Spade from the sixties."

"Oh my. Why don't you wear that?"

"It's a lunch date." And then she added glumly. "I can't fit into it anyway." As Audrey stared at the dress hanging on the closet door and spotted a mark on it. "And it has a stain," she said.

"You sound surprised? Did you not see it before?"

"I didn't," Audrey admitted, running her finger over the brown mark near the hem. "I wonder what it is."

"Have it cleaned. But I still can't get over you saying you can't fit into anything. You must be dreaming."

"It's more like a nightmare. But I've been swimming. I'll be back into my clothes by the time I get back."

Mandy laughed. "You aren't coming back. Call your mom and have her send your clothes. In the meantime, if your aunt had that in the closet, maybe she has something else you can wear for your lunch date."

Audrey thought for a moment and realized her friend had a good idea. After they ended the call, Audrey threw the phone on the bed and went looking for the Lilly Pulitzer dresses. Maybe one of them would fit. There was a fourth bedroom across from the master that she hadn't spent much time in. When she opened the walk-in closet, the dresses stood out in their bright colors and patterns. She pushed them back to get a good look at each one.

"Aren't the colors yummy?" Sally asked, standing in the door of the closet. "I couldn't resist them. Patrick never complained, but I know he wasn't happy about me buying out Lilly's store each time we went to Palm Beach."

Sally giggled and walked in closer to Audrey. "But all that money he put into golf was no different than me buying the dresses."

Some of them were the usual sleeveless shift dresses but then Audrey stumbled on a pink and lime green floral halter dress. Audrey stared at it a long time.

"Oh, that's a wonderful dress. That would look great on you." She could feel Sally smiling behind her.

Audrey hung the dress on the opposite side and continued looking. When she reached the end, she took a glance at everything else in the closet.

"I know it's silly that I have multiple closets filled with clothes," Sally said. "How I love clothes! I can see your father in you. And that means I see a little of me in you."

Just then, Sally turned and saw the dress Audrey had chosen hanging on the outside closet door. She ran her fingers across it before she walked away. Audrey watched her a moment, taking a break to look at a pink crepe dress.

Audrey tried on the pink and lime green halter, kind of glad Sally had turned away so she wouldn't see what Audrey had allowed her body to morph into. But when she slipped into the dress and pulled her hair up to tie the halter, she stood in front of the mirror and smoothed it out. Audrey turned several times to survey the scene, sucking in her stomach.

"Not bad," she murmured. "I'll get back there but it does a good job hiding everything in the meantime."

And with an ironing, the dress would look new.

Sally had returned and was standing behind Audrey in the mirror. "I knew it," she said, smiling. "Those patterns hide everything you worry about."

She disappeared after that comment. Audrey was beginning to realize that Sally only appeared when she needed to say something. Sometimes Audrey poked her head into the laundry room expecting that Sally would have worked on the painting or stuck her head out the sliding glass doors by the master bedroom thinking Sally would be in the pool.

But Sally only appeared when Audrey was doing something related to her, as if she were helping Audrey to learn who she was.

*****

While Audrey was nervous about lunch on Tuesday, she tried to act like it wasn't a big deal.

"It's just lunch," she told Betty, who stopped over that morning to wish her luck.

"It's a date!" Betty reminded her, looking like a proud mom. "And you're coming to dinner tonight because we all want to hear the details."

Audrey shook her head as Betty left the house.

But lunch did mean more casual and she knew Vince would be coming from work. She pulled on the dress, now freshly laundered and ironed, and tied her hair back in a ponytail. Audrey found her strappy white sandals and slipped her feet into them. When she looked at the mirror she smiled, finally seeing a glimmer of her old self.

As she stood there looking, reflecting back on where life had taken her and where she was now, she wondered if she wanted to be that person from before. Maybe it was possible to take aspects of the person she used to be and remake herself now. There were things she didn't want to repeat although she wasn't sure how to change them.

After all, what did she miss in her marriage? She had thought they were doing so well. Sometimes Audrey thought about her dad, glad he died before it fell apart, but also wondering what he saw that she didn't.

45

"It all looked good to me," her mom had said shrugging her shoulders. "Sometimes people don't show their true colors until later. Maybe we should give him an Oscar for his acting job."

Audrey tried to stop the thoughts. Her old life wasn't worth brooding about. Mandy was right: she had a new life. Her mom was right: Audrey needed to take this opportunity and make something out of it.

But that didn't mean she was staying in New Mexico. After all, what would she do? While she was used to summers off, it was too late to look for a teaching job. And she didn't really want to write a book. That had been a high school dream. The painting was interesting. But it wasn't enough.

Audrey turned around to see it was 11:10. She and Vince were set to meet at 11:30. She was now running late, but she wanted to make sure he arrived first anyway. That way she could breeze in and slide into the booth rather than awkwardly wondering where to sit while she waited for him.

As she drove downtown, Audrey was nervous. She tried to look cool but inside she was afraid she might vomit. She tried not to put all her hopes into this date. Everyone was excited but she was cautious: what if they found out some detail about each other they couldn't stand?

And there was something she didn't dare mention to anyone: had she healed enough from her pain for this?

Chapter 6

Audrey did breeze into Ida's just the way she had planned, saying a little prayer that she didn't trip on anything. Vince was sitting in the same booth he'd been in last time. He looked up at Audrey and smiled when he realized it was her.

She smiled back as he placed the phone on the table and stood up to greet her.

"At last a planned meeting," he said, giving her a slight hug on her right side.

"Hi," she said, feeling confident.

"You look very retro," Vince teased, "like you belong here." He looked around the room. "Are you sure you know what year it is?"

"And you look like you're in your work uniform," she teased him right back. But she didn't say how much she liked the light blue long-sleeved shirt, sleeves rolled up into the forearm, a tie around his neck.

"I never know what I'm going to have to do to a sick person," he joked.

"You're a doctor?" Audrey raised her eyebrows.

"I didn't tell you that?" he asked, leaning toward her over the table.

"No, I thought you cleaned bedpans."

"Yes, in a tie after years of medical school."

The waitress, the same one from last time walked over to them. "Looks like you two are sitting together this time. That's nice." She turned to Vince. "I know what you want." And then she turned to Audrey. "What would you like?"

Audrey ordered a water while the waitress disappeared.

"You come here that often?"

"About once a week," Vince admitted. "I try to get out of the hospital and see what the normal world looks like."

Enjoy your time with him, the voice inside Audrey's head kept saying. She tried not to analyze anything. She wanted to ask him a million questions about his past relationships forgetting that she was divorced and fair game herself.

"Sometimes I forget about my own past," she would say to Mandy sheepishly later.

"Are you going to order the green chile grilled cheese again?" Vince asked as Audrey scanned the menu.

"Well," she said, looking up, "do you have anything better you recommend?"

"Actually no," he told her, smiling. "I'm going to have the same thing."

Just then the waitress returned and Audrey finally caught her name tag: Nora. "So you'll have the regular?" she teased Vince, tapping her pencil on her small notepad.

"I will." He grinned.

"And you? The same thing as last week?"

Audrey looked at both of them as she handed Nora her menu. "Does everyone in here order the same thing?"

"Only the regulars," Nora said, taking the menu. "If someone comes in here and orders something different we know they are visitors."

"But what if I decide I want to try something else?"

"Would you try something else at your mom's house if she made you the best grilled cheese ever?" Vince asked.

Audrey thought for a moment. "No,"

"I rest my case."

After Nora left, they continued their conversation. "I guess my mom's midwestern grilled cheese sandwiches were nothing compared to what people eat here."

"I grew up here and so did my mom but she never made grilled cheese."

"Really?" Audrey raised her eyebrows.

"I had one at my best friend John's house in elementary school but his mom was an Anglo so I thought it was white people's food."

"OMG," Audrey started to laugh. "I'm so not used to this culture thing."

"That's because you and Toto grew up in Kansas."

"But there is no Toto," Audrey said, "And Dorothy wasn't blonde anyway."

"Are you named for Audrey Hepburn?"

Audrey laughed. "She wasn't blond either." She paused and added, "No, my mom just liked the name. No great story to that."

"Everyone made fun of me growing up," Vince said. He leaned forward on the table. "Vince is Italian you know. But both my parents are Hispanic."

"So who were you named for?"

"Vince Lombardi."

"The football coach?"

He nodded.

Audrey thought for a moment. "But those were the days before even cable TV. How did your dad become a Packers fan here?"

"He's from San Antonio, Texas, but he joined the military after high school. He came from a family of laborers, farmers, working in the fields, and he didn't want that. After a short stint during Vietnam, he went to college at the University of Wisconsin where became a Badger but fell in love with the Packers."

As Audrey listened, she realized how much she enjoyed hearing everyone's stories, their lives, their histories. It was as if everything in New Mexico had a slightly different slant from anything she had heard before. And then there was Sally's story on top of it, the story that started it all.

"He came to New Mexico in the late 1950s, like most everyone else, to work at the labs. He wasn't sure if he would stay but he had family here and he met my mom so he made a life in Albuquerque as the city grew."

"Is he still here?"

"Playing golf almost every day," Vince laughed. "I got him addicted."

"And your mom?"

"She died two years ago of breast cancer."

"My dad died six years ago from a brain tumor," Audrey admitted. "It's not the same."

Vince shook his head.

Nora brought their plates and began to set the cobalt blue and green Fiestaware dishes on the table. "And two pickles for you as always."

"Why is he so special?" Audrey teased.

"I'll give you half of one," Vince offered.

"I'll bring her her own pickle," Nora said, rolling her eyes at Vince. "She can have two, too."

It was quiet while they ate; Audrey looked around the diner, realizing it was full and she hadn't noticed.

"You still haven't told me what brought you to New Mexico." Vince said when they finally took a break from eating. Audrey had just swallowed a potato chip. She smiled.

"Well, the short version is that I got divorced and I'm a teacher so obviously I get the summer off," she said. "And right when school ended, I got word that my aunt who lived here had died and left me everything."

Vince sat back in the booth and laughed. "Seriously?"

"Yes," Audrey said. "It sounds preposterous.."

"You must have been close to her."

Now Audrey laughed. "That's just it– I didn't know her. She left it to my dad but since he had died, it was left to me."

"Everything?"

"House, swimming pool, Cadillac."

"Had you ever been to Albuquerque?"

"I had flown over it on my way to Phoenix," she said trying to be serious.

"So you packed up and moved here."

"My plan is to clean out the house and sell it and go back to Kansas."

"Why? And leave our beautiful state?" He waved a hand around him.

"Um, I haven't seen anything beyond the city itself and I-40 on the way here."

"That doesn't count," Vince said. "Tucumcari is not the beauty of New Mexico."

"What is?"

"Taos, Santa Fe."

He thought for a minute, chewing on a chip. "Are you free on Thursday?"

Audrey laughed. "You act like I have a full life. I've been here about a month and the only friends I have are the elderly ladies in the neighborhood."

"I have the day off. Let's go up north to Santa Fe and Taos."

"You're taking a day trip with him?" Mary Ellen asked that night as Audrey sat on Esther's couch with the others surrounding her.

"Yes," Audrey asked a little tentatively. "Is that a problem?" She played with the pillow next to her nervously.

"He must like you!" Mary Ellen said, throwing her head back and laughing.

Mandy was just as excited. "Santa Fe and Taos? That sounds so romantic!" She was quiet for a moment. "And exotic."

"Being from Kansas and now being here makes me feel like I am in some strange place," she joked. "Or at least everyone makes me feel like I am from the strange place."

"OMG, lucky you to be able to say you had a day date in Santa Fe!" Mandy couldn't stop gushing about it.

Audrey wrung her hands, pacing between the living room windows, through the dining room, and into the kitchen and back while she waited for Vince to show up. When she saw his black SUV pull into the driveway, she took a deep breath and looked down at her sleeveless sundress and brown strappy sandals. Was it the right outfit? Were they the right shoes? What did she know about anything other than Albuquerque?

She walked back to the kitchen so she wouldn't be right there when he rang the doorbell. Still the door flew open when she tugged on the handle, almost hitting the wall.

"Either you're that excited to see me or you want to escape your house," Vince teased and Audrey felt her face go hot. She hoped it wasn't red.

"I don't have a good comeback for that one," she said, letting him in. "When I'm not teaching, my sarcasm isn't as sharp as usual."

"I have a confession," Vince stopping in the living room.

Audrey turned toward him, afraid of what he might say. Was he gay? Did he have a wife? But there was no ring. She had come to expect the worst. Maybe it was because of what Rick did. Never in a million years did she think her marriage would end. And although she was on a good track, the past still lingered in her background.

"I live around the corner," he said, his face breaking into a big smile.

"You do?" Audrey's eyes got big. "That's why I ran into you at the grocery store?"

Vince was laughing and Audrey joined him. "I didn't think about it and when I asked you for your address, I thought the street sounded familiar but I didn't think it was here in Aspen Hills. I'll drive you by my house on the way out of town."

"It had been so long since I was with someone new," Audrey would tell the trio later, that I forgot what the awkward silences are like. "You get so used to being with the person . . ."

Before she could finish, Betty did for her. "He might have left me for someone else but there is no way I could adjust to being with someone new," Betty said. Audrey saw a hint of sadness in her eyes. She wanted to tell Betty that she could still have that relationship, but Audrey knew that after twenty-some years with the same man, Betty didn't want to start over.

Audrey was glad she didn't say anything. It was easy to tell someone else what they could have yet inside herself she was still doubtful of what she deserved. Part of her wondered if there was some reason she got what Rick gave to her. She went back and forth through her life, exploring any moment that karma could affect. Nothing.

"This was your aunt's house?" Vince asked, looking around.

"It explains the décor," Audrey laughed. "She had nice things but my style is a little different. Not so frou-frou."

Now as she climbed into Vince's car, she could take a long look at him. She had tried not to stare but there was something so appealing about him. He wore khaki shorts and a polo shirt, a red Wisconsin Badgers one, of course. But it wasn't just that. He made her laugh, he was interested in her. Traveling in the car all day together would be a good test.

"That's my house," Vince said, pointing at a stucco territorial style house around the corner with white trim. "I've only lived up here about a year."

"Is it a big house?" Audrey asked, knowing that all the houses in Aspen Hills were big.

Executive houses, Esther had said. "Everyone who lived up here had some sort of big position in Albuquerque or Santa Fe."

"I don't think any of the houses are under 3,000 square feet unless they were built much earlier."

"Or later," Mary Ellen piped in. "The houses near the ravine are much smaller than ours."

And the three women set into a debate about when the houses were built.

"I thought we'd have lunch in Santa Fe," Vince suggested, as he turned his car north from Interstate 40 to Interstate 25. "But it will be a little early. Is that okay? We can always walk through the plaza first?"

Audrey had no idea what he was talking about. As he drove out of the city, she watched the landscape change. The barren land north of the city was dotted with tumbleweeds and sage. Not a cloud in the sky. Mountains jutted out of the city on the east side. Audrey didn't think she could drink in enough of it to satisfy for her.

And Vince telling her what he knew.

"I grew up here and I don't think I have explored every nook and cranny of this state," he said, putting on his turn signal to pass a car.

They passed several pueblos, reservation land, and finally civilization began to form again: Santa Fe.

"I can't even remember the last time I was on the plaza," he said, looking for parking.

Audrey still couldn't take her eyes off the scenery. The brown soil and brown buildings against the green trees were like nothing she had ever seen before. And at the 7,000 foot elevation, 2,000 feet higher than Albuquerque, the air was crisper and cooler. She slipped her sweater on and let Vince lead the way.

Along the plaza, Native American artists sold their jewelry, people hovering over their blankets filled with silver and turquoise necklaces, bracelets, earrings, and other pieces.

"I have never seen anything like it," Audrey said. "I could just stand here and watch people."

Vince laughed and took her hand, guiding her through the crowd.

On the far side of the mass jewelry showcase, Vince pointed to a restaurant: Cecilia's Café. "Let's get something to eat and then we'll go on to Taos."

Audrey couldn't stop staring. If she wasn't looking at the people, she was looking at Vince. But she didn't feel able to carry on a conversation. There was too much to take in.

When she ordered enchiladas, the waitress immediately asked, "Red or green?"

Audrey looked at her, then at Vince, then back at the waitress.

Vince leaned toward the waitress. "She just moved here from Kansas. She thinks you're asking what color she prefers at Christmastime."

The waitress started to laugh and Audrey gave a teasing pout. "But I have no idea," she insisted.

"I know you don't," Vince teased her. He pointed at a dish at the next table. "That's red chile." And then he craned his neck to look for another dish, this time pointing to one behind him. "And that's green chile. Do you want red or green chile sauce on your enchiladas?"

"No one ever asked me that before," Audrey said. "I just want the enchiladas."

"That's how we do things here," Vince told her. He turned to the waitress. "Bring her Christmas so she can try both."

"Why does a state that professes to have a simple life making eating so difficult?" she asked Vince when the waitress left.

"Because we have the best food anywhere."

After she finished, stopping with only half her plate clear, she sighed. "That was so good."

"But so good you're not going to finish it?"

Audrey put a hand out in front of her. "I'll take it home. I'm trying to cut back and all this cheese isn't helpful."

"At least it wasn't a grilled cheese," Vince teased her.

She took her fork and poked around. "But I think it has just as much cheese in it."

As they drove out of the plaza and through Santa Fe, Audrey still couldn't stop staring. "I feel like I'm gawking, but it's so different from anything I have known."

Vince laughed. "My dad always said it was like a foreign country when he came here in the 1950s because everything was so small. Even Albuquerque was rural. We have World War II and the bomb to thank for the growth out here."

"The Redo. What kind of store is that?" she asked, her head still turned toward everything around her.

"It's a secondhand store like you've never seen. Want to stop?"

Audrey shrugged her shoulders. "Sure."

"Don't be fooled," Vince whispered, "keep walking. Each time you turn a corner there's more."

The store was filled with clothing, more clothing than Audrey thought a shopping mall might have. And it was organized in such a way that must have taken years to figure out. In one section, a sea of blue jeans hung on racks while around the corner with cowboy boots filled a whole wall, waiting to be tried on.

And then there was the jewelry. Audrey stopped at the case filled with vintage turquoise and silver.

"The real deal," Vince said, pointing at the large necklaces. "Those are the squash blossoms from when people sold on the side of the road, not through a store like today."

"How did they end up here?" Audrey asked. "They look strong, like they are just waiting for a second life."

The silver had been polished and the rows of bracelets, necklaces, earrings, watches went on and on.

"Would you like you to see something?" a man with a silver moustache asked, walking behind the case.

"Oh no," Audrey said. "I'm good."

"Hey, don't speak so fast," Vince teased. "I want to see something."

Audrey looked over to see what he would pull out. He pointed at a silver cuff bracelet with several turquoise stones running across the top of it.

"Ah, that's Navajo," the man said, taking it out and handing it to Vince. "I believe it's from the fifties."

Vince fingered it and held it in his hand. He handed it back to the man.

"It's very simple," Audrey said, seeing a bunch of vintage dresses hanging in a corner. She walked toward them and saw the room again transform from western cowboy to a woman's dressing room. Along one wall stood an old dressing table topped with colored brushes and small bottles of perfume.

Audrey stood for a moment, feeling as if she were stepping back into Sally's life before Aspen Hills,

"You're right," Sally said. Audrey looked in the mirror and saw Sally standing behind her. "I did have one when I had a small house with several other girls downtown. That was before. . . ."

And she trailed off. Audrey turned to her right and saw Vince walking toward her. She figured Sally disappeared because Vince appeared. "Find anything interesting?" he asked.

Audrey smiled. "There's probably more to take in here than there is outside."

She looked through the dresses, feeling as if it were an extended version of Sally's closet. "My aunt left a lot of clothes behind. And there were a lot of clothes from the fifties and sixties."

Vince laughed. "Must be a woman thing. My mom's closet was stuffed, too. My dad made my sister clean it out. He said he wouldn't know what year to start."

Audrey continued to look at each dress even though she knew there were several closets filled, waiting for her back at Aspen Hills.

"What did your mom die of?" she asked.

"Lung cancer. Lifelong smoker."

Audrey wrinkled her nose. "And everyone did it in those days, but now it seems gross."

"My dad never smoked. He was always the exercise guy. Mom was more about having a martini in the evening and smoking all day."

"I'm ready to go," she said, turning toward him.

"We can stay longer," Vince said. "There's still plenty to see."

"I'm about seed out," she said. "And that's not even a word."

As they drove out of Santa Fe and north toward Taos, the mountains surrounded them. Vince pointed toward the river off to the left. "This is the best part about this drive. The water." Audrey craned her head to see over him without getting in his way. "We never have enough water here but we always have enough up here for river rafting."

"That terrifies me," Audrey said, shaking her head.

"Really? It's a lot of fun. "You've obviously never done it if you think it's scary."

"We had cornfields, remember? We ran through sprinklers in our front yards."

Vince laughed and pulled the car off the road where they could get close to the river. She followed him down the dirty path and he took her hand. "Have a seat," he said, pointing to a big rock.

The bubbling and rushing of the water soothed Audrey. She sat, mesmerized, and thought of the pool back in Aspen Hills. The pool was hypnotic, too, but in a different way.

"I used to come up here when I was in med school," Vince said, looking mesmerized himself. "It was hard to get away but I did it because I needed to be away from that routine. Some people never do it and it takes a toll. But I believe it saved me."

Audrey watched him as he spoke.

"I'd drive up here and sit in this very spot. I'm not sure how long I would stay, just long enough that I felt as if I could face the world again. And then I'd head into Taos and stop for an ice cream at the Flippin' Cow before I went home."

"The Flippin' Cow?" Audrey raised her eyebrows.

"Yep," he laughed, taking her hand. "And in a little while, I'll be taking you there."

Audrey smiled and he squeezed her hand; she squeezed it back.

"There was another piece to it, too," he said. "I was married at the time and it wasn't going well. We met in college and I thought we were meant to be together but as I went through med school, she made it clear she wanted someone to spend more time with. That wasn't going to be me so she found someone else."

"How awful," Audrey said, shaking her head and looking at the water. "People like to hurt people and I don't understand why."

"You mean why can't we all just get along?" Vince asked with a smile.

Audrey looked at him and laughed.

"Do you want to tell me what happened to your marriage?" he asked turning toward her. "You don't have to."

Audrey laughed uncomfortably. "I realize it goes with the territory." She paused, collecting her thoughts while she pulled her dress down from riding up her legs. "I'm not even sure what to say." She shrugged her shoulders. "I thought I had the perfect marriage. I thought he loved me as much as I loved him. We had parties, we had friends, we had careers. And then one day he told me he had never loved me. And he left."

Vince squeezed her hand again.

"I've gone back and forth for a year trying to figure out what I did wrong, what I missed. I told him I would fix it. And he would just look at me. He said he wanted to move on."

Audrey felt herself get a little teary and instantly felt embarrassed. "It's okay," he said.

"I don't know you well enough to cry around you," she joked.

"Well," Vince said, "everything is always easily solved with ice cream."

Audrey almost fell off the rock from laughing. "And that's coming from a doctor."

"Who sees plenty of people suffering the effects of eating much ice cream," he added. He stood up and held out his hand to help Audrey stand up. "Let's go to the Flippin' Cow."

They drove through Taos, a smaller version of Santa Fe but looking much the same with a busy plaza of restaurants and small shops. On the north end of town he pulled into the parking lot of a small brown building, looking like all the others.

"That Flippin' Cow," Audrey read the sign out loud. "I thought you made it up."

"Great name isn't it?" Vince asked with a laugh. "And it's not even a burger place. It's all ice cream and shakes."

"So either you flip the cow or you think it's a flippin' cow," Audrey joked as Vince took her hand while they walked across the sandy parking lot.

The short line gave them time to explore the chalkboard menu above the counter.

"The shakes sound good," Audrey whispered.

"Then have one," Vince whispered back. "But we're not in a library."

Audrey laughed and caught her breath before she spoke. "I forgot," she whispered. Vince squeezed her hand.

She tried not to analyze anything, to be in the moment, to treasure the time that Vince wanted to spend with her. She also tried not to think ahead too far, like about what would happen when they parted ways after returning home. Be present, she kept mumbling in her head, holding up a billboard for herself to see.

"I really want the coffee shake," she said, this time speaking a regular tone. "But the maple sounds good, too." She tapped her finger on her chin.

"Hmmm, how about you get the coffee and I'll get the maple and we can compare them?"

"And I get to finish whichever one is better." Vince shook his head and looked away But Audrey knew he was laughing. Slowly, she was beginning to feel more comfortable with him.

"Well, I would hope you did after spending the day with him," Mandy said later on the phone.

When she and Vince were seated with their shakes, each took a sip and then passed it to the other one. Audrey wrinkled her nose at the maple. "That's not very good. Where did they get the maple? Is Vermont too far away?"

Vince had just tried the coffee. "Robust," he said. "Very good. And the maple: so-so."

"So I get the coffee back," Audrey said, reaching across the table to the one Vince had but he grabbed it before she could get to it.

"After I get a few more tastes since I won't see it again."

Audrey pretended to pout and returned to drinking the maple shake, feeling as if she were simply having milk and ice cream.

After Vince had passed the coffee shake back to her to finish, he asked, "I've been thinking about your aunt and I can't get over the fact that you didn't know her but she left you everything."

"Well, if my dad were alive, it would all have been his," Audrey reminded him.

"But that must be strange to walk into the house of someone you didn't know and it's all yours."

Audrey laughed. "It was. It still is."

"And you know nothing about her?"

She finished swallowing. "I didn't. She and my uncle had distanced themselves from the family but no one seems to know why. It's weird. The neighbors tell me what a great lady she was and what a great life she had yet I had no idea of any of it."

Vince stared out the window by their table at the mountain view across a pasture.

"But I found her diaries," Audrey said, brightening up. "This may sounds weird but there are many times I feel like she's there with me talking and sharing. It's like she comes to me to share."

"Have you learned a lot?"

"There are a pile of them and I'm still in the 1950s, when she came to Albuquerque to become a nurse." Audrey paused. "She's dating a man she is clearly in love with but it's not my uncle."

"You know that because the names are different?"

Audrey nodded. "Exactly. I haven't reached the point where the relationship ends. His name was Reuben and my uncle's name was Patrick."

"My dad's name is Reuben but that's a fairly common name, especially for Hispanics of that time."

When they reached Albuquerque following the drive home, Vince pulled into Audrey's driveway and she felt a light of happiness inside her when he didn't just pull away, he got out of the car and walked to her doorway.

"Are you in a hurry to get home or do you want to come in?"

"I'm in no hurry," Vince said, smiling. "I need to get home to my dog at some point though. But she's used to being home alone all day while I'm at the hospital."

"I want to show you the diaries."

While Vince waited in the living room, Audrey grabbed a few from the bedroom and led him outside to the pool area. It was nearing 6 p.m. and the sun was beginning to lower in the sky, making the shadows longer in the backyard.

"You have a pool," Vince said. "Very nice."

"By default," she joked. "Don't you have one? It seems like all the houses up here do."

"No," he said, settling into one of the wrought iron patio chairs next to Audrey. "I wouldn't have bought a house with one since I'm alone with my dog."

Audrey nodded and opened one of the diaries she had already read. "She left Kansas for New Mexico in mid fifties. I left Kansas for New Mexico several weeks ago but it wasn't quite the same."

Vince laughed, looking at the pages that Audrey held open for him. "It's definitely more metropolitan than it was then. Then it was pretty much a sandy mesa."

"He's very cute," Sally said, as if she had been with them all along. Audrey glanced over the table, not wanting Vince to see that Audrey saw Sally there. "Tall, dark, and handsome. Don't let him go."

"This is incredible," Vince said, taking the notebook into his hands. All the detail about her outfits and the food. And everything." His eyes glanced up and down the page.

A beeping sound came from Vince's pocket and he pulled out his smartphone to look at a text.

"One of my patients is in the hospital. He had a heart attack and it appears he's taking a turn for the worse. I better get down there."

Audrey didn't want to show her disappointment that Vince was leaving as she walked him to the front door, following him out to his car.

"I don't want to leave," he said, reaching his arms around her before she had a chance to analyze it. He kissed her on the cheek and moved to her lips before pulling away. "If I didn't have to go to the hospital, I wouldn't."

"Hi!" Betty called from across the street where she was conveniently checking her mail.

"Do you have time to say hi?" Audrey asked. "The elderly ladies on the block were very excited about my date with you."

Vince nodded. "It's okay. Let's make her day."

They met Betty in the middle of the street.

"Did you two have fun today?" she asked, her eyes looking like they might burst out of their sockets.

"We did," Vince said, reaching to shake Betty's hand.

Audrey stood and watched, feeling as if she was introducing him to her mother.

Betty peered at Vince. "Aren't you the doctor who lives around the corner?"

Audrey looked at Betty, somewhat embarrassed, but when Vince smiled and burst out laughing, she did, too. "Nothing gets by them," Audrey said, shaking her head.

"We wanted to set her up with you," Betty exclaimed, a look of extreme happiness unrolling across her face. "Thank you for making it happen."

Vince held his hands in front him as if he needed to hold Betty back. "I just ran into her in a few places."

"It was meant to be! Wait until I tell the girls!"

"The girls?" Vince asked, glancing at Audrey.

"The trio," Audrey mumbled. "Her friends."

"Mary Ellen lives across the street and down three houses from you. I need to go tell them." Betty started to walk away. "We want to have you two over for dinner. I'll call and arrange it with you," she said, pointing at Audrey.

"How do you know the date went well?" Audrey called to her. "Maybe we hate each other."

"You were in the car together all day today," Betty said, stopping at the curb in front of her house, "and you didn't kill each other. That's a good sign."

She disappeared into her front door.

"Well, that was interesting," Vince said. "I didn't realize the ladies on the block knew who I was. I thought I was incognito coming and going."

"You better go," Audrey said. "You need to see your patient."

Vince waved her off. "He's stable in the hospital. It's not like he's going to break out of there."

They walked back to Audrey's driveway where they stood for a moment by Vince's car. "How about you come over Saturday night and I'll make you some authentic home-cooked New Mexican food?" he offered.

Audrey felt her face light up.

"It was just nice knowing he wanted to see me again," she told Mandy later.

And after getting a "yes" from her, he was gone soon after, leaving Audrey alone.

Until she called Mandy to tell her about the date.

But as they chatted, Audrey heard the phone in the kitchen ringing. She ignored it and continued her conversation with Mandy.

"Is that a phone I hear? Like an old-style push-button phone?"

Audrey giggled. "It is."

It stopped ringing. And then started again.

"And with no caller id."

"Who can live without caller id?" Mandy asked, sounding confused by the concept.

The phone started to ring again.

"Someone who never had it," Audrey said. "And one day we'll be like Sally and Betty and the others– wondering about all these new fangled things we won't understand."

"You better get the phone because that person isn't giving up," Mandy said.

Audrey walked to the kitchen from the dining room where she was sitting and took the handset off the cradle. "Hello," she said, knowing Betty would be on the other end.

"Oh goodness! We are so happy for you! I've talked with the others. Find out when he is free for dinner."

60

"What if I'm not free?" Audrey asked.

"We know you are, dear. You're new in town. It's *him* we want to get to know. We need to make sure he is just right for you."

"Who was that?" Mandy asked when Audrey returned to their call.

"My neighbor across the street. I think these four women kept their landlines just so they could talk to each other."

*****

When Audrey woke up the next morning it took her a moment to remember the events of the day before. And when she did, she lay there for a moment, letting the peace and happiness settle over her before she stretched to start the day with her swim.

Later that morning she checked her email and saw one from a friend she hadn't talked to since she moved to her mother's house.

"Hi!" it read from Emily McLeod. "I thought you might be interested to know that Rick got married a few weeks ago. I found out from my sister-in-law whose sister was the photographer for the wedding. The link below has all the photos."

Audrey's heart sunk. Her peace and happiness slid away. Why did she have to be reminded of the past? And how could she not look at the photos?

She thought about deleting the email but she knew she'd find it in the trash. Just look, she said to herself. Just look. It will be a good way to know it's really over

But her head took her in directions she didn't understand. She knew it was over. Why did she need to look? She knew Rick was long gone. Yet the idea of him with someone else still hurt.

Audrey clicked on the link and it took her to a photographer's web site where she called Rick and Jennifer's wedding "the most beautiful" she had ever been to.

And then the photos. Rick in a tux, Jennifer looking like an overgrown ballerina, in a seafoam green dress with a tulle skirt and wide silver belt.

She had heard rumors he had a girlfriend but in her effort to try to move on, she had tried to block out any information offered her. And when she moved to her mother's house, she was almost an hour from where they lived.

While Kansas City had been big enough for them to co-exist, Audrey now knew something. She took the laptop and pulled it into her lap, sitting on the floor in the living room. Sally had kept a box of tissues on the end table. Audrey thought it was a stupid place for them but she never moved them. And now she knew why.

As she looked at the photos—Ricks' smiling face, Jennifer looking like the glowing bride, their families gathered around them—she started to cry. Rick had been her family at one time not so long ago. She knew now that it was over.

And she finally admitted to herself that she wasn't returning to Kansas.

The first call she made was to Mandy, to share what she had seen.

"What kind of true friend would send you that?" Mandy asked, clearly agitated. "I never even wanted to know if he had a girlfriend. Do I know Emily?"

"Probably not," Audrey told her between tears. "It's okay. Part of me is glad. I needed to see this so I can move on."

"And you have a very tall, dark, and handsome doctor who seems to have the hots for you," Mandy reminded her.

Audrey laughed. "Hopefully this pain will go away."

"It will," Mandy assured her. "You'll be just fine. Keep your butt parked in Albuquerque. You don't need to come back to Kansas."

"I know," Audrey said, quietly.

Her second call was to her mother.

"I need you to send my boxes," Audrey said. "I'm not coming back."

She heard Shirley sigh. "Oh dear. I'm glad to hear that. I was hoping you would make a new start there. I already labeled everything; I was waiting for this day. They'll be picked up on Monday."

Chapter 7

While Audrey didn't realize it at first, making the choice to stay was reflected in life around her.

She walked around the corner to Vince's house on Saturday evening, having tried on six different sundresses before finally choosing another one of Sally's Lilly Pulitzer dresses and tying her hair up in a loose ponytail.

As she walked, it was hot, but not the hot Audrey was used to: almost no humidity.

"That's why you feel cold when you get out of the pool even though it's 90 degrees," Bert had explained one morning when he was cleaning the pool. "There is no moisture in the air to keep you warm."

It felt good to walk, something she knew she didn't do enough of. Audrey tried to slither by Esther's house, grateful she had passed Betty's without Betty running outside to tell her something or ask a question, but there was Esther in the front yard deadheading her daisies.

"Where are you headed, dear?" Esther asked, walking over to Audrey with a bucket in her hand.

"Vince is having me over for dinner tonight," Audrey said, feeling proud but also wanting to get to Vince's house.

"Have a nice time," Esther said. "We'll want to hear all about it."

Audrey kept walking to the house Vince had shown her on their way out of town several days before. As she stood under the covered porch, feeling the coolness of the concrete around her, waiting for him to open the thick wood door, she took a deep breath.

"Just enjoy it," she mumbled as if something bad might happen.

What she couldn't say to anyone was how terrified part of her was—and seeing the photos of Rick's wedding had not been helpful. Maybe one day she would understand it but right now she still felt hurt.

"Those photos are the green light for you to go forward," Mandy had said. "There is no turning back. He's married; he moved on. Go have the life you're supposed to."

She heard a dog barking and Vince telling it to sit. When he pulled the door open, Audrey felt as though she had stepped into a bucket of peace. While she didn't know exactly what that would look like, seeing Vince made the pain melt away.

He wore a black Nike t-shirt and khaki cargo shorts and smiled widely at her.

"Meet Sadie," he said, pointing at the chocolate lab whose tail was sweeping across the floor quickly as if it was cleaning the tile.

Audrey took a deep breath and smelled dinner. The aroma seemed to bring her peace. Whatever it was, she wanted to curl up on a couch and stay there forever. There was no pain in this house.

"What is that smell?" she asked, stepping onto the tile floor in the hallway and letting Sadie sniff her hand. "That's incredible."

"Carne adovada," Vince said, taking her hand and giving her a hug, then kissing her lightly. As he let her body go, keeping her hand in his and leading her to his kitchen, he added, "pork marinated in red chile."

Like many houses in Aspen Hills, it was hard to tell what Vince's looked like from the outside. But as soon as one walked inside, it opened up into a large living area, more modern than Sally's cut-up house. And to the right of the sunken living room was the kitchen.

Vince led Audrey to a barstool and invited her to sit down. "How about a sangria?"

"What is sangria?" Audrey asked, feeling a little nervous as she settled onto the stool. "I'm more familiar with her sister Margarita."

He laughed and poured a glass of red liquid from a bottle into two round glasses. "Red wine with fruit. I wish I could say I made it from scratch. You'll get the bottled version here, though. But dinner will be homemade."

He slid a glass to her and held his up, Audrey following his cue. "To getting to know each other," he said.

Audrey smiled and clinked glasses with him.

Then he placed a bowl of chips and a small bowl of salsa in front of her.

"It's green salsa," Audrey said, feeling a little confused. Again. "Is that like fried green tomatoes?"

"No," Vince told her. "Your perspective is cracking me up though. It's tomatillo, a type of tomato that doesn't turn red."

Audrey nodded and dipped a chip into the bowl. After she chewed for a few moments, she put her hand in front of her mouth and said, "I don't think I even have words to describe how this tastes."

"It doesn't matter as long as you like it," Vince said, walking over to the crock pot where he stirred something.

Then he came back around and joined her on another barstool. "Anything new in Sally's world since I last saw you?"

Audrey shook her head. "I didn't really have much time to read."

"Well, something new must have happened since I saw you."

"Why do you say that?" she asked, dipping another chip after he did.

"You're new to town and exciting things always happen. Maybe you discovered the drive to the top of the Sandias."

Audrey laughed. "No, I haven't been to the top of the mountain." She shook her head.

"Then we'll have to take care of that."

"But I did have my mom ship all my clothes and shoes here."

"You're planning to stay awhile? You're going to live out of more than one suitcase," he teased.

"Yes, I'm going to stay."

"What made you change your mind?"

It was an innocent question.

Audrey turned away from him and looked out the sliding glass doors at the view from his deck. His house was situated so that he had a good view of the city and she wanted to ask how it looked at night, but at the moment all she could think about was speaking without crying. And not telling him what she had found out. She knew it wouldn't look good if she still felt so hurt after seeing her ex-husband's wedding photos.

"I asked the wrong question," Vince said from behind her. He put his hand on her back and squeezed her shoulder. "You don't have to tell me."

Audrey turned back to him and gulped. "Someone sent me the link to the photos of my ex-husband's wedding." She felt the tears coming and knew she couldn't stop them when they started. She took a hard swallow but it didn't help. "I shouldn't feel so upset about it but I do. And my friend Mandy wonders why someone would send them to me. And then I wonder why I clicked on the link and looked."

Vince stood up from his stool so he could get closer. He wrapped one arm around her, pulling her close to his chest. "Anyone who has divorced has been in your place. No matter how much time has passed, there's still that tinge of pain."

Audrey shut her eyes and let herself rest against him, feeling his heart beat.

"Don't beat yourself up over it. Don't deny it. The more you let yourself feel it, the less power you're giving it. And the less power you give it, the quicker it will go away."

She wasn't sure how long they stayed there and she didn't care. When she pulled away and he climbed back on his stool Audrey looked at him. "So you don't think worse of me because I am crying over my ex-husband's wedding?"

Vince took a drink of the sangria and shook his head before he placed his hand over hers on the granite counter top. "If you didn't feel anything, I might be more worried."

"You don't think this is a sign that I haven't gotten over him?" Audrey knew her face looked scrunched up from worry. Not a pleasant sight, she thought.

"Heck no," Vince said, getting up to stir the slow cooker again. "You loved him. You thought your life was going to be with him. And since it didn't happen that way, you feel hurt and angry."

He pulled two plates out of a cabinet and and set them on the counter near the crock pot. Then he walked back to the counter and stood facing Audrey. "I like you, Audrey, and I just want to spend time with you," he said. "There is nothing to fear."

"I'm going to have to get on a bigger diet if we keep eating each time we get together," Audrey laughed.

"I was thinking about that, too," Vince said, tapping his fingers on the side of the counter. "We can take Sadie for a walk after dinner."

Audrey nodded and let him prepare a plate for her.

"It might look messy," Vince told her as he placed the plate in front of her, the red gloppy mess in the middle with a flour tortilla folded in quarters off to the side, "but it's the best you'll ever have."

"Gordon Ramsey would ding you on the presentation," Audrey teased him as she picked up her fork.

"It's how my mom nabbed my dad."

"Over this?"

Vince nodded, picking up his fork. "She made this on their first date and he said he knew then he was going to marry her."

"So you're doing the same?" she asked.

Vince shook his head. "Each time I planned to make this for a girl, she didn't show up."

"Wait, so this was a test? Did they know what you were cooking?"

They both laughed. "I'm serious. And they didn't know what I was cooking. But I would plan these meals and they never came. I think there were five women who never showed."

"That's so sad."

"The good news is that I learned how to make really good carne in the process but my mom thought I was doomed. She died believing I couldn't please a woman with her food even though she managed it with my dad." He paused before he spoke again. "And my sister Cindy was the lucky one– each time it happened, I called her and invited her over to eat with me. She might be disappointed she's not getting a call tonight even though she lives in San Diego now."

Audrey finally took a bite of the meat that melted in her mouth. Vince showed her how to use a tortilla to pick some up and roll it into a mini burrito.

And then he spoke again. "But I think she's too busy with her husband and kids to notice anyway."

"I'm going to eat my way through this state because of you," Audrey sighed when they had finished and she took a sip of her sangria.

"You're not because we're going to go for a walk and then come back for flan."

"Flan!"

"I made the flan."

Audrey looked around. "You did? You didn't hide the container it came in somewhere?"

"Nope. Once again, you can thank Mom."

"I have to admit I've never walked around the neighborhood," Audrey said, feeling a little embarrassed as they set out with Vince holding Sadie's leash.

"Then let me show you where the best views are," he said.

"Aren't they from your backyard?" Audrey asked, pointing.

Vince shrugged his shoulders. "There are no bad views in Albuquerque."

"I have no view."

"But you have a pool."

"I can't argue with any of it because before I didn't have a view or a pool."

Vince started to walk at a faster clip and Audrey found it difficult to keep up in her open-backed sandals.

"I'm sorry," Vince said, stepping off the sidewalk into the street. "I'm used to walking in a hurry all day at the hospital."

"Everyone keeps telling me life is slower here but apparently not in your world," Audrey remarked, adjusting her sandals as they slipped under her feet.

Vince laughed and took her hand. "If I hold your hand, I might walk slower."

When they came around the corner to Audrey's street, Audrey said, "You know you're risking something by coming this way."

"You mean because the trio might nab us?"

"Exactly."

And they did. This time it was Mary Ellen and Betty who were standing in front of Mary Ellen's house.

"Oh we're so glad we ran into you two," Betty said, not even getting a chance to introduce Vince to Mary Ellen.

Mary Ellen immediately stuck her hand out for Vince to shake. "I want to hug you," she said, grinning. "We're so happy about you and Audrey."

Audrey tried to get a word in, to tell them that they weren't a couple, but the two women were too busy asking Vince questions.

What made him decide to move to Aspen Hills, what kind of doctor was he, did he grow up in Albuquerque? And Vince wasn't deterred. Sadie sat patiently while Vince dodged the questions. He didn't need to deflect them, like they were swords against his shield, but the more he answered, the faster the questions kept coming. Audrey felt like they were in a video game and each time he answered one, the sword disappeared and another one came.

"Wait, your dad is Reuben?" Audrey asked, looking at Sadie.

"Yeah."

The conversation stopped.

"The man who walks Sadie?" She pointed at the drooling chocolate lab.

"Yes. He comes up here to golf and walks her before his tee time."

"I met him the week I moved up here," Audrey said. "As I was putting out the trash."

Vince smiled. "There's something more to that but I'm not going to read into it."

Mary Ellen and Betty watched them but didn't say anything. Audrey could see the wheels turning in their brains underneath their white hair. They wanted to know more.

"You two need to come to dinner on Friday night," Betty said. "That will be enough for us to stamp Vince with our seal of approval. I hope you are free."

She glanced from one to the other and Audrey and Vince looked at each other. Audrey wanted to tell him it was okay if he was busy, that he didn't need to endure this. But Vince made it clear he was along for the ride. "I'm free. Are you?"

Audrey knew she had no choice but to say yes. "I am, too." She looked at Betty who got excited.

And Mary Ellen who exclaimed, "I can make another cake."

"We'll let you two lovebirds be on your way," Betty said, shooing them off with her hands as if they had gotten what they wanted and could move on.

They were still standing there when Audrey looked back. Both of them smiled and waved.

"That wore me out," Audrey said. "But they have been good to me."

"Worn out means time for flan," Vince said, looking both ways so they could cross the street and return to his house. Sadie went immediately to her water bowl, made a mess drinking half of it, and then lay down in the middle of the kitchen floor while Vince stepped over her to pull the flan out of his stainless steel refrigerator.

When Vince walked her home, he left Sadie in the house, still sleep on the kitchen floor.

Standing on her front porch, he slid his arms around her waist. "I keep expecting your parents to come to the door," he joked.

"I feel like I'm back in high school," Audrey added. "I guess no matter how old you are, it doesn't change."

"Maybe that's a good thing."

He kissed her. "I better go," he whispered, "before Sadie figures out that I'm not there."

Audrey sat in bed after brushing her teeth and changing into her pink nightgown. She crossed her legs and sat back against the oversized pillows Sally had on all the beds, feeling her head hit the back of the headboard, and sighed.

It should be easy, she thought. Vince was making it easy. But if it was so easy, why did she feel so scared?

She didn't want to think more about it, though, so she picked up Sally's diary, which she hadn't read in several days.

Sally sat on the side of the bed facing Audrey. "He's a wonderful young man," Sally said as if they were having a conversation in Audrey's room after getting home from a date. "Don't be scared. He's making it easy. It's been a hard road for you but you can do this and have something so wonderful."

She was gone before Audrey could ask anything or make any comments.

The next day, Audrey found it easy not to think about Vince. She still had a lot of work ahead of her and with her own clothes set to arrive in a few days, she needed to clear some closet space. But when the doorbell rang, she fully expected Betty to be standing there.

Vince.

"Hi," he said, something wrapped in foil in his hand. "I'm sorry I didn't call or text or in some way let you know I was coming over."

"You mean like modern people do, not like the trio?" Audrey said with a smile.

"Exactly. But I decided it was more important to deliver you some breakfast." He handed her the foiled wrapped package. A burrito.

"Not just any burrito," Vince said, "but a carne adovada burrito. Made by me."

"You could have made me one for each day of the week," Audrey joked, feeling it the warm foil. "And heated up."

She invited Vince in and she started to walk outside to sit by the pool with him.

"You never invite me in," he said. "You always send me walking through the house to the pool. Are you embarrassed by the furnishings?"

Audrey laughed. "No. I just love being able to go outside all the time here. They are inside with their noses pressed against the glass in Kansas now because it's so hot and humid outside. And in the winter they are doing the same because of the cold."

"Eat the burrito and then you can give me the tour," he said, pulling out a patio chair for her. "I have something to ask you anyway."

"Sure," she said.

Vince relaxed in the chair watching the sun come over the pool. "This really is an oasis."

"And your cooking is delish," she said, realizing she needed a napkin.

"Just dip your hands in the pool when you're done," he suggested.

Audrey shook her head and kept eating.

Vince leaned forward, his forearms on the table. "There is a fundraiser I go to every year; it's for kids," he said. "It's always held at a big house on Rio Grande in the valley. The Kellys are huge supporters. Anyway, it's next weekend. Do you want to go with me?"

Audrey's eyes got wide. "Really? You want me to go into a social situation with you?"

He shrugged his shoulders and sat back. "I'm the one who just suggested you wash your hands in the pool so you must be a step up from me."

"Sure," she said, "I'll go."

When he picked her up the following Saturday, wearing a long-sleeved fitted shirt tucked in but opened at the neck, with khakis, Audrey felt somewhat insecure in her little black dress with the rhinestone spaghetti straps.

She sucked in her stomach tightly, knowing she had lost weight but also not really sure she had lost enough to wear the dress again.

"That was your favorite dress!" Mandy exclaimed on the phone. "You need to wear it."

"But it doesn't fit so well," Audrey told her, eyeing the green dress hanging on the closet door. After trying on the black dress, she had tried the green dress again. She had been able to zip it up higher than the first time she tried it on, but it wasn't a good fit.

"It's okay," Audrey had mumbled to herself, taking it off and looking around at all the boxes of clothes and shoes that her mother had sent. "I will get there."

When she put on the black dress, knowing that black hid everything, she tucked her stomach in a little and deemed herself presentable in Sally's floor-length mirror.

"Oh my," Sally said. "You have the legs for that dress."

Audrey slipped into a tall pair of black opened-toed heels to complete the outfit.

"You look great," Vince said, smiling his approval.

She hadn't been to the valley yet and Vince drove slowly along Rio Grande. Lined with horse estates and looming trees, it looked very different place from Aspen Hills.

He made a right onto a gated gravel road and drove onto the circular driveway in front of the sprawling territorial home. The terra-cotta stucco was trimmed in white.

A valet pulled Audrey's door open and she stepped out, smiling.

Vince placed his hand on her back and together they entered the large house, someone pointing toward the back of the house where the majority of the guests were gathered outside around the pool.

In the kitchen they were stopped by a woman with short brown hair in a red dress and long diamond earrings. "Vince!" she cried and walked to him for a hug.

"Hi Rita," he said, then immediately introducing Audrey.

Rita smacked her lips. "You've never brought a date to these parties." She turned to Audrey. "You must be a special girl."

"We thought he was gay," a man with a silver hair and beard said, walking up and placing his arm on Rita's back while holding out his hand to Vince. "Nice to see you."

The man turned to Audrey. "I'm Chuck and I'm just kidding."

Audrey let them lead, wanting to take in the atmosphere, feeling as if she had returned home in some way: she had missed the parties.

Platters of food covered all the surfaces and several uniformed servers had taken over the kitchen, running around keeping the plates full and the drinks poured.

The energy, Audrey thought, I miss the energy. She listened politely to the conversation as Vince and the Kellys caught up on their lives.

"So how long have you two been dating?" Rita finally asked, holding her hands clasped together in front of her. "Inquiring minds want to know."

Before Vince could speak, Audrey looked at him and quipped, "We're dating?"

Everyone started to laugh, but she knew Vince caught it. "Yeah, we are."

They walked away to move on to others in the party. "Do we have to make that official? It's been a long time for me and I'm not sure how these things work anymore," he said, a drink in his hand, his other hand holding Audrey's arm as if he didn't want her to go far away.

"Me either," Audrey whispered. "So I guess we're dating."

He continued to introduce her to everyone there, and a few people he had never met before.

"I'm Laurie Baca," a woman with curly jet black hair said.

Audrey shook her hand as Laurie asked what she did for a living.

"I was a teaching in Kansas City," Audrey said.

Laurie's eyes got big. "Are you teaching here?"

Audrey laughed and waved her hands in front of her. "My aunt died and left me her house here so I've been cleaning it out."

"I'm the principal at Sagebrush High School. What do you teach?"

"I taught speech," she said. "And communication skills." Then she paused. "A lot of good it must have done since I ended up divorced."

Everyone laughed.

In many ways, Audrey felt as if this evening was her coming out after her divorce. When Rick left her, she didn't have the energy to have a party and didn't know who she would invite since most of their friends had been couples and they were forced to take sides after the divorce.

"I'm sorry," said Kelly, half of a couple they had known since before their marriage when they lived in an apartment complex. "I thought I could be friends with you and Russ could be friends with Rick but it's not working. They golf too much together."

Audrey would shake her head, take a deep breath, and tell the person on the phone that it was okay, that she understood. But when the call ended, she would cry.

"One more loss," she'd tell herself as if she were keeping a tally. She felt angry at Rick for stirring up her life as he did. She didn't know which way was up and instead had crept quietly into a corner where she stayed until moving to Albuquerque.

They were quiet on the ride home. Audrey tried not to think of it as awkward. She looked over at Vince, seeing mostly a shadow of his face in the darkness as he concentrated on the road ahead of them. She opened her mouth once to speak and shut it, thinking of things they could talk about. They were both tired, she realized, but in the back of her mind she worried that somehow it had not been a great night together. The radio played softly, Vince occasionally changing the station, looking for something more interesting.

When they reached Audrey's driveway, he pulled in and turned the car off, getting out with her.

At the front door, she asked, "Do you want to come in?"

Vince grabbed her hand and pulled her to him. "I'm a little tired." he said. "It was a long day at work. I'm going to go home."

"Oh, okay," Audrey said, feeling a little surprised but trying to act cool.

"I had fun tonight," he said, kissing her, and then pulling away enough that they were face to face. "It was good to know how well you do socially."

"Oh geez," she laughed, throwing her head back. "I knew I was being tested!"

"We were testing each other," he said, holding her tight again.

Audrey unlocked the door and opened it, assuring him she was inside, but watched his car as it pulled out of her driveway slowly and the lights led him around the corner to his house. She knew she should be happy but something didn't let her feel settled, nor did she feel better the next morning when she slipped into the pool for her laps.

She felt as if a heavy cloud hovered over her, some sort of depression. As she swam, each lap was a struggle because she wanted to lie back and do nothing.

Maybe I'm just tired, she told herself, feeling as if time was not moving quickly enough.

When Audrey finished, she wrapped herself in Sally's white crocheted robe and lay down on a lounge chair just long enough to dry off. It was going to be hot, they were saying 100 degrees, but the trees kept the shadows cool for the early morning hours.

She walked back into the house and into her bedroom, seeing the green dress. She touched the hem and wondered where she might get to wear it. Still, she had to lose more weight around her middle. Audrey looked to her right at the boxes she had yet to unpack. Her shoes fit fine, no surprise, but many of her dresses and skirts were too tight.

Grabbing the latest diary, Audrey returned to the lounge chair to read for a while. As she started at the top of a new page, she drifted off and suddenly Sally was on the lounge chair next to her.

"You looked beautiful last night," Sally said, adjusting her cat eye sunglasses. Even as an older woman, she looked elegant in her cover-up, as if the years didn't mean anything. Sally didn't look as if she were wearing an outfit that was too young for her. Instead she looked like a confident woman who knew how to wear clothes. A pair of low heels rested on the concrete next to her.

Sally picked up Audrey's sunscreen. "Now this I wish we had," she laughed. "My skin was definitely not made for the desert. I'm surprised I'm not more wrinkled than I am."

Audrey didn't need to speak; she just listened as Sally continued to talk. "What a great party! And the children's hospital is such a great cause. I used to love throwing parties like that. We had anyone who was anyone in this town over and raising money to help others was always the best kind because everyone felt like they were contributing in some way.

"And that Vince," she said, nodding her head. "He is handsome! I always loved those dark, handsome men. The Latin roots."

"But Patrick had blonde hair," Audrey said, and then realizing maybe she shouldn't have spoken.

73

"He did." Sally got quiet. "My parents came to visit, you know, when I dating Reuben."

As Audrey watched Sally, it was as if she disappeared into another time, watching the stillness of the water in the pool.

"I was so excited for them to meet the man I was in love with. Reuben and I hadn't explicitly talked about marriage but we talked about being together. We both knew that's what we wanted."

As Sally disappeared into another time, Audrey went with her. They were at Ida's Diner and Audrey was an onlooker.

"I'm so happy to see you, Mama!" Sally said, rushing up to hug her parents whom she hadn't seen since she moved to Albuquerque a year earlier. "And Papa!"

"Our little girl all grown up," her mother said, taking Sally's hands. "Stand back so I can get a look at you."

And that's when Audrey saw the dress: the green dress. Sally was wearing the green dress.

"You are so beautiful," her mother said, a black pocket book with a short handle hanging on her forearm.

"I can't wait for you to meet Reuben," Sally told them as they settled into a booth, Sally's parents on one side. She looked up and saw Reuben walking in. "And here he is!"

Reuben smiled as he walked confidently to the three sitting in the both. Sally stood up to greet him with a hug and her parents stood to shake his hand.

"Hello Mr. and Mrs. Thomas," he said, smiling.

"And then it went bad," Sally said sadly, shaking her head.

They were back at the pool, Audrey wishing they were still at the diner. She wanted so badly to know more, to see more. But Sally stopped the description and so the memory stopped.

"Why are you stopping?" Audrey asked her, she picked up the diary looking to see what happened.

It was blank for several days. And then it started again.

"It's so painful to talk about this," Sally admitted, starting at Audrey. "I had to put this away to go on."

"What happened? What was so bad?"

They were back in the diner again. Sally's parents looked surprised. Audrey watched, not knowing what was going on. Suddenly lunch became painful, although Sally and Reuben looked unaware of it.

When she began to eat, Sally's napkin slipped and she dropped a french fry smothered with ketchup on her dress.

"Oh no!" she cried, Reuben reaching for a clean napkin to help her.

Sally didn't see it but Audrey did: the looks on her parents' faces. They had turned to ice.

"I don't understand," Audrey said.

But Sally didn't speak to Audrey. Instead the scene had to play out. Sally and Reuben kept up their end of the conversation, clearly two people who loved each other and wanted to be together. On the other side of the table, Stanley and Harriet ate in silence, giving short answers to any questions they were asked.

"I need to go," Reuben said, pulling out his wallet and putting a few dollars on the table to cover his meal. "I am due back at work."

"I wish you didn't have to go," Sally told him, slightly pouting, her hands in her lap, forgetting about the stain on the dress for the moment.

"I didn't get time off like you did," he teased her.

He kissed her on the cheek and held out his hand to shake Stanley's. When he reached for Harriet's, hers was limp.

Sally watched him walk out the door into the warm sunshine and sighed. "Isn't he great?" And then she turned to her parents. And that's when she knew something wasn't right. "Why aren't you saying anything?"

They looked at each other, their food cold, each with hands on the table, and then at Sally. "He's Mexican," her mother said quietly.

Audrey let out a shriek from where she sat in the booth behind them, holding the back of the booth that Sally's back rested against. She covered her mouth and then realized no one had noticed.

"What?" Sally asked. She looked confused.

"He's Mexican," her father said, as if Sally would take him more seriously than her mother. "He's not white."

"So?" She looked at each of them, back and forth, their stares still cold. "You mean you don't like him because he's . . . ." She searched for the word. "Brown?"

"You can't be with a Mexican, Sally Marie."

"He's American, Mother," Sally said, looking irate. "He served our country in the Army in Korea. He was raised in Texas. His parents came from Mexico but he's an American. He has a degree from the University of Wisconsin in engineering and works at the labs here helping to protect our country from nuclear war against the Soviet Union."

She had started to raise her voice and her father said deliberately, "That's enough, Sally."

"No it's not enough," Sally said, hissing as she leaned forward across the table. "I find someone I love and you're not happy. You just want me to come home and live in Kansas. I thought you were happy for me, that I made a life here in New Mexico but obviously not."

"We were until we found out he was a Mexican," her mother said. "What would your children look like?" She put her hand on her forehead and looked down. "Dear Lord."

"They would be the most beautiful children ever." With that Sally, picked up her pocketbook and left Ida's, Audrey sitting there staring at the swinging door as Sally marched through it.

Audrey looked over at Sally, back on her lounge chair by the pool. Sally shook her head and pushed her sunglasses to the top of her head to dry a few tears with the beach towel that Audrey handed her. "To this day I can't believe that my parents were so racist. Reuben was the most wonderful man ever."

"But you didn't marry Reuben," Audrey reminded her, feeling stupid after she said it, but wanting to know the answer.

"That's enough for today," Sally said, placing her sunglasses back on her face and adjusting herself in the sun. She put her head back on the lounge chair and looked up at the sun.

Audrey was alone again, waking up in sun that felt much hotter than when she fell asleep. She took her things inside, including the journal, and spotted the green dress out of the corner of her eye as she walked down the hall.

She went into the bedroom and stood in front of it, fingering the hem near the stain. "Ketchup," she mumbled realizing that meant Sally had not worn the dress since that day.

But why not? As Audrey showered and dressed she thought about what could have caused her to end up with Patrick. She was starting to read more in the journal when Vince texted her and asked if he could come over.

"My swamp cooler broke and the guy can't come until tomorrow to fix it."

"Yes!" Audrey typed back. "And bring Sadie."

"Ah, nice and cool in here," Vince said when he arrived, motioning to Sadie on her leash.

"Let her go," Audrey said with a shrug of her shoulders. "The carpet needs to be replaced anyway."

"You don't like pink carpet?" he asked.

"It's rose," Audrey corrected him, pointing at the lush but dated fibers on the floor. "It's quality stuff that would last forever if the color didn't look so 1980."

He dropped Sadie's leash and at first she stood and looked at him, confused. "It's okay," he said, "you're free."

But the first thing Sadie did was paw at the sliding glass doors in the den. Audrey slid them open and they followed her out. She stood at the short wrought iron gate by the pool and wagged her tail, staring at them.

"You want to go by the pool?" Vince asked. "You never want a bath."

"Oh, but that's not a pool," Audrey giggled, giving the okay for Sadie to get in the pool if she chose.

They sat under the umbrella, Vince stretching his body revealing his belly button under his t-shirt and above the waistline of his shorts. Audrey tried not to let him know she was looking. "It's nice and cool in there," he said, pointing toward the house. "Out here feels like my house."

"It's going to be a hot one today," Audrey added.

Sadie wandered around the pool, taking a lick of the water, then backing up as the water moved.

"It's a giant water bowl," Vince said, laughing at his dog. And then he turned to Audrey. "I took my dad to the airport early this morning. He always goes to visit my sister in California for a month."

"Does she like it there?" Audrey was surprised.

"She married a guy from San Diego and he wanted to go back there. My dad stays for a month and plays with the grandkids." He paused. "As well as golfing, of course."

"I read more about Sally," Audrey said, not wanting to change the subject so much as she was still locked on trying to figure out what happened between Sally and Reuben. "Were you ever not allowed to date a girl because she was white?"

Vince laughed and sat forward. "That was random. Are you kicking me out?"

Audrey laughed at herself and thought about how much she liked his smile and the way he looked so happy when he laughed.

"No!" she said, as if she needed to emphasize it. And then she backed off, sitting back in her own chair. "Sally's parents came to visit and Sally was so excited for them to meet Reuben. But when they found out he was Hispanic, she was told she couldn't be with him."

Vince's eyebrows went up. "I guess I shouldn't be surprised. That was the fifties. And it happened in the movie *La Bamba,* remember?"

"I don't remember that," Audrey said.

"It made me afraid I could never marry an Anglo girl," he laughed.

"And did you?"

"Of course not. She was Hispanic, too. But my parents, especially my dad, didn't care who we brought home. I had friends from all sorts of backgrounds. My best friend, Darin, is Anglo."

77

Audrey shook her head. "I'm still trying to wrap my head around it. She was so in love with him. And then her parents give her icy stares when they meet him."

"So is that why she didn't marry him?" Vince asked.

"I don't know. I haven't gotten that far. I also don't know if it's why she cut off contact with the family."

They were silent for a few moments. Audrey didn't consider the awkwardness of it, her mind busy processing what had happened to Sally. They both watched Sadie as she walked around the pool, looking tentatively at it, as if it might bite her.

"My dad's name is Reuben," Vince said randomly.

Audrey looked over at him. "It is. You told me that before."

He shrugged his shoulders. "Just a coincidence."

"Yeah," Audrey said.

They were scheduled to have dinner at Betty's that night and Audrey thought it was time she told the trio what she had found out about Sally.

"You've been at Audrey's house all day," Betty said to Vince with a big smile when she opened the door and greeted them.

"My swamp cooler is out," Vince said with an even bigger smile.

"Likely story," Betty said, stepping back so they could walk inside. "But I'll give you credit for creativity rather than just admitting you like the girl."

As the three of them walked down the hall to the kitchen, Esther and Mary Ellen appeared with big smiles themselves. Vince didn't get a chance to hold out his hand to them, they each grabbed him for a hug.

"We're so glad to meet you for multiple reasons," Esther said, looking like a little girl who might start jumping up and down. She clasped her hands in front of her. "You've brought so much excitement to Aspen Hills."

"First when you moved in," Mary Ellen chimed in. "We heard rumors about you being the handsome doctor. We had so many handsome doctors back in the day, but everyone is old now. It's so good to have this new, youthful energy."

Betty handed them each a glass of white wine, not even asking if they wanted one. "It's time for a toast!" she exclaimed, "To Audrey and Vince and new beginnings!"

"And may Sally rest in peace," Mary Ellen said quietly.

They clinked glasses and each took a sip.

"And then when we heard you and Audrey started dating." Mary Ellen looked away as if she were going to cry. "Well, it's just been a long road for everyone. And we don't even know your story. Maybe you have your own long road."

Betty brought out a round basket lined with a green fabric napkin and filled with chips, followed by a bowl of salsa. "It's the store-bought stuff," she admitted. "But it's my favorite now."

They all gathered around Betty's kitchen counter, and the women began to pelt Vince with questions.

What made you decide to move to Aspen Hills? Where did you go to medical school? What kind of doctor are you? My foot hurts, do you have any idea why?

Audrey found herself turning away, trying not to laugh. They were relentless.

"I'm sorry, "Audrey would say later when they crossed back to her side of the street in the dark. "I didn't know Mary Ellen would ask about her random foot pain."

"It's okay," Vince said, locking arms with Audrey. "I'm used to it. It happened at the party the other night, too. If healthcare weren't so messed up, people would probably actually go to the doctor."

"You could be your own question and answer line," Audrey suggested.

Vince laughed. "They're good women and they mean well. We're giving them something to talk about."

He was patient at dinner, passing the Spanish rice while telling his life story.

"So your parents must know the Marshalls," Esther said. "Their son is about your age and he went to Mesa Hills High School, too."

When there was a lull in the conversation because everyone's mouths were full, Audrey took advantage of the opportunity. "Patrick wasn't Sally's true love," she said. Simple and clear.

The chewing stopped for a moment. Vince looked at her. And then the puzzled looks started.

Betty was the first to finish chewing and speak. "I don't understand," she said. "How do you know this?"

Audrey started from the beginning, explaining that she had found Sally's diaries and had been reading them. "I just reached the point where her parents came to visit and told her she couldn't be with him."

"Why on earth?" Mary Ellen asked, dropping her fork on her plate and causing a ding to be heard around the dining room. "I can't imagine even telling my children they couldn't be with someone of another ethnicity."

"Think about this for a moment," Esther said, looking at her two friends. "Did any of your children ever bring someone home of a different ethnic group?"

Betty and Mary Ellen shook their heads. "You don't know what it's like to face it. But remember, when we were growing up, it was different." She pointed her head at Audrey and Vince. "We know that Vince is Hispanic but we don't see color nor do we care."

"I'm really a Martian," Vince teased, the women laughing and Betty swatting her napkin at him.

"We've lived here so long," Betty said, looking off into the distance as if she were looking back in time. "But Sally's parents were farmers from Kansas. They probably had never seen a Hispanic person before."

"Why didn't she marry him?" Vince asked.

"That doesn't make sense," Mary Ellen said. "She never talked about her family. So if she never saw her family again, she should have just married Vince."

"She always seemed so happy with Patrick," Esther said, shaking her head.

The mood changed at the table after that. As Audrey watched everyone eat, she worried a little that maybe it had been a mistake to tell the trio.

Betty soothed her fears in the kitchen when Audrey followed her to help serve the ice cream. As Betty scooped the strawberry dessert out of the paper carton and into individual bowls, she said, "I'm glad you told us. I have to be honest, I always wondered a little about Sally. We all have secrets."

She finished dishing the ice cream and held the scoop in her hand, resting it on the counter. Audrey watched it melt and drip onto the countertop, Betty not paying attention.

"Everything always looked perfect from the outside in Aspen Hills," she said. "We have beautiful houses and live wonderful lives. But our past follows us wherever we go. And now I know what Sally's past was."

"But why didn't she marry Reuben?" Audrey asked.

"I don't know," Betty said, putting her lips tightly together. "I always thought they were perfect together but maybe it just looked that way and Sally never told us what was really going on. And maybe it was why she was able to live so long alone after Patrick died. By then she had resigned herself to the idea that she would never have what she really wanted."

"Or maybe it wasn't what she really wanted? Maybe in the end she was glad she and Reuben never got together?"

"I guess we'll never know unless you discover it in her diary." Betty pick up the tray with the dishes and motioned for Audrey to grab the spoons. "We better get this out there before it melts."

Chapter 8

"I have plenty of guest rooms," Audrey offered after she and Vince had walked back to her house. "Even Sadie could have her own."

Vince laughed and put his arms around her. "Maybe my swamp cooler really is working," he said slyly. "Maybe Betty's right, I made it up."

"Then maybe we should go check," Audrey offered, smiling.

"We can if you'd like," he said, holding out his hand to her.

"I believe you," she said. "I'm sure it was really a ploy to spend more time with me."

"Actually, that's not far from the truth," he said.

Audrey felt some anxiety wash over her and started to do a little dance on the polished flagstone in the hall where they were standing.

"Your face just changed," Vince said, looking at her closely. "What's wrong?"

Audrey looked around the room as if the answers would be there. "It's not that I don't want to be with you," she said and then paused. "No, that's what I mean." It was as if minutes were going by and she didn't speak.

Vince didn't say a word; he patiently stood there and watched her, holding her hand.

She shook her head.

"It's okay," Vince reassured her. "I wasn't thinking that at all. I'm happy to sleep in your guest room."

Audrey was embarrassed. She led him and Sadie down the hall to one of the other guest rooms and started to remove the stack of Sally's clothes from the bed. "I have so much to sort out still."

"I didn't even think about it," Vince said thoughtfully, grabbing a stack and placing them on the overstuffed chair by the end. "You have a houseful of her life."

"Way more than the diaries," Audrey joked, placing a pair of high heels on the dresser. "And she had some really nice stuff, some that I actually could wear."

"Those are quite the shoes," Vince said with a whistle, looking at the gold heels.

Audrey laughed. "Are you one of those men with a shoe fetish?" Before he could speak, she added, "I've heard about your kind."

Vince picked up the shoes. "We'll get to that another day. It can wait."

Audrey looked at him and walked to him, placing her arms around his waist. He wrapped his arms around the outside of their circle.

"You don't have to explain anything," he said. "I know the past took its toll. We'll get through it together."

She nodded, even with her head resting against his chest.

Back in her room, Audrey shut the door and climbed into bed, feeling drained but not exhausted enough to turn out the light and sleep. She looked over at the diary at the side of the bed and picked it up, hoping to read just a few pages. She wanted to skim through it to find out what happened to Reuben, but she felt as though she had to take her time or she might miss something.

"Now you know," Sally said. She was sitting in the chair on the other side of the bed.

Each bedroom had a chair and ottoman, pink in this room. "I love this chair," Sally said, running her hand across the velvet. "You know, you should always have a place for your houseguests."

She looked over at Audrey. "And now you know," she said again.

"Not really," Audrey told her, crossing her legs in front of her, not sure how long Sally would stay. "I don't know what happened to Reuben, why you didn't marry him."

"You'll find out soon enough," Sally said. "You need to be patient and it will reveal itself." She was still running her hand across the chair arms. "My family never came to visit after that. In fact, I never saw any of them again."

When Audrey looked around again, they were in the train station, Sally's father standing by a bench with Sally's mother sitting on it and their luggage in a pile next to them.

Sally came running in with her nurse's uniform on, cap and all, looking around for them, finally spotting her father with his hands in his pockets.

"I wanted to see you before I left," she told them, out of breath from running down the street on her lunch break from the hospital.

"Sally," her mother said quietly. "If you intend to marry that man, we shall disown you."

Sally stood back and looked at both of them. She saw sadness in her father's eyes but her mother was cold, looking ahead to the train platform outside the building.

It was as if all the zest in Sally's life had been sucked out of her. She continued to stare at them, not sure what she wanted to say.

"This isn't happening," she finally cried out. "I don't know who you are. You don't have to disown me because I don't want anything to do with any of you."

Her father started to speak, stepping toward her, but she stepped back as he came at her.

"No," she said. "As far as I'm concerned you're all dead to me."

She turned and ran out of the train station as quickly as she had come in.

Audrey found herself wanting to run after her, to find her, to tell her that it was okay, to go marry Reuben and be with the man she loved. But she was paralyzed in her seat on the next bench, as if she had a front and center vantage point for everything in Sally's life.

Everything went blank after that and when Audrey woke up, it was morning. She could hear the swamp cooler whirring overhead, keeping the house cool, and see the sun streaming into the windows. But there was a smell in the house.

She sniffed as she stretched. What is that? She wondered, realizing it was bacon.

Vince, Audrey thought, finding her swimsuit and putting it on.

She stood in the mirror for a moment, not liking what she saw. Audrey knew it was better but still not great. She sucked in her stomach.

"Don't I have a black one-piece?" she asked herself out loud looking around the room at the boxes she had yet to unpack. She knew black would hide what pink would show.

She found it bunched up in a corner of the bottom of one box and slipped it on. Audrey sighed. "Presentable," she said, missing the confidence she always felt in her string bikinis. She pulled the crochet cover up over her and walked into the kitchen where Vince was busy preparing breakfast. Sadie was on the floor snoozing, just like she did at his house.

Audrey quietly watched them for a moment before she announced her presence. She felt as if she was at her mother's house in Kansas on a Sunday morning.

"You've made yourself at home," Audrey said.

"Yeah," Vince said, walking over to her with a spatula in one hand and leaning toward Audrey to kiss her. "The swamp cooler guy is coming at ten so I took the morning off."

"Won't your patients be mad?"

Vince shrugged his shoulders. "I've learned I need to have a life, too. The nurses do a great job running interference. Someone taught me a long time ago that a good nurse, especially an assertive one who can stand her ground, is worth her weight in gold."

He stirred the eggs.

"How did you find everything in here?" Audrey eyed all the items on the counters: bowls, dishes, even the food. "I bet that bacon is way past its expiration date. I certainly didn't buy it."

Vince laughed. "I checked. It's okay. It was in the freezer." He picked up a plastic bag from the sink with something green inside it. "Along with the green chile. I like Sally."

"The trio loves their green chile."

"Sit at the table," he said. "I'll serve you."

"I feel like I'm at my mom's house. Or like I slept over at a friend's house."

Vince brought her a dish that looked like a big gloppy mess. And bacon. "Huevos rancheros," he said, setting it in front of her. "I didn't have any beans though. I almost went across the street to get some from Betty but I was afraid I would never make it back and you'd think I ditched you this morning."

"Because I was such a slut last night," Audrey laughed, taking a bite of the bacon.

The eggs were covered with green chile and cheese. "Maybe a gloppy mess but a tasty one," Audrey said taking a bite.

"My cookbook is rather large."

"Especially impressive for a bachelor," Audrey teased him.

They ate quietly, Sadie snoring around the corner, the sun streaming through the sliding glass doors. Audrey looked up at Vince and he looked up at the same time, picking up the brown mug of coffee at his place setting.

"This is nice," Audrey admitted, feeling a little nervous about saying it.

"Feels like we've been doing it every day."

"As roommates," she teased.

Vince took a drink and put the mug down, moving the newspaper in case he spilled the coffee. "Please don't feel bad about last night. I know it's been a year since you got divorced but anyone who has been there, anyone who has wanted to make herself better because of what she has been through, doesn't rush into bed with someone else."

Audrey sat up and nodded.

"It took me about four years before I even thought about looking at a woman again," he admitted. "Of course I was in my residency so I really was too busy anyway. Still, it's a journey, and I'd rather take this slow and make sure you feel ready than rush in and lose you in the long run."

"Thank you," Audrey said quietly, her hunger gone. She crossed her legs on the wood chair and folded her hands in her lap.

"Are you upset?" he asked, peering at her. "You look upset."

Audrey looked outside and then at him. "I'm not upset at you. I feel petrified, honestly. A lot has changed. And then things were not what I thought they were. Now I feel scared to even take a step forward. It's like there's a ledge there and I wasn't looking and fell off it once before. Now I'm terrified of the same thing happening."

He reached his hand across the table and motioned for Audrey to give him hers. He squeezed it as he leaned over the table. "We're going to take our time."

They sat there a few minutes when Audrey looked up and saw it was nearly 10 a.m. "You better go," she said quietly.

Vince glanced at his watch. "I better or I might never leave," he said, picking up some dishes to take to the sink.

"I'll get those," she said. "I'm going to swim and then I'll do them."

Vince rounded up Sadie on her leash and while Audrey went out back, he walked out the front door.

As she swam, she thought about how lucky she was to have met Vince. And then while she continued her back and forth journey in the pool, Sally was suddenly there with her.

Sally wore a swim cap with pink and yellow flowers on it, one that Audrey hadn't seen. And she didn't have on her usual navy blue one-piece suit either. This one was yellow on top with a white skirt at the bottom. Her skin looked younger, as if she was coming to Audrey from another time.

Together they swam side by side in silence, Sally gliding along with her head above the water, as if she didn't want to get it wet even in the swim cap. And Audrey doing her backstroke, looking at the sky. She had learned how many strokes it was before she hit the side of the pool.

"That's helpful so you don't hit your head," Vince had joked one day. "I don't want to see you when I'm walking by the ER."

Audrey rubbed her head. "That hurts just to think about."

She wanted Sally to speak; she tried to be patient. She wished her time would end though, figuring Sally would start talking then.

As they reached the stairs, out of the corner of her eye, Audrey saw Sally finish and sit on them, taking a moment to catch her breath.

"Keep swimming," she told Audrey. "You want to wear that bikini again."

She's harder on me than my own mother, Audrey thought, waiting for the alarm on the side of the pool to go off. When it did five laps later, Audrey pulled up next to Sally who looked serene, watching the water wash over her as she moved her arms around.

"I always wished I had been born at a different time," Sally said. "So many things would have been different. I didn't really want to be a nurse. Don't get me wrong, I loved the energy of the hospital. But I had no choice if I wanted to leave Kansas. If I became a teacher, it would have been a life sentence."

She sighed. "And no daughter of my father's was going to be a secretary."

There was a sadness in Sally's eyes. "But becoming a nurse meant I could leave. I wanted to go to California but New Mexico was the compromise I made with my mother."

She was silent for a bit; Audrey waiting patiently for her to speak again.

"And if I had been born later, then Reuben and I could have been together."

Audrey bit her tongue, wanting so badly to speak.

"His family was so good to me. His parents came to visit once from Texas and they didn't speak much English but it didn't matter. We all sat at one long table in his aunt's living room, eating bowls of beans and chile and tortillas. Everyone laughing. They were so proud of Reuben because he had accomplished so much." She laughed, a sarcastic laugh. "And I know they were proud that he was with me. But my family? They thought he was an alien."

Sally walked out of the pool and grabbed her towel on the lounge chair, disappearing inside the house, leaving Audrey sitting there alone, still with no answers to her questions about Sally and Reuben.

Chapter 9

It was hot again on Sunday.

"The weather people here are clueless," Betty said at the front door that afternoon, shaking her shirt to keep cool. "You'll find we can predict the weather better by looking out the window. I'm going to get in my pool when I go back across the street.

"Friday night though, we want to tell you more about Sally. We realized that while you have learned something about her that we didn't know, we know a lot that you don't know." As she turned away, she added, "And you can bring Vince, too, if you'd like. We aren't an exclusive all-girls club. We rather miss the male sort."

Audrey walked into the laundry room to retrieve a load of clothes from the dryer and saw five paintings leaning against each other and slid into a cubbyhole that Audrey hadn't noticed before. She left the clothes half out of the dryer and pulled out the paintings. They were nearly the same size and of the same scene: the pool in the back yard. Something was different about each one though. Some were darker than others: one looked as if it were nighttime; another looked stormy. And one portrayed the typical sunny days that Audrey was beginning to love about New Mexico.

She looked at the right corner to see that Sally had not only signed her name but dated them. 1970–74. Each one was a different year.

"The way she felt that year?" Audrey wondered, taking them to the living room and setting them on top of the couch, leaning against the wall in order starting with 1970 on the left.

"Coming out of the darkness into the light?" Audrey mumbled out loud, hoping that Sally would hear her.

She waited for a moment but nothing happened. Audrey returned to the laundry room to wash her clothes that had been boxed up for over a year. With all these "new" clothes she had to find space and ended up spending the rest of the day reorganizing the closet in the master bedroom.

"If I'm going to stay, I should act like it," she told Vince when he called that night.

"And you should sleep in the master bedroom," Vince suggested. "Not the guest room."

"You're probably right." Audrey got up from her bed in the guest room and walked down the hall. "I need to paint it, though. I'm really not a fan of the wallpaper."

"You mean you don't like pink flowers on long vines talking to you while you sleep?"

Audrey laughed. "Not really. So maybe you should come over and help me remove it so I can sleep in here at night."

"I had someone do all the work at my place," he said, "but for you, I will scrape wallpaper."

"I have no clue how to do it," Audrey said. "My mom never had wallpaper. But we should probably start with a smaller project, perhaps the bathroom, first."

"We'll do it together. I'm sure there is a YouTube video that shows how to remove wallpaper."

When Vince showed up at the house on Friday, all the necessary tools in his car, Audrey had already cleared the bathroom and was busy taking down the paintings in the hallway and hanging the five paintings she had found in the laundry room. She leaned the discards against a wall in the living room and was surveying her work in the hallway when the doorbell rang.

Vince strolled in with several Home Depot bags in his hands. "I probably should have asked you if you had any of this stuff," he said.

"I have no idea what's in the garage," Audrey said, shaking her head. "It might be better to start over."

As he carried everything down the hall to the bathroom, where Audrey had set plastic over the carpet, he laughed.

"Are you trying to save the carpet?" he asked.

Audrey moaned. "Who puts carpet in bathrooms? Really! But I wasn't sure what to do. I'll need someone to replace it."

Vince pointed at the gold light fixtures. "Don't you think it's time for a bathroom remodel?"

"And you're up for that?"

"I can't do tile but I have someone who can and we can do the rest of it."

"Knowing that I don't have a lot going on right now, sure," Audrey said. "And knowing that I have no clue what I'm going to do for the rest of my life, why not?"

Vince put his hands on his hips and surveyed the scene. "Let's get the wallpaper down and then we can deconstruct the rest of the bathroom."

"I didn't realize you knew how to do all of this," Audrey said, surprised.

He laughed. "My dad made sure I had all these skills. Even though he was able to get a college education, he knew he wasn't that far from being a laborer like the rest of his family."

"But you didn't do all this work at your house. At least that's what you told me."

He shook his head and put one hand on the pink countertop. "That's because it was just me. Helping you is very different." He looked around and added, "Let's get started."

She followed Vince back down the hall and he stopped when he saw the paintings. "Hey, these weren't here when I left."

Audrey laughed. "They weren't. I found them in the laundry room."

Vince looked at each one and Audrey could see he had figured out they were the same scene painted five different ways.

"Was she experimenting with color?" He peered over each one, getting close to them to see them better. "Isn't that the pool in the backyard?"

"It is," Audrey said. Audrey pointed in the corner where Sally had painted her initials. "Look at the years. One right after the other."

Vince stepped back and looked at each one. "It's as if they are painting a mood."

"Exactly."

"What year are you in the diary?"

"I'm still in the fifties."

"Then you need to read some more, for Pete's sake. We all want to know what happens."

"You and me both," she said.

"And the trio," he joked.

Vince showed her how to scrape the wallpaper after he applied a solution with a sponge and they each set to working in a different corner of the bathroom.

"Are you sure you want to do this with me?" Audrey asked again.

He stood up from the corner by the bathtub where he was working. "We're in, my friend. And now we won't stop until it's done."

And they didn't. Sadie layin the hallway, alternately watching them and napping.

That night, after Vince left, Audrey sat on the countertop in the bathroom and looked around, ready to climb into bed and read. She had set her phone on the diary beside her.

Sally walked in and started to inspect. "It was time for a makeover," she said. "I thought about it but I never got around to it. With Patrick gone, it wasn't the same." She sighed and sat down on the side of the tub, facing Audrey. "This is your house now, your life. Please don't be afraid to change anything."

Audrey waited for her to speak more, Sally wasn't looking at Audrey. Once again she was somewhere else.

"It broke my heart that my parents didn't accept my relationship with my Reuben," she said. "I know that times changed in the years ahead but none of us saw the sixties coming. We didn't see Kennedy's death coming either."

She did a slight laugh.

"How times have changed!" Sally shook her head. "I thought my parents could still run my life. I didn't have the wherewithal to tell them to buzz off. I tried for a time to stay with Reuben but after that it was too hard. I broke up with him a few months later.

Audrey gasped. Sally didn't notice. She left the room, leaving Audrey feeling sad, as if she had broken up with Reuben herself.

"She broke up with him," Audrey whispered to Vince on the phone that evening.

"I'll be right over," he said, arriving with Sadie in tow, and together they sat on the couch as if someone they knew had died.

"Why am I so upset?" Audrey wondered out loud. "I feel so connected to this yet I can't explain it."

"It's penetrating your own losses," Vince said, stroking her hair. "Everything you have felt about loss is right here wrapped up in this loss now."

"That's messed up," she said, sitting up and looking at him.

He shrugged his shoulders and held her hand. "Yeah, but it's reality. We all do it. I did it when my mom died. Everything from my marriage bubbled up and I was a mess."

"But you knew your mom," Audrey reminded him. "I never met Sally."

"Her story is affecting you, though. You feel a connection to her."

"It's still messed up," Audrey reminded him.

Chapter 10

Vince had asked Audrey to meet downtown for lunch on Tuesday.

"I have to stay close to the hospital," he explained. "But meet me across the street—you'll see the benches."

Audrey was early and sat down, opening the diary to read while she waited. Within a few moments, Sally was beside her.

"Oh, this bench," she said brightly as she sat down. She was wearing a navy blue shirtdress, the kind with the tie in the middle that had made a fashion comeback. Audrey thought how elegant Sally looked; she always seemed to have her act together. Sally must be hot in the dark fabric, though, Audrey wore her yellow halter dress, one more item she found that fit. Slowly she was beginning to fit into her clothes again but she also was discovering that some were loose enough that she could get away with wearing them.

Sally looked around at the people passing by, many of them coming and going from the hospital to the main part of downtown, mostly to lunch.

"Reuben and I used to meet here," she said. And then her face turned dark. "And this is where I ended it with him."

Audrey leaned forward and turned her head to Sally.

"It was a day just like this," Sally said, looking around but her hands rubbing at the fabric of her dress in her lap. "I didn't want to do it but I couldn't put it off any longer. It was getting harder and harder.

"The worst part was seeing the sadness on his face. He didn't understand, and I couldn't explain." She turned to look at Audrey. "Life is so different for you. Don't let go."

Let go of what? Audrey wanted to say but as she began to open her mouth, Vince sat down on the other side of her, a white paper bag in his hand. "Who are you watching?" he asked.

Audrey leaned over to greet him with a kiss and when she looked back, Sally was gone. As always.

"This is where Sally broke up with Reuben," Audrey said.

"This park?"

"This bench."

"Oh." He paused and looked around for a moment. "You aren't planning to break up with me here, are you?"

"I just found you," Audrey reminded him, putting her hand on his knee. "I'm not ready to get rid of you."

"Great! Then I have some lunch for you. There is a woman who sometimes makes burritos and sells them for the staff. The second? third? Tuesday of the month." He shrugged his shoulders, and opened the paper bag and handed her a roll covered in foil. "I got you the red chile because it appears to me that you haven't experienced enough red chile."

Audrey smiled, feeling limp.

"We can go sit on another bench," he suggested.

"No," Audrey said, waving her hand. "Let's stay here. The feeling will pass. I just can't imagine a time when someone felt they had to break up with someone over skin color." And then she realized she was being a hypocrite. "That's not totally true. I don't think I could have brought home a black boyfriend. Hispanic I'm not sure."

Vince raised his eyebrows. "Then maybe I can't meet Mom?"

Audrey laughed. "Oh, not today! My mom is so happy about you. She's afraid of me being alone. And yet I'm afraid of her being alone since Dad died. But she says she's old and had a long, happy marriage. She wants me to have that, too."

They unwrapped their burritos and Audrey took a bite of the red chile pork wrapped in a flour tortilla. "Carne adovada?"

"Yes," he said. "You like it? It's not as good as mine."

"It's different."

"It's more bitter; she uses the northern red chile."

"But I like it," Audrey said.

They sat for a few minutes and chewed, not talking. It was a comfortable silence, not the kind Audrey had worried about at the beginning of their relationship. She liked that they had reached the point where they were relaxed enough to not have to talk all the time. She had missed that part of a relationship: just being with someone. It was as if simply knowing someone was in her corner, there to support her, made her feel secure.

"I'm sorry I can't spend more time with you today," Vince said, holding out his hand for the foil wrapper.

"It's okay," Audrey said. "I'm the lame one who has no job." She thought for a moment. "But I'd be off for the summer anyway."

"School is just around the corner," Vince noted, crumpling everything in his hand.

"I saw the school supplies section at Target," Audrey remarked.

"Nothing like starting in August when it's still hot, not like after Labor Day when at least it seems a few degrees cooler."

He stood up and held his hand out to her to help her up, and they parted ways with a hug and a kiss. As Audrey walked away, looking for where she had parked her car, she thought about Sally.

"It was the start of a very dark time for me," Sally said, falling in step with Audrey. "I missed him so much, but I knew there was no turning back."

Audrey knew this from reading the diary. Sally didn't date much after that the breakup, choosing to take extra shifts at the hospital to keep busy. Reuben contacted her a few times, and she asked her roommates to intercede.

"I can't talk to him," she wrote. "It's just too hard. I hope one day this pain will go away."

The woman that Audrey had begun to know, the one who seemed so happy and fun loving, was gone. It was as if Sally had given up. She continued through life, she got up each morning and went through the motions. But it wasn't the same.

In some ways, Audrey could relate to it. When her marriage ended, she had felt broken and empty.

"We had no idea," Mary Ellen said, once again slapping her hand to her chest after Audrey told them what she had recently read. Vince sat next to Audrey, holding her hand beneath the table.

"How sad," Esther said, "that she felt she had to end it. But I guess now we know what happened."

"I think it does explain some things," Betty added, looking at the two women before turning back toward Audrey and Vince. "There were times when she just didn't seem happy."

"But, you see," Mary Ellen said, pushing her pizza away, "We all went through those kinds of things. Everyone thought because we didn't work, because our husbands made enough money for us to stay home, that we were these happy women who spent all day playing cards and drinking wine."

"The wine was true for a few," Esther chimed in.

Betty looked at her and let out a laugh. "It was for Lois, wasn't it?"

Audrey and Vince looked at each other and shrugged, not knowing who Lois was.

"But they were lonely times in many ways. The children went off to school; we had cleaning ladies. We were told we weren't going to work, both by tradition and our husbands."

"And even in a good marriage, there were lonely times," Esther said, pointing her head at Mary Ellen.

"There were. Life was different for couples."

"And Sally didn't have kids like the rest of us," Betty reminded them.

"She didn't talk much about that. Patrick was so into his golf," Esther said.

"That's why she took up painting," Mary Ellen added.

Everyone at the table was silent for a moment. Audrey tried to piece it all together but something wasn't fitting. Maybe it was simply that she felt sad for Sally and she was mourning her own loss right with Sally's.

"I'll get the ice cream," Betty said, taking a deep breath and getting up from the table. As she left the room, Audrey's eyes followed her but she didn't see anything.

"Why would she give up such true love?" Mary Ellen asked, talking to no one in particular.

"But she seemed so happy with Patrick," Esther said, adding, "at least most of the time."

Betty came back with the tray that held a half gallon of strawberry along with five glass dishes and spoons. "I forgot the scoop," Betty said, looking at the tray after she set it down. She left for the kitchen and came back with it in her hand.

"My mom used to say ice cream makes everything better," Vince said, looking around. After a brief silence, everyone burst out laughing.

Betty began to dig out a serving for everyone.

"Don't you have some of those vanilla cookies, too?" Esther asked, taking a dish from Betty.

"My goodness!" Betty teased her friend. "Strawberry ice cream isn't enough?"

Esther looked over at Vince and winked. "Well, it would be even better if I could have a cookie with it."

Betty left for the kitchen again.

"Amazing how we thought we knew someone," Esther said. "And then it turns out there was this whole piece we didn't know."

Mary Ellen turned to Esther and asked, "What secrets are you harboring?"

"'She has dead bodies in the garage," Betty said without missing a beat.

Audrey started to laugh and found she couldn't stop. She was sad for Sally, she was sad that Sally didn't get to spend her life with the man she obviously loved. And she was sad for herself that her life had not turned out the way she wanted.

But sitting there with the three women and Vince, she realized how lucky she was to have them. If Sally's life had been different, she might not be in Albuquerque in that moment with the life she was just beginning.

As she and Vince walked across the street that evening, Audrey stopped and looked up at the sky. "I still can't believe how bright the stars are here," she said, mesmerized. Vince squeezed her hand.

"Amazing, isn't it?"

"Yeah." And she said a silent thanks to Sally.

Chapter 11

Audrey stared at the blank canvas. She sat on the stool in the laundry room with the easel in front of her and the paints set out on a palette, on top of a small, stained wood table. A brush in one hand, Audrey sighed.

"You always wanted to write a book," her mom had said before she moved. "Now you have the time to do that."

It was one of the few things her mom hadn't gotten right about her. That had been a junior high dream, one that had long died and that she had no plans to resurrect. Reading Sally's diaries was enough for her. She didn't feel the need to tell any stories.

She took the brush and swiped the turquoise across the right side of the canvas horizontally. Maybe she would paint her own version of the pool.

"What am I going to do?" she asked out loud, feeling a little bored. Vince was right: school was getting ready to start, and Audrey was starting to get back in the mode to prepare for the new school year. But she was in Albuquerque with no New Mexico license. It was too late anyway.

"I can't stay home all day," she said, continuing to paint what looked like a swimming pool in her mind but wasn't working on the canvas.

Audrey hadn't told anyone how sad she felt ever since finding out Sally had ended the relationship with Reuben. There were no photos; what did Reuben look like? Was he still alive? Or maybe they met in heaven when they died.

What bothered her was that it felt like a missed opportunity. Sally had thrown away the love that Audrey would die for.

"Don't put too much thought into painting," Sally said, walking behind Audrey and looking on as Audrey continued to paint the pool. "Just let your emotions create it. That's what I did."

It was a one-way conversation. Audrey didn't want to push Sally away, but she wished she could ask her some questions. While there had been a few times when she had been able to speak to Sally, something had changed, and she felt as if Sally were ignoring her now. Sally kept coming to Audrey but it was on her terms. Audrey's phone buzzed and she walked across the room to the top of the dryer where she had left it.

"Do you remember Laurie Baca from the party in the valley?" Vince asked in a text.

"The school principal?" Audrey texted back.

"Yes."

"The kinky black hair?"

"Yes."

"I do."

"She wants to call you. She has a job she needs filled immediately."

"Teaching?"

"Yes."

"Um, okay."

Audrey gave up on the painting and walked into the kitchen. Within five minutes, the phone rang. She stopped loading the dishwasher and stared out at the pool.

"Hi, is this Audrey? It's Laurie Baca," said the excited voice on the other end. Audrey could picture her kinky hair bobbing all around as she spoke. "I hope you remember me from the party."

"I do," Audrey said.

"I'm not sure what Vince told you but I need a teacher at Sagebrush." She talked a mile a minute. "Our main communications teacher broke her hip and decided to retire since she'll be out for several months. We need to replace her before the school year starts. Are you interested?"

"I don't have a New Mexico teaching license," Audrey reminded her.

"Don't worry about that," Laurie assured her. "We'll waiver you and get that taken care of. School starts in two weeks and I need a teacher. I just need you to come in so everyone can meet you, but you'll be hired." She paused. "Unless of course you have some weird criminal history."

Audrey laughed. "No, don't worry about that."

"Good, because Vince never brings any women to those fundraisers, so you must be special if he brought you."

Audrey's heart skipped a beat and her excitement grew. She smiled as she looked out at the pool. "What time should I be there?"

Sagebrush High School, home of the Scorpions, sat on the west side of the city. "It's almost as far away from Aspen Hills as you can get," Vince joked with her later over pizza when they celebrated her new job.

"It's a newer school," Laurie said, greeting Audrey at the front door. "But the West Side has cheaper housing so we have a lot of kids whose families starting out. We're about seventy-five percent Hispanic and what you'll find is many of these parents are struggling making a living and raising their kids. They moved to the West Side for the housing, and now they are trying to keep it together."

She led Laurie down three hallways and up two flights of stairs. Audrey kept looking back, wondering how she would find her way around.

Prairie Valley was just as big, she reminded herself, recalling the school she'd been teaching at for fifteen years. You can do this.

Laurie stopped and opened the door of a classroom between two sets of lockers. "And this is your room."

The big windows gave her an incredible view of the mountains. That alone was reason to teach.

"It's a great view, isn't it?" Laurie said, slowing down for a moment, her arms wrapped across her chest.

"Laurie, Ted needs you," a bald man said from the doorway.

"John, this is Laurie. She's going to replace Dana."

"Oh, great," the bald man said with a smile, holding out his hand for her to shake. "I hope Laurie told you we might make you wear bubble wrap when you walk down the stairs."

"That was so not politically correct," Laurie said quietly, a smile on her face.

"Always saying what you're supposed to say," John said, "but really thinking something else."

After an hour of paper work, Audrey wandered back to her classroom, mostly to make sure she could find it, a set of keys in her hands. She sat at the desk in the darkened room with the light filtering in from the hot summer day, the air conditioner humming full blast.

"I'm a little worried because I need to start over with so much," she admitted to Vince later. "I don't have all my stuff here. I left it in my classroom and when I decided not to return, I told a few of my teacher friends to take what they wanted."

"What did you think you would do?"

Audrey shrugged as she chewed her pizza. "I'm not sure."

"Then start over. It's not a bad thing."

"I know." She put her half-eaten slice of pizza back on the plate. "I do want to do some things differently. I want to focus more on communication in relationships. I missed something somewhere in my marriage."

"And now you can help others build stronger communication in relationships?"

"Why not? It might go in one ear and out the other but at least I can give it a try."

With two weeks before school started, she put Sally's diaries aside and used a few notebooks she found in a kitchen drawer to start drafting her lesson plans. Audrey moved the china off the dining room table, still undecided if she wanted to keep it, and laid out the pages she tore from the notebook.

"You know, you could use a computer for that," Vince said.

"I need to get a printer," Audrey told him. "I don't think computers were Sally's thing. There was no internet in the house when I moved in."

He looked over her lesson plans one evening and then walked into the kitchen where she handed him their place settings for dinner. "I have something I'd like to ask you."

"Hmm," Audrey said, taking the chicken casserole out of the oven.

"My cousin is getting married next weekend. Do you want to be my date?"

Audrey set the casserole down on the hot pads and looked up. "Really? How old is your cousin?"

"She's twenty-two," he said, sitting at the table.

Audrey joined him. "Yes, I'd love to go."

"That's good because I already sent in the response card saying you would," he said laughing. "And I have something else."

Audrey served each of them and then pointed for him to get some salad.

"We kind of lost our way with the bathroom."

"Yeah, we did." She laughed. "I'm thinking we don't really have the time for it."

"I know. I'm going to get my contractor over here to finish the whole thing." And before Audrey could say anything, he added. "I'll pay for his time."

"I have the money," Audrey told him.

"I know," Vince said, holding his hands in front of her as if he needed a barrier from her. "But I'm the one who got you started on the project, not realizing that it wasn't something we couldn't do. Think of it as my gift to you for getting a job here. If you're going to stay, you need to get moved into the master bath."

Audrey got up and walked to him. He pulled his chair out and she climbed into his lap and kissed him. "Thank you," she said quietly, remaining tangled in his arms for what seemed like a few minutes.

"You're welcome," Vince told her, pinching her thigh. "Now please get off my lap so I can eat dinner," he teased.

"Yeah yeah yeah," Audrey joked.

Rodrigo showed up the next morning with a clipboard and pen.

"I heard you're the best," Audrey said. He laughed, his mouth opening wide as his face.

"He is the best," Vince had told her the previous night as he called Rodrigo and asked him to stop by and see Audrey. "His tile guy is not the best on being there on time though so I want to get this done before you start teaching."

"So he thought he could start a job but couldn't finish it?" Rodrigo asked, surveying the bathroom with its bare walls.

Audrey laughed and together they set to planning the new bathroom, the plan to gut it down to the wallboard and put in new everything.

"I like pink, but I'm not really into pink toilets or sinks," Audrey joked, pointing at the fixtures.

As she left the bathroom to return to her lesson plans, letting Rodrigo take notes, she thought that maybe it was time to do more than clean out the house.

"You should remodel," Sally said, sitting at the dining room table with a cup of tea, even on a warm July morning. "I made this house into what I wanted. Now it's your turn to make it into what you want."

Audrey looked around. She knew it meant new furniture, too.

"And that's okay," Sally told her, putting her cup down after taking a sip. "This is your house, and I want you to be happy. And I've left you plenty of money to do that."

Weren't you happy? Audrey looked at her. Sometimes she felt like Sally could read her thoughts.

"I never had the chance at happiness that you have. Maybe I'm glad the money went to you rather than my brother. I mean, I know it would have been fine, but I get to watch you rebuild your life and know that I gave you this opportunity."

"That's all for today, "Rodrigo said. "The dumpster will be dropped off later this afternoon and tomorrow I need you to meet me at the tile and plumbing stores to pick everything."

"You're having your bathroom redone?" Betty asked when they both happened to be at their mailboxes later that afternoon. "And you got a teaching job?"

Giddy, Audrey thought. She's giddy.

Betty hugged Audrey. "I'm so excited! The girls will be so happy to hear, too. We had such a good feeling when you moved in. I just knew you'd stay!" She stopped for a moment, thinking. "Now we need to get you and Vince married."

Audrey opened her mouth. Nothing came out.

"Oh, not today," Betty said, seeing Audrey's fear. "But one day. The sooner the better though. You never know what tomorrow will bring, so don't put it off."

Betty took her mail and waved good-bye, rushing back into her house. Audrey knew Betty could hardly wait to call Esther and Mary Ellen.

"What do I wear to the wedding?" Audrey asked Vince the next evening after they surveyed the demolition that Rodrigo's crew had accomplished.

"Clothes, I hope," Vince teased.

"That is so not funny," she said giving him a playful glare. "I haven't been to a wedding in a while and this is a New Mexico wedding. Are they as stuffy as Kansas weddings?

"We are not stuffy, especially compared to you Midwesterners," Vince said. "That's why all of you drink: it's the only way to get unstuffed."

"That's pretty much the truth," Audrey agreed, leading him to the guest room where she had hung her dresses in the same closet with the ones she was keeping of Sally's.

"What about this green one?" he asked, pointing at the dress hanging on the door.

Audrey moved her feet uncomfortably and looked at him. "I'm a little fat for it."

"You aren't fat," Vince said, looking at her.

"I am compared to what I used to be" she said. "Some people gain that freshman fifteen in college? I waited for the divorce fifteen." She instantly felt not just embarrassed but sad. "I was really cute, and then after Rick left, I just didn't care. Now I'm looking back and I can't believe I was so stupid and gave him that much power over my life and let myself go."

"I think you're beautiful," Vince said, taking her hand and pulling her to him. He ran his hands over her back and across her backside. Audrey tried not to think about the very fat he was feeling. "Relax," he said whispering in her ear. "I'm not going to bite."

Audrey started to laugh. She felt her body shake against Vince and then she had to pull away to hold her stomach.

"What's so funny?" he asked.

"You telling me you don't bite," she said, doubled over. "If I thought you would bite me, I would never have invited you into my house."

"But you always act that way when I hold you," he protested.

She stopped and sat down on the bed, feeling sad again. He sat next to her, Audrey pulling her legs up in front of her while Vince stayed on the edge of the white bedspread. "I can't believe how much divorce messed me up."

Vince took her hand. "It messed me up. But I'm here to tell you that I'm not going anywhere. I'm happy to spend time with you. There won't be any drama. Just let me be part of your life."

They sat for a few moments in silence and then Vince said, "I want you part of my life. And right now that means we need to pick a dress for you to wear to my cousin's wedding."

Audrey wiped her eyes and walked back to the closet.

"When the green dress fits, we'll find a place for you to wear it," he said.

Audrey looked back at him and smiled.

"But I'm counting on you to tell me when it does fit."

Audrey smiled again, nodding.

"Can we please pick a dress for Maria's wedding now?"

Audrey laughed and patted his knee. "You still haven't told me what kind of wedding it is. A pig roast in your uncle's backyard or the big Catholic do?"

"The pig roast of course," he said, teasing as she walked back to the closet. "No, we only do big Catholic dos, especially on my mom's side."

Audrey held up several dresses, two that belonged to Sally and two that belonged to her. And then she held out the spaghetti-strap short black dress. "I always worry that wearing black to a wedding is like saying you're going to a funeral and don't think the marriage will make it."

"Black is timeless," Vince said.

"And hides my fat," she added.

But she settled on a turquoise sleeveless dress that Vince liked and she knew she would feel comfortable wearing.

Audrey spent more time worrying about her hair for the wedding than she had on all their dates combined.

"It's probably because you kept running into him without planning it," Mandy said from Audrey's phone on speaker as she did her hair. The phone sat on the bathroom counter while Audrey curled her hair and then pulled it back into an updo. "You didn't have time to worry about your hair, and you knew he saw you however you were at that time."

"These are all the relatives," Audrey reminded her friend.

"You'll do fine. Besides you said they're serving enchiladas. What more could you ask for?"

"His aunt's cooking is what he said."

"That's a whole lot better than the hotel standard here. At least it has character."

"I know," Audrey agreed. "We were so culture-less growing up."

"Corn, that was our culture," Mandy laughed.

"And we grew up in the suburbs. We didn't even live near a cornfield and our culture was corn."

"Is there any culture in Kansas?"

They were quiet as they thought for a moment, Audrey trying to curl the back of her head and Mandy most likely folding laundry.

"Barbecue," Mandy finally said. "I had some last night. That place down south on Second and Grass Creek."

"The hole in the wall run by the black family?"

"Yeah, remember Miles was in our graduating class."

"He was very cool."

"And he definitely had more culture than us."

The doorbell rang and Audrey ran to it, nearly finished with her hair. When she threw open the door, Vince stood in front of her in a suit with a purple tie. "Hi," he said.

"Hi," she said, staring at him.

"You've seen me in a tie," he said, walking toward her. "You act surprised."

"For some reason you look more handsome than usual," Audrey told him.

"You opened a bottle of wine already?" he teased, kissing her. "Besides I could never be cuter than you."

Audrey rolled her eyes and walked down the hallway back to the bathroom. "Please come help me. I need you to curl the back of my head."

She didn't miss a beat, she didn't think about it twice. She just asked.

"I'm not so sure I'm the one to help you. Why don't you ask Betty?"

"You're here. I'm serious. I'll explain what to do. You can see better than me. I missed out on the eye behind my head that other teachers have."

Vince scooted next to her in the bathroom and she explained which way to curl to avoid the crease, handing him the curling iron.

"Are you sure?" he asked, looking nervous. "I don't want to ruin your hair, or hurt you."

"You're a doctor," she reminded him. "You stick needles in people. And I'm sure you've done a few surgeries in your time."

"Not recently," he said, grabbing a section of her hair and wrapping it around the hot iron. "Curling hair wasn't something we learned in med school."

She watched him in the mirror, struggling to figure it out, knowing that he was still doing a better job than she could have on her own head. And she liked knowing he was willing to try. He didn't question it. At least that much.

Outside her heels clicked against the concrete and the sun kissed her skin.

"It's on the warm side," she said, happy to get into Vince's air conditioned car.

"You're going to see varying degrees, shapes, sizes, and ethnicities of my family," Vince said as they drove to the church. "We are not all equal."

The wedding was in the valley, the part of Albuquerque where many of Vince's relatives lived.

"I don't understand," Audrey said, looking at him.

"You will," Vince said.

"Why didn't your family live in the valley," she asked as they neared the church, the steeple obvious in the distance.

"My dad wanted something better than he had. I wouldn't say he wanted us to be white so much as he tried to hold onto our culture while also giving us a very different life. If it hadn't been for the Army, he always said he would still be in San Antonio and my sister and I would have been sharing a room."

"So where did you live?"

"I'll take you on a tour before the reception," he said, pulling into the parking lot.

Once they began to walk across the parking lot to the church, she started to see what he meant about the varying degrees: while Vince wore a suit, some of the men wore jeans and polos.

"That's just New Mexico," he said, waving it off as they neared the entrance of the church itself. "That's not specific to my family."

His cousins greeted him, one in jeans, one in a suit. "We keep thinking the next wedding will be yours," the one in the suit joked. And then he looked at Audrey, "Nice to meet you. He never brings anyone to family functions so he must be secure enough to have you around us."

Vince laughed with them and they walked toward the front of the church, the pews decorated with oversized white tulle bows. At the front, flowers overflowed around the altar.

"Is there room for the priest?" Audrey whispered. "That's a lot of flowers."

"That's Maria," Vince whispered, waving to another cousin. "Everything is larger than life, including her."

When everyone was seated and the organist began to play, Audrey looked around, mostly to see how full the church was behind them. She realized she was one of the only blondes in the room. The other two had dark eyebrows.

"Isn't anyone in your family blonde?" she whispered as quietly as she could.

"We aren't that varied," he joked back. "It's more economics and a lot of it economics by choice."

The traditional brown stucco church with wood floors wasn't huge and it had filled up quickly, making the crowd look bigger than it really was. People continued to greet Vince, and Audrey smiled as he introduced her.

She felt welcome, she would tell Mandy later. There was no doubt about that. While they sat quietly, everyone waiting for the ceremony to begin, Sally appeared on Audrey's right.

"Oh how beautiful," she whispered to Audrey.

You're getting bold, Audrey wanted to say to her, looking around, including at Vince, and realizing no one had any idea that she was there.

"Reuben and I came here for a wedding once," she said. "It was one of his cousins. Oh, they were good to me. I was so different than them but they didn't care. And we ate and danced the night away in the hall next to the church." She looked toward the stained glass windows, thinking for a moment. "I think it burned down and they built something new. Hmmm. It doesn't matter. It was such a fun night."

Audrey tried to be partial but she thought Sally looked sad, as if she missed out on something because she had married Patrick instead.

Where were you and Patrick married?

Sally shook her head. "I didn't care. It wasn't such a big deal to me by then. We went to the courthouse one day at lunch, me in my nurse's uniform and him in his suit, and married." She laughed. "It was a Friday so we both took the afternoon off and drove up to Santa Fe for the weekend." She shrugged her shoulders. "I never had the wedding I thought I would."

She is sad, Audrey thought, watching her. Didn't her friends see that? Or did she hide it well?

The organ began to play and Sally disappeared, a slew of bridesmaids and flower girls entering the church, and overflowing the altar area on the left, each wearing a fluffy pink tulle dress.

Audrey looked at Vince. "I told you," he whispered, "that's Maria. All Maria."

And then it started. The wedding march. Everyone stood and looked to the back where Maria and her father, Vince's uncle, entered through the doors that had been flung open by ushers on the other side.

Vince's uncle, his mother's brother, was in his seventies, but he and his wife Victoria had seven children, Maria being the youngest. She was born when her father was fifty.

"An oops," Vince had explained. "My mom said Aunt Victoria thought that because she was forty-two, she couldn't get pregnant anymore."

"Seriously?" Audrey couldn't believe what she heard.

"I'm serious"

"No one explained to her?"

"Apparently not," Vince laughed, with Audrey.

"And you're a doctor?"

"That's my mom's family. My parents weren't like that."

Maria was larger than life. So large that she spilled out of her dress, the tops of her breasts looking like they were going to pop out of sleeveless white satin.

Some women shouldn't wear sleeveless, Audrey wanted to say, putting her hand over her mouth to make sure it didn't really come out.

She couldn't take her eyes off Maria, though. She smiled wide, her dress hitting the pew on the left side as she walked down the aisle, her flowers covering her front and that of her tiny father who wasn't much taller than her.

Audrey looked at the front of the church to see a dark-haired man with a goatee smiling back at her, their eyes connected, the love obvious between them.

"He really loves her," Vince said later. "I think my uncle was more than happy to pass her on to Javier because that meant he doesn't have to deal with her anymore. And that's why he gave her the wedding she dreamed of, right down to thousands of dollars' worth of flowers."

Maria's train was several feet long, and at the altar her sister Melinda bent down to straighten it, almost popping out of her own sleeveless pink dress. Maria didn't look back. Her eyes were locked on Javier as the priest began the ceremony.

Audrey knew that her father's family was Methodist, even Sally. Her mother was Catholic, and she had been raised Catholic, making all the sacraments. But once she finished confirmation, her mother had said, "I did my job. You can do whatever you want with it."

And they didn't go to church again.

She knew what to do in the Catholic Mass but felt rusty at the kneeling and standing and a little out of place .

And when the priest began to speak, Audrey knew something was wrong.

"I forgot to tell you it would be in Spanish," Vince whispered, gritting his teeth and shrugging his shoulders.

"Minor detail," Audrey whispered back.

She watched in awe, the wedding in Spanish like nothing she had seen before. "Sacred" was the word she kept thinking of. It was very much unlike the beach wedding in the Bahamas she and Rick had had with just their closest family and friends.

At the time, it was what they wanted, but through the years Audrey felt she had missed something. She never knew was it was. Until now. And maybe that was what Sally had missed as well. That extra piece: it wasn't just a legal connection, but something sacred and being in a sacred space was the way to tie it together.

And it was clear that Maria and Javier were ready to join together on one journey.

Driving to the reception, Audrey said to Vince, "They are so young. And we never know what life will bring. I mean, when I married I thought it was for life. It devastated me that it wasn't."

"Me, too," Vince said. "We have an hour so I'm going to take you on a tour of where I grew up."

"Maybe it's better we don't know what's ahead," Audrey said quietly looking out the window as Vince turned the car onto the freeway.

She thought of Sally and how she didn't take that chance. She could have stayed with Reuben but something kept her from doing so. And she didn't have the life she really wanted. How sad, Audrey thought.

Vince exited and drove north, turning off a main street into a neighborhood.

"I have no idea where we are," Audrey said, looking around.

"Yes you do," Vince said, teasing her. As usual. He pointed to the mountains. "They are always to the east."

"But in Aspen Hills we can't really see them since we are so close to them," she said.

"That's because you've been spending too much time at the house." He made several turns and Audrey was really lost. "Being at Sagebrush will help."

"Spending my days keeping kids in line," Audrey joked.

Vince pulled up in front of a tidy-looking house. A black car sat in the driveway, and flowers lined the walk.

"It's a nice house," Audrey said, craning her head out the window. It was white with a blue trim and a big bay window in front. "It has a good feel to it."

"My dad did a lot of work on it. He added a room in the back, and the lawn always has been perfect."

"He still lives here?"

"I think he'll die here," Vince joked. "My mom wanted to live in the valley and be close to her family but my dad wanted to put us in better schools. His goal was to give us what he never got. The Army was the answer for him but he didn't want that for my sister or me. His experience in Madison taught him that college was the answer."

"So he must be really proud that you became a doctor," Audrey commented.

"He would have been disappointed by anything less." Vince opened his car door. "We might as well go inside and make sure everything is okay. I usually come by once a week while he's gone but I didn't have time to stop on my way home from work yesterday."

The inside was clean, there was no doubt about that. But like Sally's house, it was stuck in an earlier time. "Your dad and Sally have something in common," Audrey joked, walking past the fake plants in a built-in planter by the front door.

"I know," Vince laughed. "It was so modern and cool then but now I feel like I'm in a time warp. It makes me think I'm back in high school when I come here."

The house was dark and cool, even with the heat outside.

They walked to the back of the house where a lush green lawn was shaded by a big green tree with a thick trunk. "He is proud of me," Vince said. "Sometimes he tells me the only thing is that he wishes I could have a family but then he adds that he wants me to truly love the person I spend my life with."

"That doesn't sound like he's totally in love with your mom."

"He was." Vince watched the birds in the yard. Then he thought for a moment before he spoke. "I don't know. There have been a few times over the years that he's said things and I'm not really sure what they meant. But I do know that he worked so hard for us to live here and in this school district. Some of my mom's siblings' kids haven't finished college or ended up pregnant while they were still in high school."

"That could happen anywhere," Audrey pointed out. "I taught at a school with a lot of money, and I had a few pregnant girls."

"You're right, but your chances are better when you're surrounded by people who are smarter than you and have more opportunities."

They stood together for a moment. Audrey reached over and took Vince's hand, feeling for it without looking. He squeezed, and she squeezed back.

"I guess we should go," he said after a few minutes. "We don't want to miss Maria's big entrance into the reception."

The hallway outside the hotel ballroom was hopping when they arrived, people everywhere, a bar set up, and chips and salsa on several long tables.

"This is . . . ," Audrey said, looking around.

Before she could answer, Vince asked, "Extreme?"

"Yes. Did your uncle have the money saved or did he mortgage his house?"

"I think he started to save when she was born. She made quite an entrance then; it was obvious what they were in for."

People began to walk toward him.

"Vicente!" an older man with graying hair in a black suit said, his arms outstretched as he walked toward Vince.

"Hi Uncle Diego," Vince said, hugging his uncle.

"And who is the *chica?*" his uncle asked, giving his hand to Audrey. "I'm Vicente's Uncle Diego." His handshake was warm and strong.

"This is my girlfriend, Audrey."

"Hi," she said, smiling.

"Welcome to the family. It's quite an event you're attending." He turned to Vince and they laughed. And then he said, "I'm sorry your mom isn't here. And I hear your dad is visiting your sister."

"As always this time of year. It's his excuse to golf."

"You're representing your family well," Uncle Diego said. "Your mother would be proud."

He put his lips together and gave Vince a pat on the back. Audrey bit her lip: both had tears in their eyes.

"I'm sorry," Vince said quietly, looking down when Uncle Diego had walked away.

"No," Audrey said quietly. "I've been there, too. It's just not as recent for me."

They didn't have long to talk before others walked up. "Everyone wants to meet your girlfriend," his cousin Suzanna said, taking Audrey by the hand. "We've all been hoping he'd spend enough time out of the hospital to meet someone."

"I just went on with my life," Vince told her, looking slightly uncomfortable.

"Maybe you'll be next," Suzanna said, singing the words and checking to make sure her hair, piled high on her head, was still in place.

"I'm sorry," he said when she had left.

"Why?"

"I don't want you to be uncomfortable."

Audrey waved him off. "Everyone I know has been trying to marry me off since I got divorced. I think it's human nature to want to couple people up." She paused and looked around at the crowd before speaking again. "They want you to be happy."

"I am happy," he said, sliding his arm around Audrey's waist. "And I'm happier with you."

She smiled, feeling like a giggly girl for a moment as his fingers tickled her arm. "But everyone forgets that you can be happy without being part of a couple."

Several hotel employees dressed in white shirts and black pants opened the double doors leading into the ballroom revealing a ballroom filled with flowers and purple balloons towering over the tables.

"Oh my goodness," Audrey said, her eyes growing big.

"I know," Vince laughed. "That's an understatement."

"I thought this stuff only existed on that TLC channel on TV, not in real life."

They walked in with everyone else. "It exists in my reality," Vince whispered, leaning into Audrey.

In the back of the room, two long tables held an enormous buffet.

"Let's go see the food." Vince grabbed her hand and led Audrey there. The tables overflowed with bowls and platters filled with items Audrey couldn't name. She saw black beans in a bowl, rice somewhere else,. something smothered in red chile and something else in green.

"I have no idea what all this is," Audrey joked, shrugging her shoulders.

"This is a true Mexican American fiesta," Vince said, pointing items out. "Those are enchiladas. I'm guessing you know that's a taco bar at that end."

"A taco bar? Like a salad bar?"

"Yes, we don't do salad bars. We do taco bars."

She put her hand on her face and shook her head.

"There's more," he said, taking her to the opposite end. "You should know that's the carne adovada. And these are tortillas, not flying saucers."

"You so aren't funny," she snapped teasingly.

He ignored her purposely. "And these are corn tortillas. I'm sure you've actually had these."

"No," she corrected him. "Only when they were folded and fried for tacos."

"Well, you'd think in the cornfield you'd have corn tortillas."

"Does she really not get it?" a man dark hair slicked back and a goatee said from behind them, laughing.

"She's from Kansas," Vince replied, giving the man a hug.

"Great to see you, man."

"You, too. Do you even know where Kansas is?"

"Seriously?" Audrey added, looking at both of them. "Who doesn't know where Kansas is?"

The man, probably Vince's age, and Vince looked at each other and laughed. The man said, "We pretty much just know where New Mexico and Texas are. And how to get to Mexico."

The three of them laughed and the man reached his hand for Audrey's. "Since he's not going to be polite and introduce you, I'm Vince's cousin Edward."

"I don't think I've met anyone who isn't a cousin," Audrey told Edward.

"Then you've met the family. Except for Maria. Hopefully they'll get here soon." He looked at Vince and took a swig of the beer in his hand before he spoke. "I hope she gets done with all those photos soon. I'm hungry."

As he finished speaking, the DJ spoke. "Everyone please take your seats. It's time to introduce your bride and groom!"

"Is this a basketball game?" Audrey asked, following Vince to a table where he waved to a few people and pulled out a chair for Audrey.

"Not too far off," Vince told her.

Everyone came through the door: parents, grandparents, godparents, the entire bridal party. Audrey eyed the cookies on the table, wondering if it was okay to eat them before the party started. It felt like they'd been waiting two hours for the bride and groom to arrive.

"Those are bizcochitos," Vince said, watching her. "I dare you to eat one."

"That's bad form," Audrey said, thinking about how her mother would have slapped her hands away if she tried to do that.

"Oh no, I dare you to eat one because you won't be able to stop." Vince held out his hand, palm up. "Go ahead."

Audrey took one. When she bit into it, the cookie crumbled everywhere.

Vince couldn't stop laughing.

"Why didn't you tell me?" she asked him, holding her hand over her mouth until she was done swallowing and then sweeping the crumbs off her dress. "Those are incredible. They melt in your mouth."

"Lard, flour, and anise."

"That's it?"

"Pretty much," Vince said, taking one for himself and handing her a second cookie.

The lights in the room went down low, the disco ball lit everything in purple and a spotlight illuminated the doorway. Maria and Javier strolled in, Maria smiling broadly, Javier looking a little more reserved.

"Is he questioning it?" Audrey asked Vince.

"Nah, he's a heating and air conditioning guy. I'm sure the tux is making him itch."

They walked right to the dance floor, and a song by Selena started to play.

"We're never going to eat, are we?" Audrey asked, half kidding.

"We'll eat all night once Maria gets her moments in."

There were more cousins to meet as well as aunts and uncles. And the bride's family.

"I'm so glad you're here," said his Uncle Chuck, Maria's dad, with a sad look in his eyes when he came by the table after they had gotten their food. "Your mom was always so proud of you."

Audrey felt a lump in her own throat as she watched the two men embrace, smashing Uncle Chuck's boutonniere.

"And thank you," he said to Audrey, shaking her hand.

"It's quite a party," she told him.

Vince leaned over and whispered, but loud enough for Audrey to hear. "She's from Kansas."

His uncle didn't care and looked around the room. "I hope Maria is happy. This is the last thing I'm going to do for her and I gave her all that she wanted."

"Did your sister have a wedding like this?" Audrey asked when his uncle had moved on and they had sat down again to return to their food.

"Oh no," Vince said. "My dad wouldn't have allowed this. She was given a budget and she and my mom made it work. It cost a third of this and was at least as nice. If not nicer."

As the evening went on, people continued to come by and when the dancing started, Vince led Audrey out to the floor even as she protested.

"I don't know how to do all these Mexican dances," she told him.

"Can you polka? People from the Midwest can polka."

"That's the upper Midwest," she reminded him. "We had no culture in Kansas unless you count corn. Corn was our culture. In Milwaukee they polka after they eat sausage and drink beer."

Vince wrinkled his nose and placed his arm on her waist and took her other hand. "I'll teach you."

Audrey tried to protest again but realized it wasn't working and instead focused on following Vince's steps. She thought she was back in junior high learning to square dance with boys she liked, her stomach letting her know she was scared. She wanted to show Vince she was up for the challenge but moving around a dance floor was something at which she was woefully inexperienced.

At weddings and other gatherings, Rick liked to sit with his buddies and drink beer while the women stayed at another table and talked about how they didn't get to dance. Audrey had long given up on the dream that she would glide across a dance floor with the love of her life.

And here Vince was trying to do just that.

She tried not to get frustrated with herself; she wasn't aware of the other people around them. Audrey looked up at Vince, deciding watching his feet wasn't helpful, and he smiled at her. He didn't care. She relaxed and it started to flow.

"There you go," he said, looking proud.

Audrey smiled back and the song ended.

"It's time for La Marcha!" the DJ called, Vince and Audrey still standing on the dance floor holding hands.

"You have to do this!" Vince told her, a big smile opening up across his face. "Then you'll really have experienced a New Mexican wedding."

Slowly, everyone began to gather on the dance floor, dancing and stomping their feet to the music that played, which was heavy on trumpets.

"What are we doing?" Audrey asked, feeling tentative but soon getting caught up in the excitement as everyone made a line behind Vince's aunt and uncle and Maria and Javier.

"Did Javier have a few beers?" Audrey asked Vince, trying not to ask too loud in case someone heard. "He looks a lot more comfortable."

"I'm sure there was some tequila involved as well," Vince joked, clapping to the music.

Maria and Javier led everyone first around the ballroom and then outside into the hallway and then through the double doors into the big courtyard where the pool was. As Audrey and Vince followed, they could still hear the music playing in the ballroom. The warm night air was flooded with light, and the entire group followed the leaders around the pool and then back into the ballroom where they marched underneath the arms the couple held up, joining them so everyone could do the same.

Audrey watched: some of the faces looked entranced with the music; others smiled and laughed.

The song didn't end and everyone kept going, finally making a circle around the bride and groom to complete the march. When it finished, the group clapped and Audrey laughed, shaking her head.

"You had a good time, didn't you?" Vince asked.

Audrey laughed and nodded. "It helped me burn off a few of those bizcochitos."

"It's getting late," Vince noted, looking at his watch as they sat down again at the table. "We can go anytime."

The crowd had begun to thin out and Audrey nodded that she was ready. It took another ten minutes for them to leave, everyone wanting to talk to Vince one last time. And Audrey made the mistake of telling his Aunt Carmen how much she liked the bizcochitos.

"Then you must take some home!" She exclaimed, pointing at them not to leave and returning with a Styrofoam to-go container filled with them.

"I will never lose any weight at this rate," Audrey groaned. "I'll have to start swimming twice a day."

"They'll be gone by dinner tomorrow," Vince promised.

At last, they met up with Maria at the ballroom doorway where she was coming back from the bathroom.

"I'm so glad you came," she said, holding her dress up to walk. "And you brought someone!" Maria looked at Audrey and smiled.

"Congratulations," Audrey said.

"Thank you. I'm so excited! We're going to dance all night!" She stopped for a moment. "Well maybe not all night." Maria looked to her left and saw Javier sitting at a table with several of the groomsmen, beer bottles in front of each of them.

It felt good to be away from the music and the hubbub as they walked out of the hotel and into the late night holding hands. Vince jumped on the freeway to take them back to Aspen Hills and it was quiet, just like the night they drove back from the party on Rio Grande.

This time, however, it didn't feel so awkward. And Audrey felt herself want to be bold. "Do you want to get married again?" she asked, looking at him, and then out the window at the freeway exits.

"I do." He answered quickly and decisively. Vince reached over and took Audrey's hand. "Do you?"

"It scares me," she admitted, still looking out the side window. "I thought I was going to be married forever and then Bam! that changed one day. And I had no say in it."

Vince squeezed her hand. "Life is all about taking leaps of faith."

They were quiet as Vince turned the car onto Sandia Drive, the exit that led into Aspen Hills.

He isn't scared, Audrey thought. She reflected back on the day and watching Maria and Javier bring their lives together. While she had been to enough weddings to see when the bride was excited about the dress and having the day revolve around her, and she knew that Maria was excited about that too, still, there was the sense that Maria was most excited about starting a life with Javier.

And what would that life be? The unknown lay in front of them, just as it had for her and Rick on that beach in the Bahamas, what seemed like all those years ago.

It didn't matter, Audrey reminded herself. They had wanted to do it, and she knew she would do it all over again. She was still angry at Rick in some respects, but she wouldn't change anything. This was the life she was supposed to have. As Vince pulled into her driveway, she looked at him and wondered if she would have met Vince if she hadn't married Rick.

"I would love to stay with you," he said, turning the car off and taking the keys out of the ignition, "but I need to get home to Sadie."

"I know," Audrey said, understanding. As much as she wanted to be with him, she needed a little time alone to process the evening.

"I'll walk you to your door," he said, opening up his side of the car.

They stood together at the front door, their arms wrapped around each other. Audrey didn't want him to let go.

"I feel like your parents are inside waiting for you," he joked. "Is it past your curfew?"

Audrey looked at her watch and saw it was almost midnight. "Yikes," she joked. "I'm going to turn into a pumpkin in a few minutes. Are you sure you want to see that?"

Vince laughed and kissed her lightly several times. "I'll come over tomorrow." He stopped. "Unless you don't want me to."

"Of course I do," she said. "Let's swim and have lunch?"

"Sundays are good for that." He kissed her on the cheek and let go. "Sleep well. Don't eat all the bizcochitos until I get there."

"Yeah, right. You better come over early then."

Audrey dropped her pocketbook on the couch in the living room, setting the container of cookies on the glass coffee table, and removed her heels. She sat back for a moment, realizing she was tired but not sleepy. There was too much to think about. Sally's diary was on the coffee table in front of her where she had left it earlier that day.

"Did you have fun?" Sally asked, wearing a bathrobe over a light nightgown. She sipped a cup of tea from her side of the couch.

Audrey nodded, knowing that Sally wasn't really interested in her. Or maybe it was that she wasn't really interested in telling Sally anything. She wanted to know what Sally had to say.

"I love weddings. Mmmm." She held the cup, letting it warm her hands. "I remember one time Reuben and I went to dinner at the Crest Hotel downtown. We'd been dating several months and he got a promotion at work that came with a raise so he wanted to treat me to a nice dinner. What a beautiful, grand hotel that was."

Audrey shut her eyes, imagining the scene.

"So there we were sitting at dinner when we saw a wedding cake travel by on a cart outside the restaurant. Oh, how I love cake. And it was so beautiful with delicate pink flowers on the white icing. I told Reuben how much I loved wedding cake and he promptly got up and excused himself from the table.

"I had no idea where he went but he was gone much longer than I thought he should have. Wouldn't you know, when he came back he had a slice of wedding cake on a plate with a fork and napkin for me!"

She laughed at the memory and Audrey's eyes flew open. "He got a slice of wedding cake for you from someone's wedding? A wedding where you weren't invited, didn't even know the people getting married?"

Sally was still laughing and Audrey smiled, watching the happiness that the memory brought her. Sally set her cup on the saucer on the coffee table, afraid it might spill because she couldn't stop shaking from laughter. She shook her head. "That was Reuben."

Wow, Audrey thought, no wonder she loved him.

Sally was gone quickly, the room quiet again, and Audrey caught herself drifting off to sleep. She got up, quickly readied herself for bed, and climbed into it, not waking until daylight and the noise of a text from Vince.

"Are you up? I had a great time last night."

Audrey burrowed under the comforter and smiled. Then she looked over at the green dress hanging on the door and remembered she needed to swim before Vince came over.

Once in the pool, she let the cool water wash over her and gave herself a chance to think back and process all the events of the previous day.

"Going to a wedding is a big step in a relationship," Mandy had told her when they had talked a few days before.

Audrey wasn't sure how it happened or where it came from. But as she swam, she developed severe anxiety, like something was going to go wrong. She kept swimming, hoping it would go away. She panicked. She was scared.

It was all about Vince.

When her time was up, she sat on the steps for a few minutes before she was ready to get up and take a shower. Vince was going to pick up everything they needed for burgers and they planned to eat lunch and spend some time by the pool.

"I was scared, too," Sally said, finishing her own laps and sitting next to Audrey on the steps. She adjusted her swim cap. A tendril of her brown curly hair had escaped and had plastered itself to her cheek. "But I wasn't scared until my parents came to visit. I thought I was the luckiest girl in the world to have a man like Reuben who cared about me so much."

She looked out across the pool at the water that was becoming still while they sat. "It never occurred to me that his skin color would be a problem. You're lucky to be growing up in the time you are." She looked at Audrey. "You're scared because you don't know what the future holds. None of us do. But it's obvious to me that Vince cares very much for you. In fact, I'm sure that he loves you. Don't do what I did and let him go."

Audrey opened her mouth to speak, unable to believe that Sally had just spoken to her. And then nothing came out.

"Don't let your fear of the unknown keep you from what's most important. Life is about love. I had a wonderful marriage to Patrick but it wasn't anything close to what I would have had with Reuben."

Sally stopped for a moment, her eyes focused again on the diving board. "There was a richness with Reuben that I never had with Patrick. Patrick loved me and gave me everything he could but inside me, a part of me was never the same after I broke up with Reuben."

Before Audrey could recover enough to say something, Sally got out of the pool, put on her cover up and disappeared into the house as she took her swim cap off and shook her hair out.

Audrey sat there for a little longer before looking up at the sun-shaped clock on the wall and saw it was 10:30.

How long had she been in the pool? Vince and Sadie would arrive in about thirty minutes, and she needed to get her act together. Forget the shower, she thought, walking down the hall, looking for another swimsuit to wear.

As she stepped into her room, the old guest room, the sunlight from the master bedroom caught her eye and she walked down there. Rodrigo's crew had put up the tile in the master bathroom and were waiting for it to dry so they could grout it. The bathroom had been transformed. While it still wasn't finished, it was a long way from the closed feel of the flowers and striped wallpaper with pink fixtures, sink, and carpet. It was a little sterile without the finished products but it was taking shape into something that reflected Audrey's taste, with glass blocks and soft brown paint.

"Going with brown I can change up the towels and accents." she had told Vince. "I wanted something neutral enough."

"You get bored often?" he had joked. "Does that mean when you get bored with me you'll put me in the closet and pull out another man?"

"Oh please," she teased him. "I'll put you on the curb with a free sign. Surely someone will want you."

The towels, rugs, and a few other items waited patiently in plastic bags on the bed in the master bedroom.

"We should be done by next Friday," Rodrigo had told her a few days before.

What then? Audrey wondered as she found a box she hadn't opened yet, knowing it held not only her purses but also the bikinis. Part of her wondered why she had chosen to keep them with the weight she had put on.

"Don't get rid of them," Mandy had warned when she helped her pack. "You'll get back there. You're just stuck right now but one day you'll be that cute little thing everyone is envious of again."

Audrey was sad that she had chosen not to be that cute little thing anymore. Why had she given Rick that power over her life? But it took Vince to come into her life to see what she had wasted. She found a bikini that had a lot of fabric, "Full coverage" she remembered the tag saying.

It was green, and when she slipped into it, she looked in the mirror and realized she didn't look so bad. The top looked like a sports bra. Her stomach didn't look as poochy, a word she always used with her closest friends as in, "I look so poochy."

She ran her hands over her body, feeling better. Maybe she was losing some weight. Maybe the swimming was making a bigger difference than she thought.

"That's nice," Sally said, coming up behind her the way she always did when Audrey looked in the mirror. "Very sporty."

Audrey smiled and wrapped her brown and gold sarong around her waist just at the doorbell rang and she heard the click clack of Sadie's nails on the slate floor. "We're here!" Vince called.

Audrey walked quickly down the hall and met both of them in the dining room where Vince was headed to the kitchen with several paper bags in his hands.

"You look great," he said whistling. "And even after eating bizcochitos."

Audrey blushed. It had been a long time since she had heard that from a man. "Thank you," she said, taking the package of ground beef from him and placing it in the refrigerator. "Will you help me map out a plan on this house remodel?" she asked.

"Sure," he said. "Are you really ready to have your house in chaos for months?"

"No," she laughed. "I've never done it. I am ready to make this house my own, though."

"You'll be at school all day anyway," he said, handing her a package of cheese.

They sat by the pool, wanting to spend time outside before it got too hot, and worked through a list of what Audrey wanted done on the house.

"You know," she said, as they took a break, "I feel a little sad. I mean I know that Sally is gone but it's become kind of comforting to be here in her house." Audrey looked around and held her hand out toward the kitchen. "The green countertops are growing on me."

"That figures," Vince teased. "You have the opportunity to change and you become resistant to it."

"Like your patients who are overweight and won't help themselves?"

"Exactly. They say they want to change and you hand them all sorts of info and resources and they look at you and you know they are going to throw it in the trash on the way out the door."

"They might make it home to the recycle bin," she offered.

"I'm not sure these people recycle."

"Let's finish this up so you can talk to Rodrigo about it," Vince said, snapping his fingers. "You start work this week."

Audrey sat up in her chair. "You mean I become a productive citizen of the world again."

"It's about time."

When they were done, Audrey walked over to him and hugged him where he sat, putting her arms around his neck, and kissed the top of his head. "Thank you," she murmured into his hair.

He held her right forearm and whispered, "You're welcome" right back.

She sat back down and then blurted out, "I'm really scared."

Vince looked confused. "Of remodeling the house? Why?"

"No," she said, realizing she hadn't made a transition to him, only in her brain. "I'm sorry. I meant about us."

He patted her knee. "Why are you scared?"

Audrey looked out at the pool and shrugged her shoulders. "I know I shouldn't be but I'm so afraid what happened before will happen again. I never thought it would happen to me, and since it did, I worry it will happen again."

"And then it might not," Vince said, holding up his half-full glass of iced tea.

"You make it sound so easy," Audrey told him. She wasn't acting mean, she was simply being truthful. Vince did make it easy for her.

"It shouldn't be difficult," he said, taking a drink of the iced tea.

They were interrupted by Sadie, who was tentatively putting one paw on the top step of the pool.

"Um, has she done that before?" Audrey asked, pointing her head toward Sadie.

Vince looked over. "Wow," he said softly, leaning forward. "She hasn't done that before around a pool."

He got up quietly and Audrey watched. Sadie pawed the water. It was clear she wanted in but she wasn't sure what to do. Vince took off his shirt, wearing just his swim trunks so as to be pool ready, and talked quietly to Sadie. "Good girl," he said, not wanting her to get scared, or think she was in trouble. Sadie looked at him and then right back to the water.

"She wants in," Audrey laughed quietly herself.

Vince slid into the side of the shallow end, and walked over to her. "Come on girl, you can do it." He held his arms out to her.

Sadie wagged her tail, her entire body shaking at she did. She looked like she wanted to say, "I want to get in but I'm just not sure how to do this."

Vince was patient. Audrey watched from the middle of the pool deck where she sat cross-legged.

Finally Sadie took the leap of faith into Vince's arms. But she didn't stay long. While he praised her, she slipped out of them and swam across the pool, right by where Audrey sat on the side, and then turned back at the deep end. She looked as if she had been gliding across it for years, as if swimming was something she had been born to do. She reached the steps and found some difficulty putting her legs underneath her, but climbed out and instantly shook, fur and water flying everywhere.

She ran around the pool, smiling and looked as if she had accomplished something huge. Both Audrey and Vince celebrated with her. Audrey ran into the house to get her a few treats as a reward.

"It doesn't look like she wants to get back in," Vince sighed after urging her for a while.

Audrey lay down on the diving board and he swam a few laps.

"Hey!" he called, Audrey opening one eye lazily and looking at him. "I forgot! There is something in the bag I didn't finish emptying for you."

"From the grocery store?" she asked. "Do you not like my food selection?"

Vince laughed. "Don't judge before you see it."

As Audrey climbed off the board and walked inside, she saw fur on the pool surface and jokingly said, "You might want to skim the pool. Sadie left quite a bit of herself in the pool."

"I do, too," he said teasingly. "You just can't see it."

Inside, Audrey found the paper bag on the counter and reached inside. She felt two plastic packages. When she pulled them out, one of was a blow-up float for the pool and other a blow-up ring. She laughed and took them outside.

"Well, you're right," she admitted. "I have been lacking in the pool toys department."

"I'll blow them up," he said, motioning her to bring him the packages. Vince sat on the steps and Audrey took off the plastic packaging.

"You are full of hot air," she teased.

"If it's enough to blow these pool toys up, then you will be grateful when you're floating around on the ring all afternoon."

"I'm not sure my midwestern skin can handle all that sun," she reminded him.

Audrey sat next to him and dipped her feet in the pool while he struggled with the ring. It was close to noon and getting hot before the trees would bring shade in the late afternoon, blocking out the bold sun in its peak hours.

She thought about watching Sadie try to put her paw in the pool, knowing something was there but not quite sure knowing exactly what it was. Audrey looked over at Vince.

And then she noticed a shadow to her left. Sally.

Audrey looked up and Sally smiled at her. "We all have to take that leap of faith," Sally said. "Don't be scared like I was. Moving here was a leap of faith for you and look what happened. You can have something even greater if you don't let it go. I only made it halfway: I moved here, but I was too scared to hold onto Reuben."

Audrey nodded and Sally walked back into the house.

"There," Vince said and Audrey turned her attention back to him. Vince let the ring float on the water but didn't let go. "I'll hold it if you want to get on."

Audrey smiled and let him do that for her.

Why? She wondered as she lay on top of the water, the plastic float keeping the middle of her body above the waterline, did she think a relationship had to be so difficult? Vince was making it easy and that was a good thing. Yet somewhere in her mind she felt that she didn't deserve it.

Chapter 12

With just a few days before she had to be at school full time, and a week before the students showed up, Audrey wondered if she had too much on her plate.

"Well, I'm not sure that starting a new job and remodeling the house at the same time are the best things," Mandy pointed out on the phone. Audrey could picture her friend shrugging her shoulders. "But why not? Life is short. You've been teaching for years. This should be old hat."

"I was at the same school for fifteen years!" Audrey reminded her friend, running her fingers across the newly grouted tile. They would seal it the following day and put in the vanity and toilet the day after. And then start work on the hall bathroom. Slowly, they would work their way across the house to the kitchen and laundry room.

"We can do the kitchen last if that's what you want," Rodrigo had told her looking around it. "We can enter directly from the garage so we don't disturb what we've already done."

Audrey hoped by then she would be ready to let go of the dated kitchen and what it stood for. But she also knew she would be tired of remodeling.

"I'll make you dinner every night at my house," Vince had offered. "There will be a delay somewhere, there always is, but Rodrigo is quicker than most contractors. Even my dad was impressed, and it takes a lot to impress him since that's what his family does."

She felt as organized as she could be when she showed up for the first morning of new teacher orientation. Most of it would be the same for her; Mandy was right: she wasn't new at this. At the same time, though, Audrey had left her old school under challenging circumstances. As she drove into the Sagebrush parking lot, looking for her space, 129, much of the past came floating back.

"It would be much worse if I were still in Kansas," she reminded herself, parking the car and looking out at the mountains in front of her. "I can do this. I'm going forward."

When the students showed up on Wednesday for a shortened day, almost everything was the same except for one thing: Audrey was one of just a handful of blondes in her classroom. In Kansas a dark-haired student would have been the outlier but here in New Mexico she felt distinctly in the minority.

She struggled with their names. Gurule? She looked for another teacher in the hall to help her. I might never get that one, she thought, wishing she could mumble and the student would know she was talking about him.

And Cerros?

"You need to roll the Rs," the English teacher Luis Medina said, giving her an example.

"You just rolled them all down the hall," Audrey said, looking past him, "but I can't get them out the door right here."

Luis laughed and the bell rang. "You'll be fine. The students are used to it," he assured her.

As Audrey closed the door and her students stopped talking, staring at her and turning to face forward at their desks, she realized there was no turning back. She couldn't leave Albuquerque now. She had signed a contract, and even though she realized many of her students wouldn't care about communications skills or speech, she couldn't let them down. Already Laurie the principal had lost one teacher, and Audrey was determined to hang in there.

You're stuck with me, she thought looking at them, some looking happy to be there, the girls with their notebooks open, pen in hand, some of the boys looking bored with their hands in their pockets and slouched in their chairs.

It was going to be an interesting year, she thought. "Isabel Armijo," she began.

*****

"They're high school kids just like you taught back in Kansas," Vince said that Friday night with a shrug.

"They're not the same," Audrey argued. "Their lives are different. Yes, they are still high school students, but there are differences. And it's going to make a difference in how I teach."

They both reached for the salsa at the same time. Vince retracted his chip. "Ladies first," he said, bowing to her. "I'm sure their backgrounds are different, but you'll get the hang of it." He ate his chip and then looked at her. "And you know what?"

"Hmmm," Audrey said, picking up her water and squeezing the lemon into the ice. He didn't speak so she finally looked at him. He was leaning over the table toward her.

"I'm glad you got the job."

"You are? Any particular reason why?"

"It means you're staying here, and I kind of like having you around." Vince smiled at her and squeezed her hand. "Because you're too far across the table to kiss."

"Thank you," Audrey said quietly, saying thank you silently as well.

The waitress brought their food, balancing the large brown tray in her arms.

"Why so many dishes?" Audrey joked looking at what was on the tray. "It's just the two of us."

122

"The sopas, the sides, it always goes on forever," said the Hispanic girl with her long dark hair pulled back in a ponytail. It shook each time she talked or moved.

"We like to use a lot of dishes," Vince teased.

As Audrey began to eat her enchiladas, she asked, "So now that we're here, why do you pick this place?"

An older man with a graying beard and a thick mess of gray hair slicked back off his forehead walked over to them.

"Vicente! We haven't seen you in a while. Where is your papa? He hasn't been here either."

"He's in San Diego at my sister's," Vince said, placing his fork on his plate and taking the man's strong hand for a shake.

"Oh that's right," the man said. "It's that's time of year. I should know by now that he's always gone late summer."

"He'll be back next week," Vince said, holding his hand out to introduce Audrey but the man kept talking.

"I miss seeing him. It's time to discuss football, you know, especially those Lobos."

"You mean how the Lobos should play the Badgers and how the Badgers will kick the crap out of the Lobos?"

"He does that with you, too?"

"Of course," Vince said. "I am a Lobo. Even my medical degree is from the University of New Mexico."

Audrey put her fork down and watched them banter back and forth.

The man laughed, opening the door for Vince to introduce Audrey. "This is my girlfriend, Audrey."

"I'm Jesús," the man said, holding out his hand for Audrey. Hers looked like the hand of an eight-year-old girl's next to his, and she watched it engulf hers.

"Hi," she said.

"It's nice to see Vicente bring a girl around. I always thought my cooking wasn't good enough so he stayed away and only came with his dad. Is my cooking okay with you?" Before Audrey could answer, he leaned in and said quietly, "Really, I don't cook any of it anymore. But they are my recipes."

Audrey laughed. "It's great," she said.

"She moved her from Kansas a few months ago so I've been introducing her to New Mexican food."

"Nothing better," Jesús said.

Someone walked up and called him away. He waved at them and Audrey and Vince returned to their dinners.

"You've come here a long time?" she asked looking around at Sandoval's, the small restaurant in a strip mall where they were. A sign hung proudly in the window that said, "Open since 1974."

"When we moved into the house we started coming here," Vince said, taking his sopaipilla and dipping it in the green chile sauce on his plate. "My dad told me later that this was his replacement for Ida's, which had been his favorite place, but it was too far from where we lived."

"Your dad ate at Ida's, too?" Audrey asked, her eyebrows going up.

"Yeah," Vince said. "Are you surprised? You know how good the food is."

"Sally loved that place."

They looked at each other and before either one could say anything, Vince's phone rang.

"That's odd," he said, looking at it. "It's my sister." He tapped the phone and held it to his ear and Audrey kept eating. "Hola."

Audrey couldn't understand the conversation, but she heard a female voice on the other end, one that sounded panicked. Vince's face turned a funny color and Audrey stopped eating. Something was wrong.

"Do you want me to talk to the doctor?" Vince was trying to speak but the female voice wasn't giving him much of a chance. Every time he asked a question, she kept talking. "Where is he now?" Then there would be pause as he listened. "I know he's in great shape." Pause. "These things happen." Pause. And then, "Do you want me to come out there?"

Audrey heard a "yes" and then crying.

"Okay, it will probably be tomorrow. It's too late to get a flight from here. I'll call you when I have it booked."

Vince ended the call and looked at Audrey. "My dad had a heart attack."

"Oh no," Audrey said. "That's not good. Isn't he in great shape?"

"Yeah," he said, putting his food to his mouth and then placing the fork back on the plate, with the food still on the fork. "Doesn't make sense but I'm not there. And it does happen. My sister doesn't cope with this stuff well. When Mom was dying, she wasn't here which was probably better but it also meant every time we talked to her, she freaked out."

"Is there anything I can do? We can go. I can take this home."

"No," Vince said, holding out his hand in front of him and shaking his head. "I can't get there until tomorrow. We'll go when you're finished."

But Vince was clearly distracted from that point on, and Audrey felt like a hindrance.

She finished part of her meal, feeling full from the stress, and pushed the plate away. "I'm done."

"You're sure?" he asked, eyeing the food still on her plate.

"Yes," she said. "You need to book your ticket. I'm ready."

The ride back to Aspen Hills was quiet. Audrey wanted to talk, but it was a moment where she wasn't sure what to do. She didn't know Vince well enough to see how he handled stress. This was one of the first stressful times she had encountered with him.

"We can go to your house," Audrey suggested, trying to be helpful.

"Are you sure?" Vince asked.

"Yes," Audrey said. "I can walk home."

"No, you're not walking home without me," Vince said.

"Isn't Aspen Hills safe?" she asked as he pulled into his brick driveway and waited for the garage door to open.

"It is," he said. "It's just not cool that I don't make sure you get home."

"Then you can walk me home after you book your ticket."

He put the car in park and squeezed her hand, this time reaching over to kiss her. He caught her by surprise and the kiss landed on her cheek.

"That was meant for your lips," he said.

"Oops," Audrey laughed, feeling stupid. "I guess I shouldn't have turned away." She looked at him and he leaned back over, this time kissing her on the lips. "You have a plane ticket to book," she reminded him.

"Yeah," I know," Vince sighed, getting out of the car. "I'm sure he's fine. It's my sister I'm not looking forward to dealing with."

Sadie met them in the laundry room, her nails tapping the tile floor. Vince opened his laptop where it sat on the kitchen counter by the bar and motioned for Audrey to join him on the couch. She grabbed her phone and sat quietly while he booked the ticket and called his sister.

After they finished talking, he spoke to Audrey. "Hopefully I'll just be gone a few days," he said. She snuggled close to him, letting her phone rest on the couch. Vince kissed the top of her head and put his arm around her.

"I'll be okay," she said.

"But I want you to pine for me," he teased.

"Oh, that was the wrong answer." She thought for a moment. "I'll stay in bed until you come home. I'll neglect teaching and let Rodrigo and his crew work on the house around me."

"That's much better," Vince said.

She didn't realize how much she would miss him, though, and she especially wouldn't have predicted her reaction when she left him at the airport the next morning, the first time she had been there.

"Why do they call it the Sunport?" she asked, as she drove up to departures. "It's the same color as everything else here." Audrey paused as she pulled into an open slot. "Brown."

"Sand," Vince corrected her. "It's sand."

"It's a shade of brown," Audrey said, insisting he wasn't right.

"You'll learn." He opened his side of the car and then pulled his bags from the backseat, setting them on the curb while Audrey came around from the driver's side.

Like the rest of the state, the Sunport was built territorial style. "Why can't they just call it an airport?" She looked around at how high it sat, giving a good view of the mountains off to the east.

"I don't think you've ever been so sarcastic with me," Vince noted, wrapping his arms around her.

"I'm back teaching," she reminded him. "That's what happens when you're around kids all day."

"So it's only going to get worse?"

Audrey let her cheek rest on the fabric of the polo shirt that covered his chest. "Yep."

Vince took a deep breath. "I'll be home Saturday morning. Take good care of Sadie."

She pulled her body just far enough away so she could see him. "I will. She's in good hands with me."

"But she'll be spending more of the week with Rodrigo than you," Vince reminded her.

Audrey laughed. "But you said she would supervise all the work at your house. I'm sure she'll be just fine." She knew Vince was up to his usual teasing.

As he walked through the automatic double doors, Audrey watched him disappear around the corner feeling sad that she wouldn't see him for a week. She didn't want him to know how much she feared he wouldn't come back.

There was an insecure part of her that she tried to keep under wraps, not wanting anyone to know it was there. She had learned early never to let her students see her as insecure. That was the kiss of death in the classroom. It was better to come on tough and ease up later.

"You'll never get their respect back if you try to be their friend in the beginning," her student teaching mentor, Lizzie Morgan, had told her.

While she had a reputation of being tough but fair in Kansas, she was the new girl at Sagebrush. And white, too.

"You're a cracker," one of her students, Adrian López said that Monday morning, slouched at his desk, his book in front of him and a pen on top, his sunglasses perched on his head.

Audrey thought for a moment before she spoke, tapping her pen on her desk. "Like a saltine?" she asked. She was glad the sarcasm didn't take long to return.

He burst out laughing and so did his buddy, Ben, who sat next to him. "Ms. Thomas, you're funny."

"That makes you a graham cracker then," she pointed out, not missing a beat.

Adrian stopped and looked at her, then at Ben who shrugged. Ben sat forward, his pen in his left hand in front of him. "She's right, man. If she's a saltine then we're the graham."

Adrian nodded his head and sat up. "It's nice to finally have a smart teacher."

Audrey shook her head and finished signing some paperwork for a football player. She knew most teachers were smart; they just went about it in different ways. But if communication was her game, then she had to find a place to meet the students.

The lesson plans were easy; she could incorporate what she had done before. But like every other school year, she found herself exhausted at the end of the day.

"It's the August blues," she sighed, talking to Mandy on her way home that afternoon. "I think it's also more taxing because the kids are different."

"How can that be? They're just kids," Mandy asked, echoing Vince.

"They're not."

At lunch several had knocked on her door while she sat at her desk eating a sandwich and asked if they could stay in her room at lunch, that the previous teacher had allowed them to do that. Audrey invited them in, three girls, and saw they had no lunches.

"Aren't you eating?" she asked them.

All three looked uncomfortable, first looking at each other and then looking down. "We can't afford lunch," one finally mumbled.

Audrey got up and walked closer and sat down at the desk next to that girl, Sylvia. She had big brown eyes and long brown hair. "What do you mean you can't afford lunch?" Audrey asked.

The girl looked up and shrugged her shoulders. The other two looked away. She knew kids were on the reduced lunch program in Kansas, not many at her school but a few, yet this was different. She walked back to her purse and handed them the cash she had, each girl got five dollars.

"You can leave your stuff here but go get something to eat," Audrey instructed. "And not candy. Get a sandwich and a cookie. And some water."

The girls walked out, still looking embarrassed, but when they returned they were smiling and laughing. At the end of lunch, Sylvia walked up to her. "Thank you," she said.

Audrey had a few moments after they left before her fifth period would show up and she sighed, putting her head in her hands. She looked out the window over the parking lot and then the mountains. The area around Sagebrush was surrounded with new houses. How could they not afford lunch? She didn't think they were playing her. They weren't those kinds of kids.

By the time she reached the house, she stood at the edge of the pool, still wearing her heels and her skirt, and looked down into the water, seeing her reflection, her hands on her hips.

You can't save the world, she reminded herself, not sure what she would do if she could do anything.

And too tired to swim.

She vowed she would get up early and swim before school, a good way to start the day. After eating dinner, Audrey curled up in bed with Sally's diary, Sadie snoring on the floor beside her.

It had been a while, she thought, opening it to where she left off: Sally working through not having Reuben in her life anymore.

"Yes, it was hard," Sally said, sitting in the chair across the room, wearing a tailored dress as if she, too, had spent the day at work. "There were many times I stopped myself from calling him. I knew if I did, he would take me right back. But I would remember that I needed to move on. I needed to be strong.

"I met Patrick at a wedding. My friend Martha married the next year and I was a bridesmaid. Patrick was one of the groomsmen and when he brought me a slice of wedding cake, I thought it was meant to be."

Maybe you wanted it to be so thoughts of Reuben would go away, Audrey wanted to say.

Sally stopped, looking at Audrey after being lost in her memory. "It was meant to be. I couldn't go back to Reuben. I had to move on. He was handsome in that white tux, his brown hair short. He was just out of college, starting an insurance business, and looking for a wife."

She sighed and Audrey shut her eyes, feeling as if she were at the wedding, not sure if she was Sally or if she watched. She tried to be Sally, wanting to love this man she looked at. Yes, he was handsome. Yes, he had a bright future ahead of him.

But he wasn't Reuben and Reuben was all of those things. And more.

"Of course Martha and Ted were so excited for us because they could tell everyone how we met at their wedding, as part of their bridal party. It turned into such an exciting time because everyone was so happy for me. They knew what had happened with Reuben."

Audrey looked at Sally in the bedroom, and she didn't see happiness. She saw a lot of sadness in Sally's eyes, sadness she knew Sally wouldn't admit to.

Sally got up and left the room as if something had come up that she had to take care of, as if the dryer had buzzed and she needed to fold the laundry. She left with a purpose. Audrey drifted off to sleep, the diary open in front of he, She woke up at 11 p.m. to a text.

"Hey, I know it's late. Are you still up? But maybe I just woke you up. Sorry."

"It's okay," she texted Vince back.

He called as soon as he got her text.

"Hi," she said, yawning.

"I'm sorry, baby," Vince sounded apologetic. "It's been a hectic day and you had school but I wanted to hear your voice."

Audrey smiled.

When the alarm on her phone chimed in the morning at 5:30, she didn't remember much of her conversation with Vince. As she put her feet on the floor, forgetting that Sadie was with her and almost stepping on the dog, she pulled on her black swimsuit, grabbed a towel, and walked groggily out to the pool.

The sun was coming up, the pool completely covered in tree shadows. She stood at the edge, Sadie curling up by the steps and falling back asleep.

"I'm an idiot," Audrey mumbled, climbing into the pool.

It was cool but not bad; she knew she'd be awake soon. As she swam, she thought of the kids at school, of the green dress that kept her in the pool, Vince, of Sally, of the path that had led her to where she was.

And what was next.

What was that?

Sally didn't come to her that morning. Audrey waited for her, thinking for sure she would show up. As Audrey glided across the pool, she jokingly thought that Sally was getting ready for work herself, knowing full well that Sally didn't work long after she got married.

When Audrey finished, she sat on the steps for just a minute, aware she had to get ready for school. Still no Sally.

Audrey walked through the house, one big mess filled with plastic and smelling like plaster. They had finished the master bath and had begun to tear out the guest bath and the hall bath and the carpet in the rest of the house, leaving just the bedroom where Audrey slept.

"Give me until next weekend," Audrey had begged.

"We have plenty to do with the bathrooms," Rodrigo assured her.

The furniture was piled in the garage, a pickup by a local thrift store planned for Saturday.

"It's sad to see it go but I know someone will enjoy it," Sally said, coming around the corner as Audrey walked into the garage to leave for school. The car had been sold a month before, making room for the furniture and her car. "It's time for the house to have a new life."

Audrey wanted to stay, her coffee in one hand, a stack of papers cradled in her arm, but she couldn't be late.

"Go, go," Sally said, waving her off. "There's plenty of time to talk furniture."

By the time she got home from school in the afternoons, Audrey felt exhausted, but without Vince there, she looked forward to settling into bed around 7 p.m. and reading Sally's diary.

"You're in bed?" Vince teased her Wednesday evening when he called.

It was 7:15.

Audrey giggled and dug deeper under the comforter. "The good news is I'm too tired to be cranky about the mess here," she said.

"You and Sadie can always escape to my place," he suggested. "What are you reading in bed?"

"Sally's diary."

"Have you learned anything new?"

"Are you bored?" Audrey asked, sensing he wanted to talk about anything other than his dad.

"Yes. My sister is driving me nuts. My dad to some extent but not as much as her. I'll be glad to get home to you."

"She met Patrick at a wedding. They were in it together."

"But Reuben was the one who brought her wedding cake," Vince remembered.

"And then Patrick did, too."

"What did Patrick do for a living?"

"He was an insurance agent." Audrey paused. "You're as nosy as me."

*****

Vince flew back to Albuquerque Friday evening and they picked up a pizza at Papa Francesco's on the way to the house, Sadie in the backseat of Audrey's car.

"She's drooling everywhere isn't she?" Audrey asked, keeping her eyes on the freeway.

Vince looked back and laughed. "All over the seat . . . all over the window . . . you might want to get your car washed after this."

"Yuck," Audrey said, wrinkling her nose. "You're lucky I like you. And your dog."

"She likes you, too," Vince said, tugging at Audrey's ear lobe playfully.

As they sat outside eating pizza, Vince looked over at Audrey and when she looked up, she knew there was something he wanted to say.

"I want you to meet my dad."

"Um, okay, yeah." Audrey wasn't sure what else to say. "Thank you." She was glad. It meant a step forward. "But you know I met him once."

"Yeah, no shit," Vince said, teasing her. "I mean, have dinner meet him. Get to know him. Let him get to know you. I'm just sorry my mom isn't here. She would have had you over for a feast, especially knowing you have been deprived of New Mexican food all your life."

"Until now," Audrey reminded him, raising her glass of lemonade as if for a toast.

Vince ignored her. "Since he'll be back on Thursday, how about Friday night? My place."

"You're going to cook?"

"I have the day off. I'm going to slave away in the kitchen all day," he said.

"Even better. While I'm at work."

Audrey wasn't nervous about meeting Vince's dad; she just wanted it to go well. There was nothing to hide, and his dad had just had a health scare. She knew that Vince was afraid he might lose his dad sooner than rather than later, like his mom, and wanted to make sure he was aware of Audrey in his life.

As she walked over for dinner on Friday evening, Betty stopped her, running out of her house waving her arm. Audrey was stepping off her front steps, careful not to trip or drop the oatmeal raisin cookies she was carrying on a platter.

"I haven't seen much of you since you started your job," she said, meeting Audrey at the curb on Audrey's side of the street. "Work does take up a lot of time." She sighed.

"I know," Audrey admitted. "We need to get together."

And they did. Audrey wanted to share with them what she was learning about Sally's relationship with Patrick. After she asked them what they knew. She was curious to find out if Sally had told them what really happened.

"Well, how about tomorrow night? You know we're always free on weekend nights." Betty chuckled. "Unless you count us being together means we're not free. We'll meet at Mary Ellen's house around the corner. And bring your handsome doctor with you."

"Mary Ellen just wants to ask about all her ailments," Audrey teased Betty, knowing it was true. Betty didn't deny it, she just laughed.

As Audrey walked away, cookies in hand, shaking her head and laughing, she realized how well she had come to know the trio in such a short time to make a joke like that.

Vince's father had already arrived when Audrey rang the doorbell, Sadie barking on the other side. Vince opened it and pulled her to him for a kiss.

"Don't drop the cookies," she warned. "I don't want to ruin Sadie's dinner."

"You don't need to ring the doorbell," Vince whispered, giving her a kiss, pulling away, and then smiling as he led her to the kitchen.

Reuben Montoya stood at the bar looking slightly annoyed but when he saw Audrey he brightened up.

"Hello," she said, offering her hand. He took it and shook it warmly.

"So you're the girl," he said, his graying thick hair looking much like many other men his age. "And one I've met before haven't I?"

Audrey smiled. "On the street—you were walking Sadie and I was putting my garbage out."

Sadie was dancing around the kitchen, looking happy because all her favorite humans were gathered in one place.

"I heard you had quite a scare," Audrey noted, settling in on a bar stool as Vince handed her a margarita.

"Yes," he said. "My daughter thought I was going to die. I explained to her I don't have time to die yet. I still have a lot of golf to play. And I need to see my son get married."

Audrey looked over at Vince who turned from where he was cutting onions. He rolled his eyes and shook his head. "Dad, when are you going to understand she's afraid something is going to happen to you?"

"And on her watch. You wouldn't have reacted that way."

"I'm a doctor," he reminded his father. "We'd send you in for tests."

"She was ready to call the funeral home." His knuckles turned white as he clenched his fists on the granite counter.

Vince kept shaking his head, his dad kept clenching his knuckles. Sadie wagged her tail from the middle of the floor where she sat watching the action.

"I might want two drinks," Audrey warned.

"Is there a hint of laughter in that?" Vince asked, carrying a cutting board filled with skirt steak, bell pepper, and onion outside to the grill on the deck.

"Yes," she said, taking a drink.

"I hear you're a teacher," Reuben said. "We need good teachers. The world isn't the same as when I was raising him and his sister. I gave them everything I could, but the teachers gave them a little more. Sadly parents today are making teachers do it all."

Vince walked back into the kitchen, grabbed a pair of tongs out of a drawer, and left again. "Dad has lots of opinions," he said as he walked by Audrey, the words floating in the air with his steps.

"I deserve to have them! I'm a taxpayer," he snapped.

And when Vince was out of reach he softened. Audrey could see it in his eyes. "I'm sorry. I'm usually not so antagonistic. My children are so afraid of me dying, though, and I'm not ready to die. None of us want me to go."

Audrey smiled and took another drink. "It's all good," she said.

"Your family is in Kansas, I hear." He came around and sat on the stool next to Audrey.

"Yep," Audrey said, always trying to be proud of where she was from, even when she knew when Vince walked back in he would make fun of her. She dipped a chip into the guacamole.

"You better eat more," Vince said as he floated behind her. "We don't want you getting drunk too fast."

His dad ignored his son and focused on Audrey. "Hmm. Kansas. I drove through there a long time ago. When I moved from Wisconsin to here." He shook his head, as if he had disappeared in time. "What a cold place the Midwest is. I'm too much of a Texas boy."

"And now a New Mexico man," Vince remarked, sliding the place settings over to Audrey to set the table.

The conversation settled into Rueben rehashing what it was like to live among all the gringos. Audrey and Vince stole glances at each other and smiled.

"I told you he would do this," Vince whispered, putting his arms around her waist as she finished placing the silverware at the last place setting.

"It's okay," she whispered back, Rueben ignoring them and eating a chip himself. "Let him share his life."

Maybe she didn't mind because she was trying to so hard to learn Sally's life and Sally wasn't there. With Rueben right there, she didn't want Vince to miss something he might not know about.

"We'll eat in about five minutes," Vince told them, retrieving the meat off the grill and setting it on counter to rest.

Audrey had climbed back on the stool next to Reuben and tried to keep herself from eating more chips. "Is there more guacamole for the fajitas?" she asked.

"Are you obsessed with avocados?" Reuben asked. "I had to live without them for four years in Wisconsin." He kept shaking his head. "Imagine, life without avocados."

"And mangos," Vince reminded him. "You always made us eat the mangos by telling us how people in Wisconsin ate cheese, not mangos."

"They were deprived," he father said, shaking his head.

"Just like all those kids in Africa," Audrey piped in. "That's what we got when we didn't want to eat our peas."

"Or your corn," Vince laughed, cutting the meat. "Everyone have a seat."

Audrey grabbed her drink and the bowl of guacamole. Reuben sat to one side of her at the square table with Vince sitting on the other side once he had placed everything on the table. His father looked uncomfortable in his chair, a mixture of wood and metal.

"All this weird modern furniture you have," he said, shaking his head and looking at Audrey. "I offer him a house full and he insists on buying new. What's wrong with a padded seat?"

"But you had all new furniture at one time," Vince reminded his dad, handing each of them a flour tortilla. "I can give you a pillow for a cushion if you'd like."

"I thought you'd want the antiques."

Audrey tried not to laugh at the banter while she assembled her fajita. They didn't need to worry about conversation. Reuben kept it going, moving from thought to thought, no filter.

"They are sixties antiques," Vince reminded him. "I think retro is the word."

His father shrugged his shoulders, his golf shirt moving each time he did.

"They are all in my garage," Audrey laughed.

"You're getting rid of the antiques? Your family must be so upset with you." Reuben tsked her before he took a bite of his fajitas.

"They belonged to my aunt, and she died. The flowers and such aren't really my style."

Reuben wasn't listening. He was looking outside at the view of the city. It was starting to get dark and the lights were beginning to come on, as if someone had dumped glitter on blue paper.

"I knew a girl from Kansas once."

"At Wisconsin?" Vince asked, looking for more cheese.

Reuben shook his head but kept his eyes on the view. "Here."

"I'm sure that's not unusual. Lots of people want to escape corn."

Audrey glared at him. "And lots of people like corn."

"They don't like it," Vince disagreed. "They are trapped."

"But I thought this was the land of entrapment?" she asked.

"It is but not because of corn."

"She came for nursing school," he said. "She never went back. At least I don't think she ever went back." He looked down at his food and picked up his fajita.

Audrey stopped, as if time stood still. She looked at Vince, seeing he wasn't connecting the dots. "My aunt came here for nursing school from Kansas," she said, looking at Reuben.

"Hmmm," Reuben said. "I'm sure there were a few. What was her name?"

"Sally Thomas."

Reuben's face went white. Vince almost leaped across the table. "Dad, are you okay? Are you having another heart attack? Dad?"

Audrey panicked watching the scene not sure what to do. Vince started to get up and his dad said. "Sally. Mi. . ."

"Oh my God," Audrey said, her stomach full, feeling shocked.

This was Sally's Reuben.

"You were my aunt's true love."

Reuben looked at her, his eyes glassy. "She was my true love."

Vince sat back down. He took a drink of his margarita, as if he needed that to cope with the news.

"We never put the names together," Audrey said, looking at Vince.

"There are a lot of Reubens here," Vince said with his own shoulder shrug.

"She died?" Reuben asked, looking at Audrey. "I used to read the obituaries. As small of a town as Albuquerque is, we never crossed paths. And then one day I stopped. Probably after Yolanda died. I just couldn't bear to think about any more loss. In my mind, as long as Sally was alive, even if she wasn't with me, I could still believe I would be with her."

Audrey wasn't excited. She thought if she learned the truth about Sally's life she would feel good about it. Instead, the more Reuben spoke, the more she feared she was actually contributing to his broken heart. It would never be mended now.

No one ate after that. Reuben began to ask questions about Sally. "I'm remodeling the house," she said, pointing toward it. "But if you want to see it, I can show it to you."

Reuben nodded.

"Shall we all go, and take Sadie with us?" she suggested, looking at Vince for approval.

He nodded, and they left the food on the table and walked around the corner. It wasn't quite dark, although the sun was down, and when they reached the house, Audrey started forward to open the door but Reuben stood on the sidewalk.

When she realized he had stopped, Vince still with him, she rejoined the two men.

"All this time she was right under my nose," he said in disbelief. "I walked Sadie by here when she was still alive. I never saw her. It was God's will that I never know, I guess."

He began to walk up the path and Audrey got ahead to unlock the front door. She let them both in and walked down the hall. "It's a wreck because of the remodel, but feel free to walk around," she called.

They didn't go far. When Audrey walked back into the living room, they were still standing there. Reuben didn't look particularly interested. His face spelled disbelief. Vince stood with him, as he were ready to prop his dad up if he fell down.

Audrey handed Reuben a stack of photos she had found. "I don't know who any of these people are but they were packed away in a box."

Most of them were in black and white and Reuben thumbed through them. One fell and Vince bent down to pick it up.

"This is us," Reuben said. His voice choked up.

"Let's go sit in the kitchen, Dad," Vince suggested, touching his father's elbow and leading him across the empty dining room.

The three of them sat down at the table and Reuben touched Sally's face on the photo. They were leaning against a car, the kind with fins. "That was my car. It was taken in my aunt's driveway. I never should have let her get away." He shook his head. "She told me we couldn't be together."

He didn't speak anymore, instead pushed each photo off the stack, putting his finger on Sally's face on each one. Finally he shoved the whole stack toward the middle of the table.

"I'm sorry," Audrey said. "I had no idea how hard this would be."

Reuben looked at Audrey and reached over and patted her hand. "No, this is good, *mijita*, my daughter. All these years I had no idea what happened, and now I know."

Audrey swallowed hard, feeling sad herself.

"I just hope she was happy. On Sundays in church I always prayed she was happy."

"Um," Audrey said with some hesitancy. "I'm not so sure about that."

Reuben looked at her.

"Come with me," she said, motioning him to the laundry room where she had placed the four paintings to protect them from the remodeling. She pulled them out from under the plastic on the counter and stood them up where they could see.

"What are they?" Reuben asked, squinting.

"Your glasses, Dad," Vince suggested quietly.

"Oh yes," Reuben said, reaching into his shirt pocket.

Once he put them on, he looked at each one.

"They're of the backyard," Audrey said. "There's a pool back there." She pointed to the date in the corner. "She did them four consecutive years. I think you can see a progression of sadness."

"Yes," Reuben said quietly. "I see." He looked for a minute before he spoke again. "He gave her a good life. She had this house, a pool. Living in Aspen Hills. I couldn't have afforded a house here. Did she have children?"

"No," Audrey said. And then she added, "I never knew her."

Reuben took a step back. "What do you mean? Didn't you visit her?"

Audrey was feeling teary herself, now that it was coming full circle. "She didn't have anything to do with our family. When she died, she had left everything to my dad but because my dad had died, it was passed down to me."

"But you never knew her?"

Audrey shook her head. "She left behind diaries from the time she moved to New Mexico. After her parents told her she couldn't be with you, she cut off the family."

"She did?"

"Yes." Audrey shrugged her shoulders. "I don't know why she cut you off, too. She should have married you, but for some reason she felt she couldn't."

Reuben walked up to the darkest painting and put a finger on it lightly, touching something that Sally had created, something that she touched herself. "All this time she was in all that pain. Was she happy with him?"

"The women in the neighborhood say she was. They never knew about you. I don't think she ever spoke of you after she married Patrick. She was only about forty when he died, I think."

"All this time she was alone."

"Dad, why didn't you ever tell us about her?" Vince asked.

Reuben took a step back and looked at Vince. "Because if I did, I knew I would start crying. I had to be strong. Your mother was a wonderful woman." He shook his head. "But Vicente, she wasn't Sally. Sally was my true love, my soul mate. She was everything to me."

He stopped talking and looked at each of them. "It was a different time. Sally and I didn't see the difference in our skin but her parents did. I had more exposure having lived in

Wisconsin than Sally did coming here. But her parents. . . ." His voice trailed off. "I don't know. It's so much better now for you two."

Reuben took a deep breath. He grabbed Audrey's hand. "Thank you." When she took it, he pulled her toward him and held her tight. She wasn't sure how long they stayed that way, but she didn't let go. It felt good to have that connection to Sally.

As Reuben walked to the front door, Sadie following, Audrey held Vince back for a moment. "Would you please stay with me tonight?" she asked, feeling awkward about her request. "For some reason I don't want to be alone."

"Sure," he said. "Let me get my dad to his car and I'll be back."

When Vince returned, Audrey was in her pajamas, a turquoise spaghetti strap tank top and a pair of black shorts with a robe thrown over her. She was sitting in bed, the diaries in front of her.

Vince walked in a bit tentatively. "I thought maybe you might answer the door and invite me to your room."

Audrey laughed. "I'm sorry. I got lost in my thoughts. Not very girlfriend-ish."

"More like married-ten-years-ish," Vince teased, getting on the other side of the bed, still in his clothes, and leaning against the pillows. Sadie made herself at home at Audrey's feet.

"But I guess my dog knows what to do."

"She does," Audrey said. "This is her house, too."

Audrey felt sad, and Vince pulled her to him and wrapped his arm around her back. She leaned against him. "I just don't want to be alone tonight. I feel pretty flummoxed by what just happened. I should be happy to know but it's almost like it hit too close to home. I mean, who knew that Reuben was your dad?"

"There are a lot of Reubens here," Vince laughed.

"I'm sorry," she said.

"Why are you sorry?"

"There your dad was talking about this woman he is clearly still in love with. And it's not your mom."

"It's okay," Vince said. "Maybe I would have made it here anyway."

"And then we would be . . . cousins."

"Let's drop that thought."

They both laughed and were quiet for a moment.

"I'm getting sleepy," Vince said.

"Me, too." She reached over to turn out the light, putting the diaries on the nightstand. Vince took off his shirt and shorts, and together they climbed under the comforter. He kissed her on the cheek, wrapping his arms around her middle section.

As she drifted off to sleep, Audrey thought about how lucky she was.

*****

In the morning though, everything didn't feel so rosy.

When she woke up, Vince still curled up next to her, she started to stretch. Vince moved around a little but kept hold of Audrey so she relaxed and shut her eyes.

It's been so long, she thought, wanting to get up but also not wanting him to loosen his sleeping grasp on her. It felt good to be held.

Thinking about the events of the night before didn't feel as good, though. All this time Audrey had wanted to know who Reuben was, and now she knew. And she felt bad about it. Reuben was so sad. Audrey worried that she had opened a door to something that had been shut because it was so painful. Maybe it should have stayed shut.

"Good morning," he said sleepily from behind her, kissing the top of her head. "It's nice to be here with you."

"And it's nice to have you here," Audrey said in her raspy morning voice. She cleared her throat. Sadie stirred on the floor, her tags jingling.

"I'll let her out," Vince said, pulling himself out of bed and putting on his clothes.

When he didn't come back right away, Audrey found her bathing suit and put it on, thinking a swim might clear her head. She found Vince in the kitchen trying to figure out the coffee maker.

"It's so easy you don't get it, do you?" she asked, pointing at the brew button where the painted word had worn off.

"I haven't seen one of these since med school," Vince joked, watching the brown liquid fill the clear carafe.

"And who makes coffee in a clear carafe anymore?" Audrey joked, pointing at it. "They're all insulated."

"Are you going swimming?"

"My morning swim. You know I do that."

She wrapped the cover up a little tighter.

He just slept in your bed and held you all night but you're going to cover yourself up? She asked herself.

It was getting better though. She didn't worry so much when he followed her to the pool, holding a brown mug with orange flowers on it. As she climbed into the pool, Vince sat by the steps and Sadie lay down next to him.

Audrey let the cool water wash over her. "I don't feel so good about last night," she admitted. "I almost wish none of it had happened."

"My dad will be fine," Vince assured her, coffee in one hand, petting Sadie with the other.

"But it made him so sad. I didn't want to hurt him."

"You couldn't have known," Vince reminded her.

"But why not?"

Vince shook his head.

"His name is Reuben. There were other similarities. I didn't pick up on them."

"Neither did I," Vince reminded her holding out his hand. "Come here."

"Why?" Audrey looked at him tentatively.

Vince laughed. "Please come here."

Audrey walked slowly across the pool and let him hold her wet hand in his dry one.

"You didn't know. I didn't know. It's okay." He looked into her eyes as if that would help get the message across.

She tried to stop the thoughts, but they lingered until school started the next morning. Once she arrived at school, she didn't have time to think about it or worry about it. And then the remodel. And swimming. And slowly life got too busy to worry about the past. The diaries went untouched for weeks, buried under a stack of clothing Audrey dumped on top of them when she was in a hurry to move things around for Rodrigo's crew.

Chapter 13

"Is homecoming that early here?" Audrey asked, peering at the kids who sat down at the table next to them at the Route 66 Malt Shop, yet another place Vince had on his list to take her to.

"Sometimes, I guess," Vince said, looking over the menu and not paying that much attention. "Do you wait until it gets freezing cold in the Midwest?"

Audrey shrugged her shoulders. "It's usually the beginning of October."

"It's not like I'm an expert in teen things since I have no kids," he reminded her.

There were six teens seated at the table, all Hispanic, and all dressed for a big night. Four boys and two girls. Two of the boys wore ties, one a bow tie, and one no tie at all. The girls had long flowing black hair in loose curls that cascaded down their backs. The girl closest to Audrey wore a soft pink dress with lots of ruffles.

Audrey looked down to see their high heels and sighed a little.

"What was that for?" Vince asked, putting the menu down and looking at the kids for the first time. "You want to go to homecoming? I can take you to the Sagebrush dance if you want."

"No," she said, playfully pushing him away. "I miss wearing my high heels."

"You like wearing high heels?" Vince asked, surprised. "I thought all women complained about them."

"I imagine the ones you work with do. They shouldn't be wearing them all day at a hospital anyway," Audrey said. "I can't say I love the way they feel but I do love the way they look. I wear low heels to school but it's not exactly kosher to wear the high ones."

"So what's the key to wearing them?"

Their waitress, a teen girl herself in a light blue and white uniform, walked up to them with a notepad and pencil to take their order.

When she had left, Vince joked, "Reminds me of Lindy's. The kids here could just go to Lindy's and get the real deal rather than having to re-create the nostalgia."

Audrey wanted to finish the heel discussion and waited until he was done with his thought. "The key is that you don't wear them all day. You pick and choose an event that lasts just a few hours, the amount of time your feet are good in heels. Unless of course you're Barbie and you can wear them all day."

"Barbie is wearing heels even when she's wearing tennis flats," Vince added. "That I know from my niece."

The waitress brought them a strawberry milkshake with two straws and Vince gave her the first chance at it.

"Models look great in them because they aren't wearing them all day."

"I didn't know you were such a heel expert," Vince noted, getting his first chance at the milkshake.

Audrey shrugged her shoulders and looked back at the kids. She couldn't take her eyes off them, although she wasn't sure why. "There are probably a lot of things you don't know about me. It's not like we've known each other that long, you know."

By the time they finished their burgers, the kids were just getting served. When Vince went to give the waitress his credit card for their meal, he said, "And please pay for their meal as well."

"What?" The girl asked a little confused. And then getting it, a big smile lit up on her face. "That's very cool. Can I tell them?"

"Sure. After you come back and we're getting ready to leave."

Audrey couldn't believe what she just heard and looked at Vince, smiling herself. "That is very cool. What made you decide to do that?"

He shrugged his shoulders. "There are always people doing for us. People did it for me along the line and I know it's my obligation to do it for someone else."

Vince was sitting with his back to the kids while Audrey could see them from her spot on the next side of their chrome table. Out of the corner of her eye she watched the waitress excitedly tell them what had just transpired.

The kids all turned back to look at Vince and one of the ones wearing a tie got up and walked up to Vince, sticking out his hand. "Thank you, sir. Thank you so much."

"Oh my gosh, thank you," the girl in the pink dress said.

"That really helps," The boy without a tie said.

"You're welcome," Vince told them. "I just ask that you do one thing in return." They waited to hear what he would say. "Do something for someone else. Doesn't have to be tonight or tomorrow. It can be any time."

They all said they would and Vince and Audrey pushed their chairs out from under the table and got up to leave, wishing the kids a good time at their dance. As they walked out of the memorabilia-filled restaurant, Audrey took Vince's hand and squeezed it.

He squeezed back.

*****

She didn't get to check her phone that often during the day, especially knowing that Vince was as busy as she was. But when she finally sat down to lunch that Tuesday, she saw a text from Vince.

"My dad is back in the hospital."

Immediately, Audrey wrote back. "Oh no. What happened?"

That afternoon she checked it as much as could, trying to be inconspicuous because she was constantly telling her students they needed to put theirs away.

"But it's a form of communication," the communication skills students would argue.

Audrey would laugh. "At the right time. And right now I'm your form of communication."

No word from Vince through the end of sixth period when she was getting ready to leave for home.

"He had another heart attack. His heart isn't going to last long."

A lump formed in Audrey's throat and she sat down in her chair, not able to function for a moment. Sally. If only she had never figured out that Sally had been Reuben's true love. He had a broken heart and it was never going to be mended.

"Do you want me to come to the hospital?" Audrey asked.

"If you can."

Instead of driving home to Aspen Hills, Audrey kept going south past the interstate that would take her east and headed downtown to the hospital where Vince worked. And where Sally had worked.

She found Vince in his office in the medical tower that adjoined the hospital.

"Hey," he said, inviting her in and shutting the door behind him. It was the first time she had been in his office and couldn't help but look around: diplomas on the wall, a big view of the mountains from the window.

"So this is where you do all the important work," she said, trying to get a look at everything without being too obvious. But as soon as the door shut, she knew it wasn't good and set to paying attention to Vince.

He didn't invite her to sit down; he pulled her into his arms and they stood there for a moment when she realized he was shaking.

Crying.

Audrey didn't move. She grabbed Vince tighter, feeling his body beneath his white button-down shirt. She waited for him to pull away.

When he started to shift, she let her arms go from his back and placed them in his hands. Audrey took a step back from Vince. Even in the sterility of his office, she could feel something warm between them. She looked up at him and saw the sadness in his watery eyes.

"His heart is failing."

Audrey leaned back against him and felt him shake. "I'm so sorry," she murmured into his shirt.

"I should have known this was coming."

Audrey pulled away again. "How would you know that?" she asked.

"He's shown signs of this for several years. I think I was in denial, and then there was Mom's death." He sighed, his body shaking as he did.

Audrey gulped. It didn't matter what Vince said, she still worried about what she had brought on with Reuben finding out about Sally.

Vince let Audrey's right hand go but kept her left hand in his and squeezed it. "He asked to see you. That's why I wanted you to come this afternoon."

Audrey's stomach jumped. She knew she was lucky that he wanted to see her, lucky that he cared that much about her. But she still worried that she had caused his heart problems.

They walked together to the elevator through a maze of hallways.

"Don't hospitals have colored lines to help people find their way around?" Audrey asked, completely confused about where they were. The only time she had any sense of where they were was when they walked by a window with a view of the north end of the city.

"Nah, that would make things too easy," Vince joked on the elevator. "I think they hire people to design these who like to do mazes. Designing a hospital is the ultimate maze. And then I think they have contests to see who can trick people the most."

Audrey shook her head when they walked off and once again, Vince pointed right, then left, then right.

And finally, the cardiac unit.

"You don't spend much time in hospitals, do you?" Vince asked, waving to the nurses at the station in the middle of the large room.

"I try not to," Audrey admitted, remembering when her father had brain cancer. She gulped, a bunch of scenes running through her head like a movie: the initial visit to the ER after he had collapsed in the shower, the subsequent hospital stays for surgery, and then hospice. Even five years later she could still recall that awful smell of death in the hospice facility.

"I wish I had brought him to home to die," her mother had lamented at least once a year since her father's death. She, too, avoided hospitals after that.

"You deserve a lot of credit," Audrey said quietly, as she and Vince stood outside the door where her father's name was written on a placard next to the doorway.

"Why?" Vince asked, half looking in the room, half looking at Audrey, his hands shoved in his white coat pockets.

"You do medicine. Your mom died of cancer. Your dad is here. This isn't easy," she said. "I can't stand the smell."

"I don't smell it anymore," Vince admitted. "It's probably because I'm too focused on saving lives."

She nodded and he stretched his right arm and hand to the doorway.

"You aren't going with me?" she asked.

"I'll be in later. I was here an hour ago. I want you to have a little time with him."

She knew that Vince had some idea of what was coming. Audrey looked at the doorway and took a deep breath before she walked in, trying to be confident. As she pushed the half closed heavy door, she saw Reuben in the bed, several machines hooked up to him.

"*Mijita!*" he said immediately, reaching his hand to Audrey from the bed. She felt as though she were going from one outstretched hand to another.

As Audrey pulled up a chair and sat down, she swallowed hard. Reuben had always looked so strong and healthy: wearing his golf shirts, walking Sadie. But now lying in the bed with wires coming out of him, he looked weak, much the way she remembered her dad before his death.

"Hi," she said, quietly, afraid to talk because she might cry.

"Don't cry," he said. "Please."

And then Audrey started to blurt it out. "But I caused . . ."

"No, no, no," he said, his voice raspy. "You did the opposite. You brought me peace for the first time in over fifty years."

"What do you mean?" Audrey asked through her tears.

"No one knows how much I suffered after Sally ended it," he admitted, squeezing Audrey's hand tighter. "I loved her more than anything in the world. I thought we were going to live happily ever after."

Audrey could see he had a tear in his eye.

"I still don't understand why she ended it."

"I know," Audrey said. "She refused to have anything to do with us anyway."

"It was so hard to wish her happiness. And I loved Yolanda with all my heart. And I love Vince and his sister. But my life was not what I thought it would be."

Audrey listened, just listened. She tried not to let her mind wander. She wanted him to know she was there with him.

"But I loved her. I tried not to look for her. I tried to move on." He paused and let out a funny sound, as if his body were releasing his feelings. "But I never did."

Audrey began to cry herself.

"And now I know what happened."

They were quiet for a moment. Audrey couldn't look at him. She held his hand tightly, and he squeezed just as much.

"Thank you," he finally said.

Audrey looked up and through her own tears, she asked, "But why? I feel like I hurt you, I made this worse by you finding out about Sally."

"*Mijita,* that's not true. You brought me peace. I can move on now because I know she is waiting for me."

"But what about your kids and grandkids?" she asked. "Are they angry at me?"

"There is no anger at me," he said. "I don't want that. What I want is for you and Vince to go forward and have the life that Sally and I never could have. Vince loves you, that I know. Finally he has found that love that I had with Sally. And he has it with Sally's niece." He paused to catch his breath. "What would make me happiest is to see you two be together, to watch over you from heaven."

Audrey was in a full-fledged cry now. She nodded.

"Don't give up. If it gets hard, don't give up. You two have something most people never get to experience in their lives. I had it with Sally only a short time but I also know that I am lucky to have had it at all."

There was a light knock at the door and a nurse walked in tentatively. "I'm sorry to interrupt," she said, her dark brown ponytail flipping around behind her. "Mr. Montoya, we need to check your vitals."

"No rest in the hospital, even when one comes to die," Reuben sighed, smiling at Audrey, squeezing her hand again.

She smiled weakly at him and they had to let go to let the nurse through to reach the machines. Audrey got up to leave and Reuben said, "No. Don't go."

And as she sat back down, Vince walked in.

"Your son is here to make sure I do my job," the nurse joked with Reuben.

Vince ignored her and walked over to Audrey. He rubbed her shoulder and they sat and watched, not paying attention to what the nurse was doing, lost in their own thoughts.

"It's too quiet in here," Reuben barked. "All this attention doesn't need to be on me."

"Your son is waiting for the results," the nurse joked again.

Audrey looked up to see Vince shaking his head. Later, he would ask Audrey, "Does it really matter? I only want him to be comfortable."

The nurse left and Audrey tried to get up to leave again. "No," Reuben told her, wheezing a bit.

"Dad, please," Vince said. "It's not worth straining yourself."

"If I don't say it now, I might not get the chance," Reuben reminded him.

Audrey got comfortable again in the uncomfortable standard-issue hospital chair. She wanted to leave yet she didn't want to leave. She was afraid that it might be the last time she would see Reuben.

"We'll let you rest, Dad," Vince said, patting his father's arm in a spot where there weren't any wires attached.

"Come back tomorrow, *mijita*," he said. "Please."

It took Audrey a moment to realize he was speaking to her, and she nodded as she got up. She squeezed his hand and turned away before he saw she was crying again.

Outside the room, Audrey walked to the right and leaned her back against the door, shutting her eyes.

"Let's go back to my office," Vince said quietly, taking her hand.

Once the door was shut, she fell apart. "It's okay," Vince said, pulling her into his lap in one of the chairs on the front side of his desk. She rested her face against his and felt wetness. He was crying, too.

"He told you he felt like it was time to go?"

Audrey nodded without pulling away. And hearing Vince say it made her cry harder. When he pulled away from her, to look into her eyes, he said, "You didn't do anything wrong. How could you have known?"

Audrey shrugged. She didn't have an answer but it all felt painful.

"I'll pick up dinner," Vince suggested without giving her much of a choice. "Sadie and I will be over at six."

When she got home, she dropped her two bags on the kitchen table filled with all sorts of other items displaced in the remodeling. She glanced at the kitchen, felt exhausted and walked down the hall to the bedroom.

Audrey lay down on her bed, curling up with her pillow. She saw the diaries on the nightstand, ran her finger along them, but didn't pick them up. Instead, she shut her eyes, wishing she could think about nothing. There were too many thoughts although she fell asleep quickly.

The next thing she heard was the tapping of Sadie's nails on the bare floors, seemingly coming and looking for Audrey in the bedroom.

"Hey girl," Audrey said, scratching her ears as she breathed on Audrey.

Vince followed a few moments later, putting dinner in the kitchen.

"Hey," he said, climbing in the bed and curling up next to her. "Are you okay?"

"Not really. So I know you're not; he's your dad."

"I'm not sure if it's harder or easier when you get have the chance to say goodbye to someone. I've seen people in the ER who didn't get that chance and they wished they did. But when you're waiting for someone it can be just as hard. You don't know when it will come and you don't know if you'll remember to say everything you wanted."

"It doesn't matter I guess." She turned to him and they held each other quietly.

"I'm glad he found peace," Vince finally said. "I had no idea about Sally. He never let on to us." He paused. "Don't feel bad ever. Maybe this was what was meant to happen."

"But I do," she said. "Here your dad is going on about this woman you didn't know about—and she's not your mother." She stopped for a moment to think. "It must make you feel like your mom didn't matter as much to him."

Vince shook his head. "No. Don't think that. My dad had a life before my mom. If there is one thing I have learned in life, it's that nothing is cut and dried or black and white. None of us knows what someone has in their history that we don't know about. We all have some gray in our lives. I feel better knowing something about my dad than watching him die and not knowing."

When he went home later, Audrey climbed into bed and started to open the diary where she left off. She looked at it, at Sally's loopy handwriting, and she shut it, putting it back on the stack.

It didn't matter anymore. She knew what she needed to know. The next day she packed the diaries in a box and put them away with some other things of Sally's she didn't want to get rid of.

Chapter 14

They sent Reuben home the next day at his request.

"That's what he wanted," Vince told Audrey via text. "At least he'll be at home."

She met Vince for dinner at Reuben's house that night. He was shuffling around, even in his golf shirt. The strong man she met in the street walking Sadie was gone. It was still hard to believe that this wasn't her fault.

"How do you know it wouldn't have happened anyway?" Vince kept asking. "You'll never know."

But each minute she spent with Reuben she tried to enjoy the time with him, and to help Vince be with his dad as much as possible.

"I want to eat enchiladas every day until I die," Reuben said at the dinner table as Vince and Audrey unpacked the brown paper bags.

"That can be arranged," Vince said, handing his dad a container filled with red chile chicken enchiladas from Sandoval's. "No reason to worry about your cholesterol now."

"But I can't!" Audrey joked. "You could live another year and I'll be as fat as a moose."

"More of you to love, *mihita*," Reuben laughed.

"But Vince won't like me so much," Audrey argued.

"He always liked his girls thin," Reuben said looking at his son.

"And here goes the dating history," Vince said, raising his eyebrows as he soaked a sopa in red chile sauce.

"I have to share all that I can now or it will be lost history," his father argued.

They sat at the table until Reuben looked like he was uncomfortable and Vince helped him to bed.

He didn't make it until Sophia, Vince's sister, flew in that weekend.

"My dad died in his sleep last night," Vince said, calling Audrey early Friday morning as she dressed for school. "I woke up to check on him, and he was dead."

Audrey felt empty all day, going through the motions with her classes, knowing she couldn't take a day off because she was too new and hadn't accumulated enough days off.

When she showed up at the house that night, various members of the family had gathered, some of them recognizing Audrey from the wedding. The kitchen table was filled with endless food. People were milling everywhere.

"My sister is a mess," Vince whispered, Audrey instantly knowing who she was by the loud crying coming from the living room. A young woman with bobbed black hair sobbed, female relatives gathered around, comforting her.

"Why couldn't he wait for me to get here?" she was crying.

Audrey gulped, watching the tears fall and seeing a stack of crumpled tissues in her lap. She wished she could take away Sophia's pain.

"So this is your girl?" an older man asked, coming up next to them.

Audrey shook herself away from watching Sophia and turned her attention to the tanned balding man.

"Hi," she said, giving him her hand to shake.

"This is Audrey," Vince said.

"I'm glad your dad knew her before he died," he said to Vince and then turned to Audrey and added, "I'm Steve. Reuben was my brother." He shook his head and looked at Vince. "He was so happy about you two."

Audrey looked up at Vince and smiled at him.

They didn't have much more time before Sophia was suddenly at Vince's side. "Are you Audrey?" she asked, sniffling.

"I am."

Sophia grabbed her and hugged her. "The last time I talked to my dad, he told me how much he appreciated you and the fact that you and Vince found each other."

Audrey looked at Vince, his sister's tight hold still on her and his Uncle Steve still standing next to them. Everyone's eyes were watering.

Sophia finally pulled away but didn't move too far from Audrey. "You brought my dad a lot of happiness in the end, knowing that Vince had someone in his life." She looked at her brother. "I can't help but think that he felt he could die because Vince finally had someone."

Audrey bit her lip and looked at Vince again. He was looking down, holding back the tears.

Later, after the house was empty except for Sophia, who had had a few glasses of wine and gone to bed, Audrey asked him, "She doesn't know about Sally, does she?"

Vince shook his head. "I don't think my dad told anyone. But what everyone is telling me is that he told them all about you and how grateful he was that you were in my life."

"But he never told them about Sally?" Before he spoke, she added, "I know it's not the time. I know it probably really doesn't matter. I can't stop thinking about it, though."

Vince nodded. "I'm not sure," he admitted. "The important thing is that we have each other. And we know he was at peace when he died."

They sat in the quiet of the room, just a table light on at the other end of the couch. "I better go home," she said, tracing her finger across Vince's forearm.

"You don't like my hairy arms?" Vince teased.

He grabbed her to pull her closer before she could pull back from him. "That's exactly it. I'm going to leave because your hairy arms are grossing me out."

As she drove home in the darkness of Albuquerque, the city lights below her, she felt sadness not just for Reuben's death but also for Sally. And yet she knew they were finally together in a way that life had not let them be.

The glittering lights weren't sad in the darkness. They were a sign that life was still happy, that even in darkness all was well. She sighed and pulled into her driveway. The house felt empty and cold without flooring or furniture. Audrey sat down in the still-untouched kitchen at the table.

"I need to go to bed," she mumbled. It was almost midnight.

At least in the morning, she knew, the light would come, the sun would come over the pool. And life would go on somehow. Rick leaving her had taught her that much. And moving to Albuquerque had brought her happiness for the first time in a long time.

Hopefully this was just a bump in the road, she thought as she pulled the covers over her body and leaned forward to turn out the light by the bed.

Chapter 15

Audrey knew her own experience of grief but not much else. She had watched her mother's sadness after her father's death, their plans cut short by a brain tumor no one knew was growing in his head. "We were going to travel. We were supposed to grow old sitting together on the front porch," Shirley would sigh, looking off into the distance of a future she wouldn't have.

Audrey knew the two white-painted rocking chairs on the front porch, bought when she was still in high school, were for that exact reason. For years her parents joked they wouldn't have time to sit in them together until Audrey was gone from home and they were both retired.

The only time they sat together on the front porch was when her father came home to die, refusing a wheelchair into the house, walking up the steps himself, arguing, "You're going to bring me out in a body bag so at least let me go in one last time by my own feet." Instead of going in the front door, though, he stopped at the rocking chair closest to him and sat down, urging Shirley to join him.

Audrey finally ushered the hospice people away. "We'll take care of it," she whispered, not knowing if they really could but realizing it didn't matter. They would figure it out.

What she knew of grief was her mother's sadness at the end of two lives together. Her mother often told her she knew nothing was promised to them when they married but they had such a good life together she never expected it to end so soon.

And there was her own grief, the sadness she felt for not having her father around anymore. That had made it somewhat easier for her to move to New Mexico. And she knew that if she left, her mother would find it easier to sell the family home and move on.

"North Carolina," Shirley sometimes said. "But we'll see."

Here Audrey was almost a half year later, and life had done a one-eighty turn. It was a good thing, even with the sadness surrounding Reuben's death.

"Cling to the happiness," she told herself throughout the day when she felt as if it all might overwhelm her. "There is no reason to be sad."

Audrey thought of Reuben holding her hand tight, and realized that not everything she felt sad about had to do with Sally. It was also about how she thought Reuben would be around, too. Maybe in some ways she expected he would be the father she didn't have in her life anymore.

But she tried to remind herself that there might be something bigger, that despite the fact that she felt as if she might have caused Reuben's death, it was about giving Reuben the peace he might not have found otherwise.

"He had a good death," Uncle Steve had said. "He died peacefully, something not everyone gets to do."

As she drove to and from school, or she found herself caught in a moment where something reminded her of Reuben's death, she tried to steer her thoughts toward how far life had come.

"I haven't seen you in a while!" Betty exclaimed, spotting Audrey get her mail one afternoon several weeks after Reuben's death.

"I know," Audrey admitted. "It's my fault. School has been busy."

"Oh we know how busy you are," Betty said. "And you have Vince, too."

"Vince's father died," Audrey added.

"Oh dear," Betty said, taking a step back as if the words physically touched her.

Audrey wanted to say more but she knew it wasn't the time. Before she could suggest anything, Betty said, "Let's get together this weekend." She paused. "Unless you and Vince are busy, of course."

Audrey nodded. That would be good, she thought.

The nights had begun to cool. A winter storm had come through the week before, dropping snow at the top of the Sandias, Audrey stood outside and looked into the swimming pool.

"Are you really going to get in?" Vince asked in a text earlier. "Like the Polar Bear Club thing?"

"I'm going to try," Audrey texted back, knowing her laughter didn't come through in the words.

She pulled the solar cover back first and the steam from the heated water rose over the surface. "It's like a giant hot tub," she mumbled, sticking her toe in lightly.

It was warm enough.

"Maybe I should get you a wet suit," Vince had suggested.

"That would be cheaper than heating it," Audrey wrote back, knowing how much money Sally had spent on heating the pool over the years. She slipped off her big fuzzy bathrobe and into the water, wearing a long-sleeved top that Mandy had sent to protect her from the sun ("I don't want you to get all wrinkly in that sun!" she had written in the note when she sent it). She felt a freedom she had missed in the few weeks she had been out of the pool, consumed by Reuben's failing heart and his death.

As she began to glide back and forth across the pool, warm in her shirt, she thought about how free Sally must have felt. Surely life in some ways had been a burden because she had to end a relationship with the man she truly loved. And then she kept it a secret. But now Audrey saw that Reuben had done the same thing.

This is why she paid all that money to heat the pool, Audrey thought, waiting for Sally to come and tell her that. And how happy painting and swimming made her.

Audrey waited, as she swam. Nothing. Just herself in the pool.

As she climbed out of the pool, her body shivering from the cold air, she quickly wrapped the bathrobe around her and ran into the house where she started a shower.

"I don't think it's economically feasible," she told Vince later when he and Sadie came to dinner.

"You mean because you have to pay to heat the pool and then take a shower after to get warm again after getting out."

"Exactly," she laughed, hearing the absurdity of it out loud.

She called the pool guy the next day to set up the soonest he could close it. "Thanksgiving," he said. "I'm busy installing wood stoves to make ends meet in the winter. And I never kept any time free this late since Sally kept it open all winter."

Until then, Audrey thought she could at least stare at it out the bedroom window and pretend it was warm outside.

That Thursday when she went into the bedroom, she saw the green dress hanging. She sat on the bed and stared at it for a moment. It had been several months since she had tried it on, mostly because she had been too caught up in everything in her life.

It's time, she thought, sitting there another moment before getting up and slipping out of the skirt and sweater she wore to school. Audrey slipped the green dress on, remembering that last time it had fit until she zipped it up.

Now she pulled the zipper slowly, sucking her middle in, realizing there wasn't as much as before. The zipper kept going, it didn't get stuck. It didn't tell her it wasn't going to budge. All the way to the top seam. Audrey let out her stomach and looked in the mirror, smoothing the dress in front of her, especially across her middle section.

It fit. She wanted to cry out but there was no one to tell. She would see Vince in a few hours and could tell him. It was a moment when Audrey wished Sally would come to see her. She looked around, fully expecting Sally to come around the corner or appear in the mirror. But nothing.

Audrey looked down at the spot on the dress. Now she could clean it. She still had nowhere to wear it though. Clean it, she told herself, walking out of the closet and looking for her workout clothes. As she did, she noticed a shoebox she hadn't seen before. Audrey thought she had been through everything at this point but somehow the box escaped her. It was probably from the sixties, black and white stripes on the bottom with a pink lid.

"How did I miss that?" she wondered, slipping off the lid to see photos and what looked like other mementos.

Instead of changing in her workout clothes, she kept the dress on and climbed on the bed realizing the photos were of Sally and Reuben. And underneath was a necklace with a silver heart, some matchbooks of various places in Albuquerque.

"Hey Baby!" a voice called from down the hall.

"I'm in here!" Audrey said, scurrying to take the dress off. She found her bathrobe and tied it just as he walked in.

"I missed you naked?" he asked, grabbing her for a kiss.

"Sorry," she said, hoping he didn't see the dress that was in a heap on the bed. She didn't care if he saw her naked but she wanted to keep the dress a surprise. Audrey immediately pointed at the box, half the contents on the bed.

"Look what I found just now." Audrey climbed on the bed, crossing her legs in front of her, and Vince sat on the side of it, both of them facing the contents.

"Wow," he said, quietly.

"I found some photos before but never these. And look." She held up the necklace, looking tarnished. "I'm guessing your dad gave it to her."

"These places don't exist anymore," Vince laughed, thumbing through the matchbooks.

"Except for Lindy's" Audrey said with a smile.

Vince held it in his hand and looked at it. Then he put it down and together they filled the box back up.

"Weird how I didn't find it until today," she said.

"Yeah." Vince lay back on the bed and shut his eyes.

"Long day?"

"They're all long right now," he said, reaching for her hand without looking.

But when they arrived at Betty's two hours later, Audrey having missed her walk to take a nap with Vince instead, it was hard not to get caught up in the infectious excitement of the trio.

"We've missed you!" Mary Ellen said, grabbing both of their hands and squeezing them. Her face went sober and she said, "But we know it's been a sad time. I had no idea that was your dad walking your dog all this past year."

"He was very handsome," Esther said, raising her eyebrows.

They stood in the kitchen while Mary Ellen poured everyone a glass of red wine. "We're having lasagna again," Betty said.

"She always cooks the same few things when she has other people over," Esther remarked. "So now we're back to the lasagna."

"But I'm relying on the rest of you to host dinner for a while," said Betty, "and then you'll forget when it's time for red chile enchiladas again."

"We have the Christmas dance next!" Mary Ellen reminded them, getting excited.

"Um, what?" Audrey asked. She looked at Vince who shrugged his shoulders and looked back at Mary Ellen.

"Oh, it's the event of the year at the country club. We use it as a fund raiser to buy gifts for children who don't get much Christmas. Mostly immigrant children."

"You two will have to be there. It's the only time any of us get to dress up," Esther said.

"Unless we go to a funeral," Betty reminded her.

"Remember when we had legs like Audrey and we wore dresses all the time?"

The three women laughed and looked down at their pants.

"I get a new pair of pants every year just for the event," Betty said.

"I guess we're going," Vince whispered.

"I'm not sure we can miss it," Audrey said, realizing she could wear the green dress that night.

When they sat down at the table to eat and everyone had been served, Audrey opened the conversation.

"I know who Reuben is," she said simply, her fork in one hand, while the women were busy unfolding their napkins. Vince had already begun to eat and acted as if he wasn't paying attention.

The trio stopped mid unfolding, except for Betty, who continued until she finished. "Do we know him?" Mary Ellen asked.

Before Audrey could say anything, Vince, who had finished chewing, quietly told them. "My father."

Audrey wondered if she could drop a pin in the room, but realized the carpet might soak up the noise. Their faces were filled with bewilderment.

"What?" Esther asked. "I'm confused. How did you find that out?"

As they began to relay the story, the women leaned in closer, their lasagna going cold.

"Betty, please pass the wine," Mary Ellen said. "I need help absorbing this."

"Did you talk to him about it?" Betty asked, passing the wine bottle.

"We did," Audrey said.

"I can't imagine . . . " Betty's voice trailed off.

The lasagna went cold. As Audrey watched everyone, she felt Vince slide his hand into hers, holding it tightly. She knew he was telling her to be strong, that she wasn't ruining anything for anyone.

That night as they lay in bed at her house, he would say once again, "It's okay. It's okay."

"Why me?" Audrey kept asking, feeling tears from her frustration. "I never meant to hurt anyone but I feel like that's what's happening."

In the dark, Vince sat up. "Why do you think you're hurting everyone?"

She looked at him and couldn't answer at first. "I'm not making anyone happy with what I'm telling them. This isn't happy news. It just leaves more questions."

"Baby," he said, touching her cheek. "You're pulling people closer together. Stop seeing this as something that's dividing people."

He lay back down and pulled the covers back over them and then reached to pull Audrey close. "I don't know," she said quietly.

"Let it go. Life is good. I miss my dad, but I know he's happy in a way that I never could have imagined if you hadn't come along."

Audrey couldn't fall asleep. She lay there trying to figure out *how* she would let it go. She had thought that nothing could be harder than the end of her marriage to Rick, but something about this was proving more challenging than she ever imagined.

After Vince left the next morning, Audrey decided it was time to take the dress to the cleaners.

"It's old," Audrey told the short Hispanic woman with glasses. "Vintage." She corrected herself.

"I might have to take the buttons off or they will melt," the woman said thoughtfully.

"And there is a stain there." Audrey pointed at it. "I think it's actually about forty years old. Ketchup."

The woman wasn't paying attention and added a stain sticker with an arrow to the garment. "I'll see what we can do."

"No hurry," Audrey said, "I'm not going to wear it until the first weekend in December."

When she arrived back home and went into the bedroom to change out of her school clothes, as she called them, she looked around and realized what a mess she had.

There were clothes everywhere, mostly Sally's. Everything from the master bedroom, which was being painted a soft cream to accent the turquoise bedding she had bought, was in the guest room where she had been sleeping.

"I don't know what I was thinking," Audrey sighed when she tried to go to bed that night.

"I was wondering," Vince said, looking for a spot to climb into the other side of the bed. The floor was lined with stacks of boxed shoes. "Don't you need to get rid of most of this stuff anyway?"

"Yeah, probably," Audrey admitted. She got into bed and rested her back against the pillows, rubbing lotion on her hands. "I've never had such dry hands in my life."

"It only gets worse in the winter," Vince said, holding out his hand for a squeeze from the tube. "It's the price we pay for not having bugs."

"Then I think I'll take not having the bugs." As she lowered her body onto the bed, she turned out the light. "I dread having to go through all that stuff. I think I've reached my saturation point."

"No surprise. Have you missed anything?"

"The garage. But I figure who needs to go through the garage, right? I'll just leave it all for the next person after I die."

The light on Vince's side of the bed was still on. He shrugged his shoulders. "Maybe someone will want to move in here with you and he might have some stuff."

Audrey's eyes were closed and she didn't get it at first. Then they popped open. "You?" She looked up at him.

"Maybe one day."

"Don't I need to ask you?"

Vince turned out the light and lowered himself until they were facing each other. "Maybe it will be mutual," he said.

Audrey didn't say anything. He was there every step of the way with the remodeling project, as if they were remodeling the house together.

"What are you scared of?" Mandy asked the next afternoon when Audrey was sitting on the bed after school, knowing she needed to tackle the shoes first, at least enough to make it easier for Vince to get to the bed. It felt like a contradiction. Had she put the shoes there purposely to keep him from staying?

"That it won't last forever," Audrey admitted. "That he will come home one day and tell me he doesn't love me anymore."

"Girl, someone needs to give you a lesson."

"How so?"

Mandy laughed. Audrey could hear she was making dinner: the water running, the microwave buzzing.

"Isn't it obvious to you that you are supposed to be together?" Audrey didn't say anything so Mandy continued. "Your lives have been intertwined for a reason. And they share history. It's the most romantic story I've ever heard."

"Maybe I should write a novel about it."

"No one would believe it if you did it as a memoir," Mandy joked. "Fiction would be a better route."

After they ended the call, Audrey dropped the phone on the bed and started to open the boxes of shoes. Sally had so much of everything, as if she could never stop at one.

"That's true," Betty had told Audrey when they met at the mailbox earlier in the week. "If she found a pair of white shoes she liked, she would also get them in brown and black." Betty thought for a moment. "And any other color they came in." Out of the blue, Betty began to laugh and looked back at Audrey. "One time she brought home these sequined heels in pink! Of all colors! And she wore them with a pink dress! Oh dear. We thought she looked like a flamingo with those long legs."

Audrey laughed when she opened a box and saw the sequined pink heels inside. She slipped them on her own feet, admiring that they fit.

"I think that was something like 1969," Betty had said.

"Vintage now," Audrey said out loud to herself, still looking down at the shoes, wishing Sally would show up so she could share the moment with her.

But the room remained silent with only Audrey standing in front of the full-length mirror to see how the shoes looked, realizing it wouldn't be overkill with a different colored dress. She didn't want to be a flamingo, too.

Down the hall she heard Rodrigo's crew wrapping it up for the evening. "Audrey?" Rodrigo called.

Audrey walked out with the pink shoes still on her feet and Rodrigo laughed "Those shoes are hard to miss."

"I know," Audrey laughed. "At least I'm not wearing them with a pink dress. You might think I'm a flamingo."

"Or the pink panther." He shook his head.

"Maybe!" Audrey laughed.

"They'll be done in the master tomorrow." Together they walked into the bare room, the cement floor exaggerating the clicking sound of Audrey's heels.

"So you'll be moving down the hall?" she asked.

He nodded. "Let me know if you see anything you want repaired." He pointed at a spot near the ceiling. "I like to do them before the carpet is put in."

After he left, Audrey looked around at the mess. Some rooms were empty, their contents filling other rooms. Her clothes were piled up in the room that must have been Patrick's, a closet Audrey knew she'd have to attack over the weekend.

"It makes me crazy," Audrey sighed when Vince stopped over with Sadie so she could show him the color in the master bedroom."

"It's a transition," he said.

She nodded, knowing he was right. It was the move from Sally's house to hers and this was the most difficult part: the mess.

After Rodrigo had left, Audrey returned to the bedroom with several boxes she found in the garage and started to fill them with shoes. A black trash bag held what she knew no one would wear or was broken.

And when she was done, the shoes cleared into the garage with the other trash and donations, she surveyed the sort of clear floor. In a week that room would be torn up, too, and the big bed and flowered sheets would be in the garage, too. She would be sleeping on her new furniture in the master bedroom.

It was 6:00 but she kept going, sorting dresses into piles. All of Sally's later clothes were easy to throw out, "Too old ladyish for me," Audrey joked to Vince.

"One day you'll be that old lady, too," he laughed.

"She was very stylish but those clothes aren't stylish for a thirty something."

"A picky one at that. One who prefers the 1969 pink sequined heels."

"They'll work in just the right setting," Audrey reminded him. "You'll be surprised."

It was easy to get rid of the later clothes, to throw out the underwear and stockings, but the closet of Lilly dresses, Audrey wasn't sure what to do.

"It's like a time warp," she said out loud, at first wanting to keep them all but then thinking maybe that was silly. Would she wear them all?

Too confused, she left them and walked into Patrick's room, another box in one hand and a trash bag in the other. Golf had been his life outside of work and the closet was filled with golf balls and hats.

When Vince arrived, he settled into the overstuffed chair with the ottoman. "Do you think you he sat in that chair and read?" Audrey asked.

"Maybe. Do you know anything about him?"

Audrey shook her head. "Honestly, it doesn't seem relevant. All I really care about is that Sally and your dad loved each other. For me, it's like her life stopped there even though she still had. . . ." Her voice trailed off and she placed several boxes of golf balls in a box. Then she looked at what was left, not saying anything. And then, "a lot of life to live."

Chapter 16

Sylvia and her friends, Ruth and Veronica, were talking among themselves at lunch when Audrey looked out into the hallway and saw some of the cheerleaders hanging homecoming signs. The girls with the long hair and navy blue and white ribbons in their hair, wearing their short skirts, were talking excitedly, a little loudly.

"I can't believe Chris Martínez asked me to homecoming!" one of the girls said.

"But you don't have to go with a date," the other girl said.

"I know but it's fun if you have one," the first girl added, smoothing out the sign. "Kind of old- fashioned."

Audrey looked over and saw Sylvia was watching the cheerleaders. She looked sad.

"Are you going to homecoming?" Audrey asked her, hoping for the answer she knew she wouldn't get.

Sylvia shook her head, looking away.

"But it's different than when I was your age," Audrey said, Ruth and Veronica ending their conversation to listen to Audrey. "We had to have a date or we didn't go."

"Did you go?" Sylvia asked.

"I had a guy friend who always took me. We were never romantic. It turned out he was gay so I think I was his cover during high school." The girls giggled and Audrey shook her head at the memory.

"I can't afford a dress," Sylvia said, looking right at Audrey.

Audrey opened her mouth and shut it. "Oh," she said quietly.

She felt stupid at first, realizing that if they couldn't afford lunch, how could they afford dresses? She turned back to her paperwork but she couldn't focus on it. The girls began their conversation again.

And then she thought of something.

"Girls," she said, getting up and walking toward them, sitting down in a desk one row over. "Are none of you going because you don't have dresses?"

They all shook their heads. "My sister has a dress but she's way taller than me and my mom doesn't have time to fix it. She's working two jobs right now," Veronica said.

"I'm afraid to ask my mom," Ruth said. "My parents are working so hard."

"I have an idea," Audrey told them. "I will make sure you have what you need."

"What do you mean?" Sylvia asked.

Audrey waved them off. "Don't worry about any of this. Show up here at 5:00 the night of the dance."

"But we can't afford tickets," Ruth reminded her.

"I'll take care of it. You're going to have to trust me on this."

The girls didn't look so sure but they nodded and agreed to show up.

That night, Audrey opened another box of her clothes and began to pull dresses out as she talked to Mandy. "I'm continuing your tradition this fall," said her friend. "We've already got ten donated for the girls at school. It makes me so sad that these girls can't afford dresses."

"Me, too," said Audrey. "And the dresses are way cheaper than when we were their age. You can find something now for fifty dollars, wear it once, and throw it out."

Audrey pulled out a pink dress, a green dress, and a black dress. And at the bottom of the box she found the shoes.

"You always looked great at your parties," Mandy said. "And the school dances. I think the kids were always shocked when you showed up looking like a model. The girls always wanted to know which dresses you donated because they knew they were the best ones. They were disappointed you didn't donate any before you left."

Audrey laughed. "When you're the speech and communication teacher, you can do things a little differently."

She placed all three dresses on the bed where she could look at them. They were nice dresses: just enough style so the girls would blend in with the others. They didn't need to be top of the line. They just needed to be nice. Luckily they were all about the same size—her size—so the dresses would fit but she added a clear plastic sandwich bag with safety pins just in case. They would make it work.

Audrey had gotten pretty good at doing this at school, making sure any girl who needed a dress got one. While she hadn't seen the same kind of poverty in Kansas that she was seeing in New Mexico, the recession had made things tight for many families, and buying extras like dresses was often out of the question.

In a box, Audrey put several pairs of shoes, not knowing if the girls would be able to fit into them, careful that she didn't select heels that were too high.

The next day, she gave the girls a little more information when they came in. "On Saturday," Audrey started, sitting next to them again, "Please bring some shoes that you can wear with a dress."

"Are we going to the dance?" Ruth asked, her green eyes getting big.

"You are," Audrey told her.

They started to ask a million questions. Audrey held out her hand to stop them. "I'm not going to tell you more. I need you to come with hair and makeup ready and a pair of shoes you can wear. Can you do that?"

"Yes," they said in unison.

Before she left school that afternoon, she stopped in the activities office and bought three tickets for the dance. "Are you planning to bring two dates?" Lee Chang, the activities director teased her. "You really don't have to pay."

"No," Audrey said with a smile. "I'm paying for three students."

The permanent smile on his face grew big and he nodded his head. "Nice," he said.

Audrey felt satisfied as she went home that afternoon, ready to give the girls something she wished she could give all her students: hope.

She didn't have to twist Vince's arm to go with her.

"Of course I'll go," he said. "It sure beats dealing with sick people all day and then going home and thinking about my dad."

"We don't have to stay," Audrey said.

He laughed. "We'll see. Maybe I like high school dance punch. It's been a long time since I've had any."

On Saturday he helped her fill the car and carry everything to her classroom. "Isn't there more security?" Vince asked as they went up the stairs.

"I got lucky on this one," she said. "They had some other activities going on today."

It was 4:55 and the girls weren't there. "What if they don't show up?" Vince asked.

Audrey ran her fingers across her own navy blue dress. "I hope they do," she said, not feeling as confident though. She had been a teacher long enough to know what teens went through. And in her own life, Rick had broken her trust like no one else. She vowed to herself that she would not be upset if they didn't come.

About thirty seconds later, the three girls walked in, their hair and makeup done and a pair of shoes in each one's hands.

"Look at all of you," Audrey said, her face brightening after seeing them.

When they saw the dresses spread out on the desks, their eyes grew big.

"As if Santa Claus had visited them," Vince joked later.

"One for each of you," Audrey said, happy to see them smiling.

They walked up to the dresses, as if they each knew which one was for them and ran their fingers across them. "They're ours?"

"They are," Audrey said. "They were mine but I'm giving them to you." She sized up their shoes. "I'm not sure what size each of you is." She pointed at the three pairs of shoes set up on another desk. "I brought a few pairs and if they fit, they are yours, too."

"We need to change," Ruth said, looking around and seeing Vince.

"I'm Vince," he said, waving his hand. "Her boyfriend."

"Go to the bathroom down the hall," Audrey suggested.

"*Muy guapo,*" Veronica giggled as they walked out the door.

Audrey looked over at Vince. "Very handsome, of course," he said, smiling. "They were referring to me."

"I bet they were," Audrey laughed, her arms folded across her chest while they waited for the girls to return.

The laughter in the hallway grew louder and Audrey and Vince stole a smile at each other. When the girls reappeared, the clothes they had been wearing rolled up in their hands, they were smiling in a way Audrey had never seen. She beamed at how the dresses had transformed them.

Ruth wore the pink one, hair long hair pulled up into a bun that Audrey could never have done with her own thin hair. Ruth touched each of the shoes, selecting the low gold heels, and slipped them on her feet starting with the left. They fit perfectly and she smiled, knowing her look was complete. The pink dress, with a cap sleeve, lay perfectly across her slender body.

"You look beautiful," Veronica said to Ruth, seeing that her feet were too big for the shoes.

"And so do you," Ruth giggled.

Veronica wore the green dress, looking vintage with the fitted top and flared skirt, a satin finish.

No, Audrey thought, it made her look mature, as if she was wearing what she should wear.

Sylvia selected low black heels to wear with the off-the-shoulder black dress. After they had finished with their shoes, Audrey handed them each a ticket.

"Go have fun tonight," she told them.

"Thank you," they each said, looking like trick-or-treaters excited to get Halloween candy.

"Can we bring the dresses and shoes back on Monday?" Sylvia asked.

Audrey shook her head. "They're yours to keep."

"Really?" Veronica looked like she might faint. "But this is an expensive dress. I know the brand."

"It's yours," Audrey said. "Enjoy it. Find other places to wear them. All I ask is that you enjoy them."

Sylvia hugged Audrey, and then the other two took turns, light, nervous hugs from girls who weren't secure in their lives. As they walked out of the classroom, Audrey placed her hands behind her back and crossed her fingers, hoping they had a great time at the dance.

"I guess we should head down there?" Vince asked, adjusting his white shirt that was tucked into the waist of his black pants with a black belt. "Do you have my ticket?"

"You're the boy, you should have the ticket," Audrey reminded him.

"That's not very modern of you," he said.

"I'm an old-fashioned girl," she said. "As if we need tickets. It will be obvious we don't belong."

Vince walked to the classroom door and held out his arm. "Did you ever go to the homecoming dance?" he asked.

Audrey laughed, recounting the story of her friend who was gay. "He used me so everyone would think he was straight."

"It was the early nineties," Vince reminded her. "We weren't as open as we are today."

"Have you been to a high school dance in the last ten years?"

"Not since I graduated."

"Then get ready for something completely different. Like same-sex couples dancing together."

As soon as they walked into the gym, decorated with colored streamers and balloons, it was apparent that it was not the couples dance they both knew from their own high school years. Groups of kids mingled everywhere, laughing and looking like they were enjoying the night. And time out of the classroom.

Audrey looked around for the three girls and when she found them, they were standing with another group of girls, pointing at their dresses.

"You might have a group at your classroom door on Monday all looking for new outfits."

Audrey laughed, shrugging her shoulders. "I'm not worried about it. They deserved this. They don't even have lunch money some days and now they have nicer dresses than the most popular girls in school."

But what also struck Audrey as she watched them was that they were . . . the trio. Because Audrey had never known all four women in Aspen Hills to be together, they were simply the trio to her. She watched Sylvia throw her head back with laughter, Veronica giggling, and Ruth running her hand across the pink dress, still in disbelief at what she was wearing.

As she watched them, Audrey hoped that life would never hurt them. That wasn't realistic, she knew, but she saw how much they had already been through at a young age. She hoped they would always find happiness, but also laughter to help them through the tough times. And that they wouldn't feel as if they needed to keep their past or any part of their life private.

She didn't think they needed to put it all on social media but maybe Sally's life would have been different if she hadn't been afraid to share her pain. Instead, she hid it from everyone. Just as Reuben had.

Audrey looked over at Vince who was sipping the punch. "Not as I remember," he joked. "I guess they don't sell Hi-C in the big cans anymore, do they?"

"Too much sugar," Audrey joked. "There would be an outcry now. It's probably lemonade with food coloring to make it red."

She took his free hand and squeezed it. "We can go."

As they walked out of the school to her car, she looked across the parking lot at the city lights glittering before them. This was the opposite view from Aspen Hills, the complete other side of the city.

"That faint light on top of the mountain," Vince said, "is the Tram House. And if you look to the right you can see the TV antennas."

They drove back to Aspen Hills quietly, Audrey thinking about the girls and life. And pain and hope. She looked over at Vince and knew he was thinking about his dad.

Chapter 17

They spent part of Sunday shopping for new living room furniture. "I have no idea what I want," she sighed, feeling overwhelmed by all the choices in the store. "I just know what I don't want."

"Flowered couches?"

She started to laugh, uncontrollably, falling onto the nearest couch in the store.

"Kind of like that one?" Vince asked pointing and smiling at her.

Audrey looked around and realized the fabric was filled with roses and petals. "Ewww," she said, starting to laugh again.

Vince flopped onto the couch next to her, taking her hand, and they smiled at each other, unaware of anyone else in the store.

"I know you met some of my dad's family," he said abruptly, "but I want to bring you to Thanksgiving dinner. I want to tell them that you're Sally's niece." Before she could say anything, he touched her mouth with his finger. "You have no say in this. You told me yourself how much Sally enjoyed Rueben's family. Now it's time you get to know them in that context."

"You just asked me that now because you didn't want me to say no," Audrey realized, turning her head toward him.

"I feel like I just asked you to prom," Vince admitted.

"That can be arranged in the spring," she teased him.

"Would you like to buy this couch?" a kind older lady with dyed red hair asked, walking by with a notepad and pen in her hand.

"No, thank you," Audrey said. "I just got rid of one of these."

"Out with the old," Vince added and Audrey began to laugh again.

*****

The week of Thanksgiving the carpet was laid in the entire house. The walls had been painted the week before. The furniture would be delivered the day after Thanksgiving.

The day before Thanksgiving, with a day off from school, Audrey stood in the driveway with her coffee cup in one hand and watched the truck from the local homeless shelter drive off with the last of the furniture from the garage. The house was becoming more hers everyday. And she could afford it. Alone.

Yet she wasn't alone. Vince was becoming a bigger part of it each day.

"Hello!" Mary Ellen called, walking up the street with a plate in one hand. She was on her way to Betty's but stopped when she saw Audrey standing in the driveway holding the tax donation slip. "I was going to take these to Betty but since I saw you, here," she said, shoving the plate of brownies into Audrey's hands.

"Oh," Audrey said, caught off guard. "Thank you." She would eat one and give the rest to Vince. She might even drive them to Vince's house as soon as Mary Ellen left just so she wasn't tempted.

"I'm so glad you told us about Sally," Mary Ellen said, a little out of breath from the walking and her excitement of seeing Audrey. "We had no idea, obviously. But I'm glad they are together in heaven. That makes me happy." That's when she started to cry.

Audrey reached out and hugged Mary Ellen.

"I'm okay," Mary Ellen said. "Don't drop the brownies to hug me." She pushed off any idea of sadness. "We all get sad when we're really happy."

As Mary Ellen went on to Betty's house anyway, Audrey watched her for a moment, the plate of brownies in one hand and her coffee in the other.

"We all get sad when we're really happy."

As the day went on, Audrey thought of those words. Maybe she was confusing sadness and happiness. What the outside looked like wasn't always what was on the inside, she knew. Everyone thought her marriage was happy; even she thought it was happy. But Rick thought differently.

She walked inside and looked around at the newly remodeled living room and dining room. The kitchen would be started after the holidays but the rest of the house was just about done. The outside didn't match the inside with all the changes.

Just like with emotions, she thought, setting the brownies on the counter in the kitchen and watching the pool guy enter the side gate to shut the pool down for the winter.

Still no Sally, she thought, having gotten used to her showing up at moments like this. There hadn't been any sign of her since Reuben died. But Audrey didn't feel the need to read the diaries anymore. Maybe she had all the information she needed from Sally and it was time to move on.

The doorbell rang– Rodrigo arriving to go over the punch list with Audrey—and she forgot what she had been thinking about.

*****

"We know it's a sad time," Aunt Sylvia said, hugging Vince in the small updated kitchen she shared with Vince's Uncle Steve. She let go and picked up a wooden spoon to stir the potatoes boiling in a huge pot. "But we're glad you're here."

"Vicente!" Uncle Steve bellowed, walking into the room with his arms outstretched.

They embraced, and Audrey watched Vince cling to his aunt and uncle, his godparents, and the people he had told her would serve as his parents for the rest of his life.

"And you brought the girl! Even better!" Uncle Steve hugged Audrey, too.

She understood why Vince felt so close to them: they were warm and welcoming, the house filled with two of their children and the assorted grandchildren along with Sylvia's mother, Anna, who was fretting over the turkey in the oven.

"Stop opening the oven door, Mom," Sylvia kept telling her mom. "You spent twenty years telling me to not do it and here you're doing exactly that."

"Oh, I can do what I want," Anna said, waving her daughter off with a potholder but grinning at Audrey when she had a chance.

"I bet Vince Lombardi never got called Vicente," Vince told his uncle.

"I'm sure his Italian relatives called him that," Uncle Steve retorted. "Besides, I believe that's what your birth certificate says."

They went back and forth for a few minutes until one of the grandchildren walked in looking for a snack.

"When are we going to eat?" asked Sylvia and Steve's son, Martin, the mother of the little girl who was wandering around the kitchen hungry. He grabbed the little girl in the red dress and held her.

"As soon as the potatoes boil," Sylvia said with a sigh. She looked over at her mother, who was standing with her hand on the oven door. "And when your grandmother stops opening the oven door so the turkey can cook."

Her mother stared blankly at her.

"I have something I need to tell you," Vince said, watching his cousin chase Miranda, the little girl, out of the room.

"You're getting married!" Sylvia's brown eyes grew big. Steve started to walk forward until he saw the look on Audrey's face.

"Well, if you're getting married, you forgot to tell her," he joked.

"That's not it," Vince said, putting his head in his hand.

"Then what is it?" Sylvia asked, peeking over at the pot of potatoes. "I hope it's nothing bad. We've had enough bad news this year."

Vince ignored her. "Do you remember my dad knowing a woman named Sally?"

Steve and Sylvia immediately looked at each other. "Oh my," Sylvia said. "He was so in love with her."

"How did you find out about her?" Steve asked. He looked confused. "He was devastated when they broke up and asked us never to talk about her. We were all so glad when he met Yolanda. We thought his broken heart had mended."

Sylvia put her hand on her heart and sighed, not looking at anyone in particular. "I remember that first holiday season. He was so sad. He was sitting in the corner at Grandma Elena's house looking pitiful. I don't even think he saw us opening the gifts. He had that stack of wrapped presents in his lap and someone had to finally remind him he was supposed to open them."

"Audrey is Sally's niece."

No one reacted right away, staring for a moment at both Vince and Audrey while they processed what she had just said.

"Sally is your aunt?" Sylvia asked, looking directly at Audrey who nodded.

"Was," she said. "She died a year ago."

"Did your dad know she died?" Reuben asked Vince.

"About a month before he died, after his heart attack in San Diego, I introduced Audrey to him and somehow the dots got connected."

"*Dios mio,*" Sylvia said. "Did he die of a broken heart?"

Vince shook his head. "The opposite. He said it brought him peace to know after all the years of not knowing."

Uncle Steve ran his hand across his face. "I saw her once. She was with her husband. I could never bring myself to tell him though. He tried so hard to move on by marrying your mom." He looked at Audrey. "We loved your aunt. She was such a good woman and they were so happy together. What happened?"

Audrey looked at Vince. She was afraid to speak, afraid to say the wrong thing. Vince placed his hand on her lower back to give her strength. "Audrey never knew her aunt. Sally severed ties with her family after she broke up with Reuben."

Audrey felt pained as she thought about what was coming.

"What happened?" Steve looked at Audrey as if she would have the answer, but Vince saved her from having to say it.

"Her family wouldn't let her marry him because he was . . ."

"A Mexican," Sylvia said, shaking her head. "It was such an awful time. Reuben was more of an Anglo than some white people I know."

"It was so bad," Sylvia's mother said, turning to Audrey and Vince. "You have no idea how easy it is now. And it went both ways. I was forbidden to bring home an Anglo man."

Audrey felt uncomfortable. One of their children had married an Anglo, Scott, who was in the next room, but everyone in the kitchen except Audrey was Hispanic. Vince held her tighter.

"It doesn't matter," Steve finally said. "That time has gone by. Reuben is happy in heaven with two women."

"Oh God," Vince said, slightly embarrassed by Steve's comment.

"We all can't be so lucky," Steve joked. Sylvia glared at him.

"You need to go confession tomorrow for that one," Sylvia warned, taking the potatoes off the stove and pouring the water out.

"What's most important is that you two have found each other," Steve said. "Now I know why your dad was especially happy about it."

Audrey tried to savor the moment and the words of so many people who supported them. Steve walked over and hugged Audrey again. "He hasn't asked you to marry him yet, but he will."

"Hey, don't I get any say in this?" Vince asked, pouting slightly.

"Not really," Audrey said, finally feeling playful enough to take part.

When they left a few hours later, Steve walked outside and stood in the driveway of the brick home with them and looked around. "Tomorrow I'll put up the Christmas decorations." The three of them stood quietly for a moment in the cool evening air, the holiday season about to start. "But I believe in the magic in the season, even after all that's happened. Christmas magic. You never know what kind of miracles will happen." He hugged them both and Vince and Audrey walked down the street to Vince's car.

Chapter 18

"The stain came out," Audrey said excitedly when she stopped to pick up the green dress at the dry cleaner.

"Yes," Marta the dry cleaner said. "And all the buttons are sewn back on. I was afraid they would melt."

Audrey happily took the plastic-covered dress home, singing "Jingle Bells" in the car, believing the dress looked brighter than when she dropped it off. She stared at it for a moment and then walked in the closet, looking for her silver heels, the shoes she thought would be perfect. As she held them up next to the dress, she smiled and nodded her head approvingly. The Christmas dance wouldn't come soon enough.

But it did.

Before Audrey knew it, she was slipping on the dress to wear it to the Aspen Hills Club Christmas Dinner. She stood in the mirror looking at herself, at how much her life had changed in less than a year.

Christmas the previous year had been a challenge, her first without Rick since they had gotten together. And while she was angry at him, mostly she was sad and felt confused, spending Christmas as a single person. Even with her mother and the relatives, it wasn't the same.

At my age I should have my own family, she remembered thinking, watching all her cousins chasing their kids, as Vince's cousins had done at Thanksgiving.

But this year everything was different. She had Vince.

Audrey admired herself in the mirror: her hair pulled back and curled, her face not looking so puffy and sad now that she had lost weight and started this new life, her stomach looking smooth from the weight loss. She touched the string of pearls she wore close to her neck, one of the many strings she had found in Sally's dresser drawers.

Then Audrey looked behind her, hoping that Sally would be there to say hi, to tell her she hoped they would have a good time. But Audrey was alone in the house until she heard the front door open.

And Audrey wanted to tell Sally how happy it made her to put such a happy time on a dress that she knew represented something so sad to Sally.

Audrey took one last look, smoothing her hands across the heavy textured green brocade fabric, smiling at the high heels, having forgotten what it was like to feel sexy in them. It had been a long time.

"Hello!"

She went down the hall to meet Vince in the updated living room, her heels clicking across the wood floor, Vince wearing a suit, smiling as Audrey walked toward him.

"Wow," he said.

For the first time in their relationship, really for the first time since Rick had told her he wanted to end their marriage, Audrey could smile and feel confident with the way she looked. It translated from the way she felt inside: the insecure side of her, the side that was trampled and stomped on by Rick, had healed. It had taken her time to like herself again, to put the effort back into the way she looked, but now she realized it had been there all along, covered up by her sadness and depression.

"You look beautiful," Vince said, taking her hand. They stood together, holding just one hand each, in the middle of the living room, a totally different room than when they had started.

"Thank you," Audrey said, taking the compliment. "And you look pretty handsome yourself."

"I clean up well," he teased, pulling her toward him and they hugged for a moment, Audrey careful not to get lipstick on his suit jacket. For a moment, they listened to each other's heartbeats and rested in one another's presence.

"We better go," he whispered. "I know a certain trio that will be excited to see you."

"Oh please," Audrey laughed, throwing her left hand out as her right hand reached for the knob on the hall closet door.

"And the dress fits," Vince noted.

"It does. Finally." She pointed at the hem. "And the stain is gone."

The snow from the previous evening had melted off the street but where it hadn't melted on the grass and shrubs, everything was lit up with the Christmas lights reflecting on the white light of the night.

"It usually takes a few extra days here," Vince said. "It's much colder on the side of the mountain than down there in the city." He pointed at the city lights shimmering below them as he pulled into the Aspen Hills Country Club.

Audrey pulled her knee-length ivory coat closer to her in the bitter air, shivering as they walked across the parking lot. "I thought the desert was supposed to be warmer than Kansas this time of year."

Vince laughed and held the door open for her. "Maybe you are really still in Kansas," he joked, then adding, "The desert gets cold at night. Not like the Midwest where everything stays the same temperature as it started."

They could hear the holiday music playing down the hall. And when they reached the open doors to the ballroom, people were dressed up, milling around, glasses of wine or champagne in their hands.

Vince slid her coat off and handed it to the woman at the coat check. Audrey kept her clutch, a white beaded one she had found in Sally's closet, and Betty spotted them.

"What a beautiful couple!" she exclaimed almost running up to them, a few chairs wobbling as she went forward. Not far behind her came Mary Ellen and Esther.

The three of them gushed as they looked Audrey and Vince over. Each one had her hands clasped in front of her.

"We are so lucky to have them here," Mary Esther said, admiring Audrey's dress.

"It was Sally's," she told them.

"Oh my," Esther reached out to touch it. "It looks so vintage."

"Vintage Kate Spade," Audrey said, proud of her own description.

"She must have kept it a long time," Mary Ellen said.

"It was in a closet with a stain on it, and I had it cleaned."

"It fits you like a glove," Betty said and the other two nodded in unison.

"It didn't always," Audrey told them.

"Really?" Esther asked.

"I couldn't zip it up when I first put it on after I moved here," she said, embarrassed to admit it, but proud of herself for the weight loss.

"I find that hard to believe," Betty added, putting her hands on her hips.

As promised, all three women wore black pants, their tops glittering and shiny, taking the focus off below the waist.

"It's true," Audrey told them.

"It doesn't matter," Mary Ellen said, waving it off. "You look wonderful. Merry Christmas! We're just so glad you're here and you're not leaving."

"How do you know I'm not leaving?" Audrey teasingly asked them.

The three women laughed and turned their attention to one of the country club staff who walked up to them with a question.

After dinner, as the dancing started, some people began to leave. Vince leaned over and suggested they walk outside and look at the view from the patio. "It's nicer in the summer when it's not so cold," he admitted, helping her wrap her shawl around her shoulders.

"Then we should stay in," Audrey said, not looking thrilled about going outside.

Vince laughed and grabbed her hand.

"The view is just fine from here," she said, nodding her head toward the glass windows.

Vince ignored her and opened the door, pulling Audrey outside with him. "I'll give you my suit jacket." He began to pull it off.

"Nooo," Audrey said, "I'll survive. Now that I'm out here though, the view is nice." She looked at the glitter that made up the city lights and walked back to the door.

But Vince held her hand tightly and led her to the edge of the patio where a low wall kept anyone from tumbling into the brush.

Audrey tried to get lost in the lights, the music playing loud enough from inside that it filtered into the cold night air. No one else was outside with them, a quiet moment in the chaos of the party.

She wasn't paying attention when Vince took her hand and slipped something on her finger. Audrey looked down to see a diamond sparkling in the night light.

"Oh." She said, starting to shake, not from the cold but from what was about to happen. She looked up at Vince and he started to speak.

"When I got married, I thought it was forever," he said. "And when it ended I never thought I would meet someone I would want to spend the rest of my life with. But in the past months, you've made me realize that we all have that second chance for love. And I know my dad believed in us."

Before she could speak—after all he still hadn't actually asked her the question—he kept talking. Audrey found herself starting to cry.

"This was the ring that my dad planned to give to Sally. He kept it all those years because somewhere in heart he still thought he would get to spend his life with her. Before he died he told me that he would find her when he got to heaven and that now he realized that he kept the ring for me. He wanted me to give it to you."

Vince's hand, palm up, rested underneath Sally's hand. She looked down, knowing that even if she couldn't see Sally or Reuben, they were both there with them.

"Will you marry me?"

"Yes," Audrey said, bursting out into laughter and then falling into his arms for a long kiss.

"Let's go inside so you will stop shivering."

Audrey couldn't stop looking at the ring. And then at Vince. She shook her head. "Do I need to pinch you?" he offered.

Audrey teasingly glared at him. "I don't think so. You'll actually hurt me."

"I just want you to know it's real," he said.

"What are you two grinning about?" Esther asked when they were inside and sitting back at their table. Audrey held out her hand.

"Oh my! Oh my! Oh my!" She clutched her hand to her heart and looked around for the others.

As she went looking for them, Audrey kept laughing, feeling as though she were on the outskirts of the scene, as the camera panned away from it, realizing that was how Sally and Reuben were seeing it.

She knew they were together, smiling down on Audrey and Vince, happy they had found each other but also happy they helped bring happiness to what had been so much sadness over a long period of time.

Audrey grasped Vince's hand and squeezed it. He squeezed it back.

"Merry Christmas," he whispered. "Just one of many we'll have together."

Audrey looked up and saw Sally, wearing a long black sequined dress, just as she knew the entire trio had dressed at one time, smiling at her. Their eyes met, and Audrey's smile grew. Reuben stood next to Sally in a tux. He gave a thumbs up.

The trio had found them and hovered around Audrey and Vince, wanting to see the ring. When Audrey looked up, Sally and Reuben were gone.

It's okay, Audrey told herself. They know. They'll always be with us.

www.ingramcontent.com/pod-product-compliance
Lightning Source LLC
Chambersburg PA
CBHW050848180626
46814CB00007B/2674